Eros Rising
By Ally Blue

Scott Jasper needs a change in his life. Stuck in a dead-end relationship with a man who manipulates and uses him, Scott wants out but hasn't found the one thing to motivate him to leave. Until the night his partner takes him to local gay swinger's club Ganymede's Grotto, where Scott meets the man who might just be The One.

Keegan Rourke—a.k.a. "Eros," the most popular stripper at Ganymede's Grotto—has been burned before. Determined never to let another man rip his heart out, Keegan doesn't let anyone get close enough to love him. Until Scott comes along, offering Keegan the gentle, unconditional love he's always needed but has never experienced.

For Scott and Keegan, the road to lasting commitment isn't a smooth one. A lot of roadblocks stand in their path—Scott's trepidation about his own dominant tendencies, Keegan's abusive past and resulting fear of intimacy. Can they can rise above past sorrows and find their happiness in each other's arms?

Café Noctem
By Willa Okati

Sint Holo, the Snake Man of Cherokee legend, is up to his mischievous games again. He lives to cause trouble, and there's no better time than Valentine's Day to toy with a few hearts.

Nicholas and Grey have been lovers for almost a year now, but all is not well in paradise. They have more than a few issues to work out around this time of year, and in their turmoil the Trickster sees his opportunity. Sint Holo has a game in mind for the two of them to play—whether they want to or not.

Caught up in the magic of Celebration de la Vie, the two lover must outwit the trickster so they can celebrate their life... together.

Warning, this title contains explicit male/male sex.

With Love
By J.L. Langley

All Devlin wants to do is find a good new home for his business and his pack. He's not looking for any complications, but he finds something he never expected—a mate. A mate with a whole lot of energy who attracts trouble like a magnet.

Laine Campbell never means to get himself into hot water, but everything has a way of getting tangled up between his feet. He needs more than just a mate—he needs a savior.

When Dev turns up at a pack get-together, Laine finds both. The two werewolves have an instant attraction, but the pack Alpha is determined to keep Laine for himself. Dev soon learns the only way to protect his mate is to fight, not just for the top spot—but for his life.

Just one small problem. His accident-prone mate is determined to help him...

Hearts from the Ashes

A Samhain Publishing, Ltd. publication.

Samhain Publishing, Ltd.
2932 Ross Clark Circle, #384
Dothan, AL 36301
www.samhainpublishing.com

Hearts from the Ashes
Print ISBN: 1-59998-346-X
Eros Rising Copyright © 2007 by Ally Blue
Café Noctem Copyright © 2007 by Willa Okati
With Love Copyright © 2007 by J.L. Langley

Editing by Sasha Knight
Cover by Anne Cain

First Samhain Publishing, Ltd. electronic publication: January 2007
First Samhain Publishing, Ltd. print publication: January 2007

Contents

Eros Rising

Ally Blue

Dedication

For J.L. and Willa, my friends and partners in crime on this anthology, and for Sasha, whose brilliant idea it was in the first place. You ladies rock!

Chapter One

"Scott, would you please relax?"

"You didn't tell me Ganymede's Grotto was a sex club, Logan."

"You wouldn't have come if I had."

Scott Jasper glared at his lover, who sat sipping an Appletini (*fucking girly drink,* Scott thought nastily) as if they were in a five-star restaurant instead of a gay swingers' club. The music boomed through the air, the heavy bass vibrating in Scott's ears.

He studied the large, dimly lit room. Tiny silver stars dotted the dark blue ceiling, which curved down to meet bluish-black walls that formed small bays along the edges of the club. The bays contained private booths in which pairs and groups of men gathered, engaged in activities Scott was rather glad he couldn't quite see. He and Logan sat in one of the freestanding booths scattered around the dark blue wood floor, facing a large curtained stage.

"Why'd you want to come here, anyway?" Scott asked, watching the crowd at the polished mahogany bar.

"I've never been here, I wanted to see what it was like." Logan widened his hazel eyes. "You wouldn't want to waste those guest passes Todd and Steven gave us, would you?"

"Don't know what made them think we'd want two guest passes to a swingers' club for Christmas." Scott gave Logan a pointed look. "You told them to get us that, didn't you?"

"I didn't *tell*." Logan took a sip of his drink. "I may have let slip that we wanted to check it out, and they've been members for ages, so..." Cocking an eyebrow at Scott, he grinned.

Scott couldn't find it in himself to smile back. Years ago, that wicked, I'm-up-to-no-good look of Logan's could melt Scott into a sticky little puddle. Then he'd figured out that Logan's mischief was usually at Scott's expense, and now that look just made him sad, missing something he was no longer sure they'd ever had together.

"I know you were curious, Logan," Scott said, keeping his voice calm and soft, "but you know that sex is a private thing for me. This place is nice, but it's not my scene and you know that."

Logan made an impatient sound. "You're always like this. So damn uptight."

It was Logan's standard comeback and Scott ignored it. He laid a hand over Logan's, trying to keep some sort of connection between them. "Why are we here, Logan? The truth."

Something passed through Logan's eyes, something Scott didn't like one bit because he'd seen it too often before. "Well, I was thinking we could, you know..."

Scott knew. With a sigh, he slid to the edge of the black and purple leather booth and stood up, leaning against the painted table. "How many times do we have to have this argument, Logan? I don't want to have a threesome. I don't feel comfortable with it. Why can't you accept that?"

Logan's expression turned hard. "And why can't you ever do what I want? You *know* the things I let you do to me, but you won't let me have this one fantasy. Selfish prick."

12

Scott straightened up and closed his eyes for a second, trying to control the mix of fear and anger and hurt roiling inside him. Nothing was that simple, and they both knew it. Logan was trying to guilt him into doing something he didn't want to do. Scott was determined not to let him.

Logan grasped his wrist as Scott started to walk away. "I'm sorry, Scott. Don't be mad at me, okay?" He gazed up at Scott with his patented kicked-puppy look, oblivious to the fact that Scott had been immune for years. "It was just an idea, baby. We won't do it if you don't want to. We can just stay and watch the show, huh? It's about to start."

Sure enough, a gray-haired gentleman in a black suit and pink feather boa had stepped up to the mic and was announcing a performer with the improbable name of Eros. Drawing a deep breath, Scott started to tell Logan where he could stick his fake-pleading eyes and his stupid ideas.

At that moment the blue velvet curtain behind the MC swung open and Scott promptly forgot what he was going to say. He stood there with his mouth hanging open, staring at the vision on the stage.

The man stood no more than five-foot-eight or so, at least six inches shorter than Scott. He was slender and graceful in sinfully tight white pants, a sheer white shirt and huge white-feathered wings. Strawberry blond hair streaked with white hung in wild waves and curls down to the middle of his back and framed a rounded, pixyish face. The silver ring piercing the man's full lower lip glinted in the light.

"Well, I see you found something you like at the dirty sex club after all."

Logan's sneering tone grated on Scott's nerves, but he nevertheless tore his gaze from the stage. Lowering himself to the edge of the padded seat, he gave Logan a guilty smile. "Sorry."

"Whatever." Logan shot him a dark look. "I'm going to the restroom."

Scott watched in resignation as Logan slid out of the booth and stalked toward the back of the room. He knew Logan wouldn't be back for a while, if he bothered to come back at all. If he cared to go look, Scott would undoubtedly find Logan at the bar, flirting with the first twink to give him the eye.

He did the same thing practically every time they went out, which was the main reason Scott didn't like going out with him. Even though Logan's behavior rarely went beyond flirting—as far as Scott knew, anyway—it still hurt.

"Why," Scott wondered aloud, "do I put up with this shit?"

He didn't answer himself, because he didn't know. After seven years, he supposed it was sheer complacency that kept them together. It sure as hell wasn't love, not anymore. Hadn't been for a long time.

Not wanting to dwell on his strained relationship with Logan, Scott turned his attention back to the stripper. Eros. The young man was dancing to the primitive rhythm of the music, his movements lithe and sensual. To Scott's shock, he found himself hardening in his jeans. He hadn't had that sort of reaction to a stranger since his teenage years.

Eros tore his shirt away, revealing lean, defined muscles and creamy pale skin, and Scott gasped out loud. Little silver rings pierced both of the man's nipples. Through the wings and the thick mane of hair, Scott caught glimpses of a huge tattoo on his back, though he couldn't quite make out what it was.

The pants came off next, ripped away in one fluid motion. *Must be those special stripper's pants,* Scott thought with the part of his brain that still worked. Eros was now dancing in nothing but the feathered wings and a gold and white G-string that left nothing to the imagination. A tattooed vine wound up the man's right leg all the way from ankle to buttock. Scott watched, mesmerized by the stripper's gracefully sexual movements.

Scott didn't realize the show had ended at first. Wild applause, cheers and a few indecent proposals from the audience snapped him out of his stupor. Eros flashed a wide grin at the audience and bent forward in a deep bow, long reddish-gold tresses brushing the floor.

Eros exited the stage with a wave, disappearing behind the edge of the curtain. Scott took a deep breath and glanced around, hoping no one could see how the show had affected him. He needn't have worried. No one was paying him the least bit of attention.

When the tightness in his pants subsided, Scott reluctantly decided he'd better look for Logan. He got up and wandered toward the bar, threading his way through the crowd. He had to deflect several offers along the way. Logan was nowhere in sight, which increased Scott's irritation exponentially.

"Good grief," Scott muttered as he slipped onto an empty barstool. "Am I the only one who's not into threesomes?"

"Not really," said a voice from behind the bar. "It just seems that way sometimes."

Scott raised his head, looking for the owner of the voice, and was startled to find himself face-to-face with Eros. The young man wore skintight jeans faded within an inch of their life and a long-sleeved blue T-shirt with Ganymede's Grotto embroidered over the left breast. His hair was wound into a single long braid. Little golden wisps escaped to curl in wild disarray around his face. Scott stared, seized by a sudden urge to tug on the silver lip ring with his teeth.

The young man grinned. "What's the matter, cat got your tongue?"

Scott blinked, trying to clear his head. "Huh?" he said, and immediately wished he hadn't. *Smooth, Scott,* he thought, mentally smacking himself. *Some great impression you're making.*

The stripper laughed. "I was just saying that no, you're not the only one who's not here for a threesome. Most guys join the club either to find other couples to swap with, or to watch the live sex shows, but there's still some looking for single guys to play with. Hot as you are? No wonder you attract 'em like flies."

Scott cleared his throat. "I'm not actually single. I'm here with my partner." He was relieved that he didn't sound flustered this time, and wondered why he cared. He wasn't exactly available, after all.

The man's gaze raked down Scott's chest. "Too bad."

Scott licked his lips. The stripper's eyes were different colors. One dark midnight blue, one pale gray, both sparking with life. Fascinating.

"You have beautiful eyes," Scott heard himself say. The blood rushed into his cheeks. "I shouldn't have said that, I'm sorry."

"What for?" Drawing a draft beer, the man slid it over to someone on Scott's right. "I think I like you complimenting me."

"It's just that I…I'm, uh, I'm with someone, and I don't even know you, I shouldn't be saying those things."

"Well, I can't do anything about you being taken, but I can introduce myself." He stuck a hand across the bar. "I'm Keegan Rourke."

Scott took Keegan's hand and shook, feeling like he was in a dream. "Scott Jasper."

"Pleased to meet you, Scott." Keegan flashed that wide, wicked grin. "There, now we know each other. You drinking?"

"Oh, um..." Scott tapped his chin, thinking. "Gin and tonic, please. With lime."

"Coming up." Keegan snatched a glass and two bottles and began pouring, every bit as graceful as he'd been on stage. He stuck a lime wedge on the rim of the glass and handed it to Scott. "That'll be five even. You want to pay now, or you want me to start you a tab?"

Scott considered. A quick look around revealed no sign of Logan. *Hell with him*, Scott thought, and favored Keegan with his sunniest smile. "Guess I'll start a tab, since Logan doesn't seem to be around anywhere."

"'K. I'll need a credit card." Keegan gave Scott a careful look as he dug his wallet out of his jeans pocket and handed Keegan his credit card. "Is Logan your partner?"

"Yes." Scott squirmed uncomfortably on his barstool. "Let's not talk about him."

"Whatever you say." Keegan ran Scott's card through and handed it back to him. "So. Did you like my show?"

Scott choked on his drink. "What?"

Keegan laughed. "Man, you gotta relax a little. I asked what you thought of my strip show. Did you like it?"

Scott held Keegan's amused gaze with an effort, wishing he could stop blushing. "Very much. You're..." *Incredibly gorgeous. Sexy as hell.* "You're really good."

"Thanks. Maybe I could give you a private show sometime."

Keegan's smile promised sex and sin. Scott gulped. "I...I, um..."

"I know, you're with Logan, wherever he is." Keegan sighed, one hand over his heart. "Don't worry, I'll get over it some day."

Scott laughed, Keegan's playfulness dispelling some of his tension. "Keegan's an unusual name. Where's it come from?"

"It's Gaelic." The young man made a sour face. "It was my grandfather's name. My mom promised her father before he died that she'd name her first son after him."

"I like it. It's different." Scott took a sip of gin and tonic. "What's it mean?"

Keegan blushed and stared at a puddle of beer on the bar. He mumbled something Scott didn't catch. "What was that?" Scott asked, leaning closer.

"I said," Keegan repeated, looking resigned, "it means 'little fierce one'."

"I like that," Scott said, holding Keegan's gaze with a boldness that surprised him. "It fits you somehow."

Keegan's eyes softened, the subtle guarded expression Scott had only just noticed dropping for a second. Before he could say anything, a young man in full leather gear called from the other end of the bar. Keegan glanced over, then back at Scott. "Sorry. Duty calls."

Scott smiled. "Of course. I enjoyed talking with you, Keegan."

"Yeah. Me too." Keegan gazed at him for a moment longer, then turned, braid swinging, to wait on the other customers.

Scott leaned against the bar and watched him work, for once not wondering what Logan was up to. Everything about Keegan fascinated him, from those captivating eyes to his natural grace to the charisma that seemed to draw every eye in the room. For the first time since he and Logan had been together, Scott wished he was single.

Not that I'd have a chance with him, he thought morosely. *He could have his pick of anyone here, what would he want with me?*

Craning his neck, Scott scanned the room once more. Still no sign of Logan. Scott settled in with a smile, not at all disappointed with his lot. A guy could do worse, he figured, than parking at the bar in an upscale club, drinking good gin and watching the sexiest bartender-slash-stripper he'd ever seen.

Another two hours slipped by while Scott sat at the bar, working his way through several more gin and tonics. Keegan stopped to talk whenever he had the chance. Scott found himself liking the young man more and more. He was intelligent, well-read and well-spoken, and had a warped sense of humor that matched Scott's perfectly. His apparent rapt interest in Scott's mundane tales of life as an accountant put Scott more at ease than he'd ever felt with Logan. The realization came as something of a shock.

Keegan was at the other end of the bar pouring tequila shots for a raucous group of men in leather and chains when Scott heard Logan's laugh ring out from somewhere to his right. It was the too-loud, slightly desperate giggle Logan used when he wanted something and thought he was about to lose his chance at getting it.

Instantly, all the tension Scott had let go over the course of the evening came flooding back. He turned toward the unwelcome sound, dreading what he might see.

It was even worse than he'd thought. Logan stood pressed between two men, one short and stocky with a shaved head and a health-club tan, the other tall and slender with cinnamon-colored skin and an expensive suit. Logan had one arm around the black man's neck, kissing him with great enthusiasm. The other man was sucking on Logan's neck, hands running up and down his thighs.

Scott's vision went red. Before he realized what he was doing, he'd jumped off the barstool, shoved his way through the crowd and yanked Logan away from the two other men.

"What the *fuck* do you think you're doing?" Scott shouted, ignoring the protests of the two men. "You said you were going to the restroom, Logan! Over two hours ago!"

Logan blinked at him, eyes wide and panicked. "Scott, baby, it's not what it looks like—"

"Don't you fucking dare say that to me!" Scott bellowed. He ground his teeth together, fighting the urge to punch that deer-in-the-headlights look right off Logan's lying face. "Where were you, huh? Where've you been all this time?"

Logan licked his lips, gaze darting around the room. "I...I was..."

"They came out of one of the viewing rooms," Keegan supplied from behind the bar. "Live sex shows, every night," he added helpfully.

Scott turned to him with a grim smile. "Thank you."

"Any time." Shooting Logan a look that Scott was glad wasn't aimed at him, Keegan went back to pouring drinks.

Scott glared at Logan, crossed his arms and waited.

Hanging his head, Logan gazed up at Scott from under his lashes. "I'm sorry, baby, I really am. I didn't mean to let them tempt me like that, but they were just coming on so strong." The men in question broke their stunned silence to vigorously protest this statement. Logan ignored them both and plowed on.

"And I'd been drinking, and the show was so hot it made me really horny, and I was disappointed that you wouldn't let us have a threesome and you were already mad at me anyway, so—"

"Stop," Scott snapped.

Logan laid a hand on his arm. "Come on, Scott, just listen for a minute—"

"No." Scott shook loose of Logan's grip and stepped back. "Don't try to make this my fault, Logan. I'm not the problem here. The problem is, you wouldn't know the truth if it smacked you upside the head."

Logan's eyes narrowed, his mouth curving into a calculating smile. "I know what you want. You can do it, you know. When we get home." He leaned closer, voice dropping to a rough whisper. "I know how much you love it when I scream for you, baby. I love it too."

Scott tuned out the murmuring crowd of onlookers and stared at Logan, into those eyes he'd have done anything for once upon a time, and all the anger drained out of him. He was sick of playing out this same scene over and over. Confronting Logan with his latest flirtation, only to be faced with Logan's pathetic excuses and justifications. It always ended the same way—Logan bent over the end of the bed, white-knuckled fists bunching the covers, stifling his cries in the mattress as Scott's well-used strip of supple birch drew hot red lines across his naked skin.

Scott hated that part more than the arguments, more than Logan's small but painfully frequent infidelities. He hated how much it excited him, and he particularly hated the person it made him become.

"I can't do this right now." Without another word, Scott turned and walked away.

Logan ran after him, spouting the usual insincere apologies and hollow promises. Scott shook off his grasping fingers without so much as a glance. Predictably, Logan didn't follow him through the front door into the cold January night. Scott was glad of it. Right then, he'd be perfectly happy if he never laid eyes on Logan again. He flagged down a cab and climbed in, leaving Ganymede's Grotto and Logan behind.

He was halfway home before he remembered the bar tab he hadn't paid. Keegan had run his credit card, but Scott had never signed for the tab.

It took him a minute to realize the tab provided an automatic excuse to go back. To see Keegan again. The thought lifted his sagging spirits and he smiled.

Chapter Two

Keegan watched the blond man out of the corner of his eye as he wiped down the bar. Larry? Lonnie? He couldn't quite remember. Scott had told him the asshole's name, but it had gone right out of his head.

Whatever the man's name was, he sure as hell didn't deserve someone as hot, as intelligent, as fun and as just plain *nice* as Scott. The jackass was still with those two sluts Cameron and Dave, pressed between them in one of the private bays. Keegan shook his head. Some people didn't know when they had it good.

He glanced up at the clock. One forty-five. The bar area would be closing in a few minutes, meaning everyone except members who'd rented a room for the night would have to leave. Keegan chuckled to himself, childishly pleased that he would get to kick out the Cheater and the Sluts.

He waited another ten minutes, then sauntered over to the shadowy booth where Scott's worthless boyfriend—*Logan, that's his name*—had his tongue down Dave's throat and his hand up Cameron's shirt. Keegan cleared his throat and the three of them jumped apart.

"Closing time." Keegan jerked a thumb over his shoulder. "Out."

Dave and Cameron wished him good night and left like good boys, arms around each other. Logan got up and stood there looking bereft.

"You deaf or what?" Keegan said, not bothering to keep the contempt out of his voice. "Time to go home. If he'll let you in, that is."

Logan's expression turned stormy. "Mind your own business."

Keegan crossed his arms and gave Logan a curious look. "Are you really as stupid as you seem?"

Logan flushed a dangerous shade of red. "What?"

"It's just that you have a great guy," Keegan continued, ignoring Logan's clenched fists and snarling lip. "He's not only incredibly hot, he's nice too. I gave him an opening and he turned me down. Said he was with someone. No one, least of all you, could ask for better than that. And look how you act. So I figure you're stupid."

"Shut up!" Logan hissed. "You can't talk to me like that."

"Funny, I don't seem to be having any trouble." Keegan smiled. "Get the fuck out of here, asshole. See there, I just did it again. Easy as pie."

For a second, Keegan thought Logan was going to hit him. Part of him looked forward to it. He itched to punch the man right in his chiseled jaw. He was disappointed when Logan elected to point a warning finger in his face instead.

"Listen here," Logan growled. "I don't know who the hell you think you are, but you can't get away with saying things like that to me."

"Sure I can," Keegan said cheerfully. "You're a lying, cheating waste of space who obviously can't see when he's got a good thing, and I don't like you."

Keegan watched with amusement as Logan gaped like a fish. *What the hell does Scott see in this jerk?*

"Well, at least I don't get naked for a room full of perverts," Logan spat, eyes glittering triumphantly.

Keegan burst into laughter, which Logan's slack-jawed confusion did nothing to dispel. "You mean like you?" he gasped, wiping tears from his eyes. "Listen, if that's all you got, you might as well give up now. I've heard a whole lot worse than that from a whole lot better than you. And now, we're closing. Leave, before I call the cops." Keegan turned his back on Logan's sputtering fury, letting him know in no uncertain terms that he'd been dismissed.

Logan's hand whirling him around was a surprise, but he managed not to show it. He cocked an eyebrow at the man. "You got something else to say, asshole?"

Logan smiled, looking for a moment like a shark. "You said you came on to Scott. Well, be glad he turned you down. You don't know a goddamn thing about him."

"True," Keegan agreed amiably, plucking Logan's fingers from his arm. "But I know one thing. He can sure as hell do better."

"And I suppose you think you're better." Logan shook his head. "You come have a good look at my back tomorrow morning, then tell me you still want him. I don't think you could handle it."

Keegan watched Logan storm out the door. The man's words brought back things he'd much rather forget. Things that still had the power to shake him deep down, even after eight long years. He shook off the uneasiness, reminding himself what Logan had been up to for the past several hours. He'd clearly say or do anything to make himself out as the victim. Shoving the dark memories back into his subconscious and dismissing Logan's appalling behavior from his mind, Keegan turned back to his work.

Within half an hour, he had the bar sparkling clean, the floor swept, the bottles wiped down and put away and the dirty glasses in the dishwasher. He counted the drawer, put all the money and credit card receipts in the special zippered bag, and headed into the back office to stash it in the safe for Earl to deposit in the morning.

That chore done, Keegan locked the office and switched off the lights at the bar. Yawning, he headed for the staff entrance in back, calling goodbye to the night kitchen staff on the way.

The service door through which the staff entered and exited the club opened onto a narrow alley in back of the building. The door remained locked from the outside and open from the inside. Every staff member had a key, enabling them to come and go at all hours. While the bar area closed between two and ten a.m., the private and group sex rooms, viewing rooms and dungeons remained open twenty-four hours a day for members who had reserved them ahead of time.

Ganymede's Grotto might be a sex club, but it was a classy one, with a rigorous screening process for potential members and a high standard of service. Keegan figured he could do a lot worse than tend bar and strip to a G-string for a friendly, appreciative audience. He even got health insurance in this job. He'd sure as hell never had that when he made his miniscule living jerking off for the peep shows in Charleston.

The people at Ganymede's Grotto were good to him. They treated him like family. Or rather like family *should* treat each other, something else he hadn't really known before coming here. In return, they got Keegan's complete and unhesitating loyalty. It was a mutually beneficial relationship.

Inside his tiny one-room-and-a-bath apartment situated above the club, Keegan stripped off his work clothes, unwound his long braid and headed into the bathroom for a shower. As he soaped himself, his thoughts drifted to Scott. He'd never met a man quite like Scott before. Big enough to be intimidating, but with an aura of gentleness that drew Keegan like a magnet.

Closing his eyes, Keegan cupped his balls in one hand, rolling them between his fingers and picturing Scott's face in his mind. Great big chocolate-colored eyes, with the sort of long, thick lashes that girls go crazy for. High cheekbones. Jaw sharp enough to cut glass. A nose that was slightly crooked like it had been broken at some point. And God, that mouth, sweet and sinful and tailor-made for long, slow kisses. Keegan moaned, imagining those soft lips wrapped around his cock.

He hadn't meant to jerk off. He'd intended to shower and go straight to bed. But the mental image of Scott sucking him off was too much to resist. He took himself firmly in hand and went to it, putting his back against the tiles and pumping his shaft hard.

It wasn't long before the familiar tingle began to spread through his groin and down his thighs. He shoved two fingers in his ass and came with a cry, picturing Scott's prick buried balls-deep inside him, Scott's hands caressing his body.

He managed to shut the water off before his knees buckled. Sitting sprawled on the floor of the tub, he had to laugh at himself. "Keegan, my boy, you really, really need to get laid."

It was all too true. He hadn't been with anyone in months, not since the last one-nighter had gotten a little out of hand. He grimaced at the memory. He hadn't realized until too late what exactly the man wanted to do. Keegan had suffered a full-on flashback when the man attempted to tie him to the bed. He'd evidently kicked the man in the face then run all the way back to the club in his underwear. To this day, he couldn't remember doing that. He'd learned of it later, when the man came to the club to complain to Earl about Keegan being dangerously unstable. Earl, predictably, had thrown the man out and told him never to show his face again unless he wanted to go to prison.

Keegan privately thought the man had gotten off easy, considering. Earl Queen, the owner and manager of Ganymede's Grotto and a substitute father to Keegan, had been livid when Keegan showed up in his office that night, half-naked and incoherent with pure blind panic. After determining that Keegan wasn't physically harmed, he'd stormed around the room threatening the man with the most hair-raising tortures imaginable. Then he'd hugged Keegan so hard he could barely breathe and called him "son" and sworn he'd rip the liver out of the next person who did such a thing to him.

Keegan had felt more loved and protected at that moment than he ever had. Eight years ago, he thought with a grim smile, it would've confused him no end. He would've been looking for a way to sabotage it, because being cared for had been so foreign to him at that time. Now, he accepted Earl's fatherly affection as the gift it was, and returned it in kind.

As always, thinking of his past made Keegan's guts churn. Shaking off the memories, he clambered to his feet and grabbed his towel. He wandered back into the main room, squeezing as much water out of his hair as he could before weaving it into a loose braid. He collapsed naked onto the bed and was sound asleep within minutes, a contented smile on his lips.

Earl waylaid Keegan the next afternoon the moment he showed up for work.

"Keegan," he called from the half-open door of his office as Keegan passed by. "Come in here for a mo, darling, I need you."

Keegan veered into the office and grinned at Earl. "What's up?"

Earl flashed a wide smile, bright blue eyes crinkling at the corners. "Two things, beautiful. First, don't call the customers assholes, even if they are. Second, there's an absolutely stunning man waiting for you at the bar. He's not a member, but I let him in anyway because, honey, if you've got a chance at *that*, far be it from me to ruin it for you."

Earl spoke in his usual breathless rush, long fingers toying with the iron gray hair that still hung thick and straight to his shoulders. He wore a charcoal gray suit paired with a pale pink shirt and a blinding fuchsia tie. A pink carnation was pinned to his suit jacket. *Looks like a gay gangster,* Keegan thought affectionately. Earl might live up to his last name a bit too well, but he'd taken Keegan in when he had nowhere else to go and Keegan loved him fiercely for it.

"What's his name?" Keegan asked. "Is it Scott Jasper? He's probably come to pay his tab from last night. He forgot before."

"Yes, that's his name," Earl confirmed, nodding. "And now that you mention it, I believe he said something about a tab."

"That was Scott's partner that I called an asshole," Keegan continued, guessing at who he was in trouble for insulting, "and he really is one. He was making out with Dave and Cameron, right in front of Scott. If he ever shows his face here again, I'll think of something worse to call him. I'm sure as hell not apologizing."

Earl tapped his nails against the desk, his features schooled into his best approximation of a stern face. Keegan

Ally Blue

wasn't fooled. He was a damn good bartender and an even better stripper, the customers loved him, and Earl knew it.

"It's a good thing for you that I love you like a son." Earl sighed and waved a languid hand in the general direction of the bar. "Go on, go talk to Studly."

"I'm going." Keegan started toward the door, then turned and frowned as something occurred to him. "Hey, Earl, how'd you know I called that guy an asshole anyway?"

"He called to complain earlier. Said he was withdrawing his application for membership because the help here is substandard." Earl rolled his eyes. "Good thing, too. It saved me the unpleasant task of turning him down and having to nod sympathetically through the resulting tantrum."

Keegan laughed. "Not that I'm complaining, but why were you gonna turn down his application? And for that matter, why'd he even apply without Scott?" Keegan's eyes went wide. "Or did Scott apply too?"

"Because his credit history is dismal, I haven't a clue and no." Earl grinned, eyes sparkling. "Not yet, anyway. I'm counting on your irresistible charm to lure him in."

"Earl, you've got to let go of these delusions about me," Keegan said, shaking his head. He leaned against the doorframe. "You know what, I wish now that I hadn't said those things to Logan. I wish I'd been nicer."

Earl clutched at his chest. "Is this true? Am I actually hearing Keegan Rourke express regret for one of his legendary tongue-lashings? Oh my God, the world must be ending."

Keegan nodded solemnly. "If I hadn't pissed him off, he wouldn't have withdrawn his application, and you'd have had to turn him down. You would've let me watch, right?"

"Darling, I could cheerfully strangle you some days, but then my life would be dreadfully dull." Earl made a shooing motion with his hands. "Now go away, I'm busy."

Laughing, Keegan shut the office door and strolled out to the bar. Charlie was tending, leaning across the bar on his forearms and talking with a couple of the regulars who'd stayed the night. Not many members came to the club before five or six o'clock, but there were generally a few who wandered out from their overnight rooms to the bar as soon as it opened.

Keegan stopped in the shadows for a moment, drinking in the sight of the man perched on the barstool. Scott looked even better than he had the night before. Low-slung black jeans clung to his slim hips and hugged the tight curves of his ass. The muscles of his arms and chest strained against his snug red T-shirt, big enough to make Keegan's heart thump without crossing the line into freakish. Keegan licked his lips.

As if sensing his scrutiny, Scott turned and pinned Keegan with an intense dark-eyed gaze. Keegan grinned and walked toward Scott, hoping the man couldn't see how flustered he felt.

"Hi Scott," he said, relieved when his voice came out nice and steady. "Earl said you wanted to see me?"

Scott smiled, that sweet lopsided smile that lit up the room. "Yeah, I did. I hope I'm not bothering you or anything."

"Not a bit." Keegan stepped closer and leaned an elbow on the bar. He was close enough to smell Scott's cologne, something soft and spicy that made him want to bury his face in the man's neck and just breathe him in. "What can I do for you?"

"I'm afraid I forgot to pay my tab last night. I came back to pay up." Scott let out a tense little laugh. "So, I guess I need to sign the credit card slip, huh?"

"Mm-hm," Keegan mumbled, not really paying as much attention as he should. Scott's voice, deep and rumbling yet almost touchably soft, was doing terrible things to his concentration. "I left it in the cash register."

Keegan scooted closer under the pretense of shifting his weight to his other foot, and was rewarded by a rosy blush rising in Scott's cheeks. "Okay," Scott said, a bit breathlessly. "Should you...um...go get it? The slip? For me to sign, I mean."

"In a sec." Keegan stuck his hands in his pockets, thinking Scott might not appreciate being felt up right then. "Look, I know it's none of my business, but I like you and I feel like I need to tell you the truth. Last night after you left, Logan—"

"Don't bother," Scott interrupted, his smile fading. "He didn't come home until two-thirty. I'm betting he didn't spend all that time at the church confessing his sins."

"I'm sorry, Scott," Keegan said softly.

Scott shrugged. "I shouldn't be surprised anymore, really."

"You mean he's done this before?" Keegan had no trouble believing that.

"He usually just flirts, but I've caught him kissing other guys a few times. This is the first time he's cheated on me with two at once, though." Scott grimaced. "Aw, hell. For all I know he does it all the time and I'm just too stupid to notice."

Keegan knew he probably shouldn't ask, but he couldn't help it. He had to know. "Why do you stay with him? What could he possibly have to offer that would make you willing to put up with all that shit? You could have anybody, you could—"

The look on Scott's face stopped him cold. A wild-eyed, hunted look. As if Keegan had hit upon a truth that Scott wished wasn't there. He stared up at Scott, trying to figure out what he'd said wrong.

"Scott?" he ventured. "I shouldn't have asked that, it's none of my business. My mouth just gets ahead of my brain sometimes. Sorry."

Scott's eyes wouldn't quite meet his. "Don't worry about it. So, um, the credit card slip?"

"Yeah."

Keegan turned and hurried behind the bar to the cash register. He felt Scott's gaze on him like a physical weight. His fingers trembled a little as he opened the cash drawer and pulled out the slip he'd saved in the event of Scott's return.

"Here," he said, sliding the paper and a pen across the bar.

Scott scribbled what Keegan assumed was his signature on the line and handed the slip back to Keegan. "There you go."

"Thanks."

Silence fell. Keegan pushed his lip ring back and forth with his tongue, a nervous habit he thought he'd broken years ago. Something about Scott put him off balance in a way he couldn't pin down. And damned if he didn't like it. A lot.

Okay, stop acting like a kid with a crush. Keegan put on his brightest smile. "Hey, how about a drink? On the house."

Scott chuckled, the sound rich and rolling, setting Keegan's skin tingling. "What the hell?" Scott said, breaking into a huge grin. "It's Saturday, I don't have to work or anything."

"Gin and tonic again?"

"Sure."

Keegan reached for the bottles and a glass and started pouring. "You could hang out here this afternoon, if you want," he suggested, watching Scott's face. "We're allowed to bring guests in, you can be mine."

Scott raised an eyebrow at him. Keegan's cheeks heated as he realized the implications of what he'd just said. "Oh shit, sorry, I didn't mean—"

"I know what you meant." Scott's dark eyes shone with amusement and something else, something that made Keegan's cock twitch. "I'd love to stay as your guest." His face clouded. "Logan probably won't even notice I'm gone."

"Asshole," Keegan growled before he could stop himself. He met Scott's surprised look with a defiant lift of his chin. "I'm sorry, Scott, but he is. You deserve better."

Scott simply stood there, staring at him hard enough to drill holes. Keegan was starting to get that hollow, oh-no-I-fucked-up feeling when Scott suddenly reached across the bar and took Keegan's hand.

"Thank you," Scott said, very softly.

Keegan swallowed. "What for?"

"For thinking I deserve better, even if I don't." Scott pressed Keegan's fingers, then pulled away, that adorable lopsided smile curving his mouth. "I needed that today."

Keegan beamed, knowing he looked too eager and not caring. "Stay for my show, yeah?"

"Wouldn't miss it."

Scott's tone was light, his smile unrevealing, but his eyes burned. Desire curled in Keegan's belly. He gazed into Scott's eyes and thought he could happily drown in them. The feeling scared him, on multiple levels. Attraction, sex, he could handle. But his gut told him that if he ever got Scott into his bed, he'd never want to let him go. And that was something he'd never felt before. Something he'd actively avoided, for lots of reasons.

Just stop it. It doesn't have to be that way. Doesn't even have to be sex. He's got a partner, and Scott's not a cheating jackass even if Logan is. Besides, what makes you think he's even interested in you like that?

Keegan tried not to notice how obvious the answer to that last question was. The smoldering light in Scott's eyes couldn't be mistaken for anything but lust, and Keegan knew it.

He shook off the uneasy knowledge and started pouring drinks for the men who had drifted up to the bar from the corners of the room, talking with Scott in between customers. Eventually the turmoil inside him died down, but it didn't go away entirely. He had a feeling it wouldn't as long as the question of what could happen between him and Scott remained unanswered.

The problem was, he wasn't at all sure that he wanted to know what might happen if he followed his heart all the way to Scott's bed.

Chapter Three

The Saturday night before Valentine's Day, Scott walked up to the front door of Ganymede's Grotto with a brand-new membership card in his hand. "Hi Patrick," he said, grinning at the tall, gangly young man at the window. "How are you?"

"Gettin' by," Patrick drawled in his honey-thick accent. He nodded toward the card in Scott's hand. "Finally joined up, huh?"

Scott laughed. "I figured I might as well, since I'm here nearly every day anyhow. It wouldn't be fair for me to keep taking advantage of Keegan like that, coming in as his guest all the time."

After that first afternoon and evening as Keegan's guest at Ganymede's Grotto, Scott had begun to spend more and more time there. Stopping in for a couple of hours after work had become a habit. He knew all the staff now and had been more or less adopted by Earl, who fussed over him more than his own parents ever had.

At first Scott had tried to pretend that he kept going there to get away from Logan's increasingly erratic behavior. But he couldn't lie to himself for long. Ganymede's Grotto was a nice club, clean and friendly with a laid-back, no-pressure atmosphere, but it wasn't a place where he would have normally spent so much time. He went there to see Keegan, and everyone knew it.

Scott continued to stubbornly insist he felt nothing but friendship for Keegan. Even he was having trouble believing it anymore.

"It made Earl pretty happy that you joined, I bet," Patrick observed, taking Scott's card to scan it. "He's been dying to sign you up ever since day one."

Scott raised his eyebrows. "Really? Why? Is it my incredible good looks, or my enormous bank account?"

"Smart-ass." Patrick handed Scott's card back. "Keegan likes you, and Earl spoils that boy rotten."

"Keegan's almost thirty," Scott said, putting his card back in his wallet. "Hardly a boy, and definitely older than you."

"Maybe, but he looks way younger." Patrick grinned at him. "Speaking of Keegan, he says come back to the dressing room, he wants your opinion on what costume to wear for his show tonight."

Scott's heart tried to jump right up his throat. He swallowed it back down. "Oh. Okay. So he's, um, he's not being Eros tonight?"

"You know he changes his act around now and then, just to keep things interesting. You've seen some of his other acts." Patrick chuckled. "Man, when are you gonna make a move already? You know he'd be putty in your hands, right?"

The blood rose in Scott's cheeks, because he *did* know it. "Come on, Patrick, don't."

"Yeah, I know. Logan." Patrick shook his head. "I'm not sayin' a word, man. Have a nice night."

"You too. See you." Scott pushed the door open and escaped into the welcoming dimness of the club.

Making his way through the already crowded bar to the tiny dressing room behind the stage, Scott smiled and spoke to the staff and a few of the members he'd gotten to know. He thought, not for the first time, that he should thank Logan for bringing him here that night. He felt comfortable and accepted here, even though he never did anything but sit at the bar and talk to Keegan. *And watch him strip,* Scott reminded himself.

The thought was enough to tighten Scott's balls. He bit his lip and forced his mind away from the memories of Keegan looking like a debauched angel in that obscene G-string and those huge white wings.

When he reached the dressing room, Scott tapped on the door. "Keegan? It's me, Patrick said you wanted to see me."

"Yeah, c'mon in," Keegan called, his voice muffled.

Scott eased the door open, slipped through and closed it again before looking at Keegan. When he did, he burst out laughing. "What the hell are you doing?"

Keegan's blue eye glared at him over a strip of black lace. "Shut up and help me, I'm stuck."

Still snickering, Scott strolled over and walked in a circle around Keegan, trying to make sense of the tangle he'd made. "What is this, a dress?"

"Yes." Keegan wriggled in a way that had Scott adjusting his crotch, and managed to get an arm through one sleeve. "It's not a tear-away, and it's really fucking tight. Could you just straighten it out in back there? Then maybe I can get it all the way on."

Scott obediently tugged on the tangle of black fabric wound around Keegan's back. Heat flared in his belly when his hands brushed Keegan's skin. He longed to slide his arms around

Keegan's slender waist and pull him close, bend and kiss the curve of his pale shoulder. He satisfied his urge to touch by tracing his fingertips over the naked, pale blue pixie tattooed on Keegan's back.

Keegan laughed and turned around, slipping his other arm into the sleeve and yanking the dress down. "You feeling up Blue Boy's cock again?"

"No," Scott said, truthfully for once. He'd been fascinated with the tattooed pixie's frighteningly large erection ever since he'd first gotten a good look at it. "I was feeling up his fangs this time."

"Yeah, well, that's another erogenous zone for him, I hope you know." Keegan faced the mirror, eyeing his reflection critically. "So what do you think? Should I put on make-up and be the Goth-Chick-With-A-Dick, or be lazy and drag out the devil costume?"

Scott considered. "I kind of like what you've got on. But how do you get it off again if you had this much trouble getting into it?"

Keegan grinned. "Tear it off."

"Oh." Scott groped behind him for the chair he knew was there and hung on for dear life. "Yeah, do that."

"Hot idea, huh?" Keegan rotated his hips in a slow, teasing motion, tongue flicking at his lip ring. "I can only rip the dress in half once, but it was only two bucks at the thrift store, so it's no big deal."

The mental image of that tight little black lace mini-dress ripping away to reveal Keegan's sleekly muscled body did not a damn thing to reduce Scott's arousal. Before he could think of what he was doing, Scott stroked a hand down Keegan's lace-clad chest.

Keegan went still, wide eyes locked onto Scott's face. "Scott? What are you doing?"

Scott blinked, shook himself and pulled his hand back. "I...I'm sorry. I don't know what's wrong with me."

Keegan smiled. "Hey, you know I wouldn't turn you down. You're the one with a boyfriend."

The mention of Logan dragged at Scott's spirits like an anchor. "Yeah, I know."

Keegan tilted his head and stared hard at Scott. "Did something happen? With Logan, I mean."

"It's nothing."

Scott heard the stubborn edge in his voice, but he couldn't help it. He didn't want to think of how Logan had blatantly propositioned the check-out boy at the grocery store that afternoon. Or how he'd turned nasty when they'd gotten home, calling Scott a spineless eunuch and worse when Scott didn't react with the anger he'd clearly expected.

Keegan crossed his arms. "You're not fooling me, Scott. Spill it."

Scott sighed. Keegan could read him with terrifying accuracy. "We had a fight. Or rather we didn't, which I think was the problem."

"I'm not following you," Keegan said, frowning.

Scott looked at his feet. "He came on to some kid this afternoon while we were out shopping. But he does it so often I just ignore it lately, so that's what I did. I just pretended it wasn't happening. And that pissed him off. He jumped all over me when we got home. Basically told me I was a pussy."

"For not calling him on what he did?"

"Yeah." Scott raised his head to meet Keegan's unusually thoughtful gaze, and decided to take the plunge. Lord knew

Keegan was the closest friend he had. "He's doing it on purpose. I don't know why, or if he even realizes it, but that's what's happening. He keeps coming on to other men just to make me mad."

Oddly enough, Keegan didn't seem surprised. "That explains something I've been wondering about."

Scott frowned. "What do you mean?"

Keegan pinned Scott with a penetrating stare. "I don't know if he told you this, but the first night you guys came here? I told him off for how he acted."

"No, he never mentioned it," Scott murmured, unsurprised.

"Figures," Keegan said, rolling his eyes. "Anyhow, I told him that I'd come on to you and you turned me down."

Scott blinked. "You did?"

"Yeah. Listen." Keegan leaned forward, red-gold curls cascading over his shoulder. "He told me that I should take a good look at his back in the morning and then see if I still wanted you."

"Oh shit." Scott groped for the chair again, swung it around and sat down heavily as the epiphany hit him like a brick. "I only ever did it when I was angry. So that's why..." He closed his eyes. "Fuck."

"I figured he must like getting some of the rough stuff, but the whole thing just felt wrong, you know? He talked like someone who was being abused, but I could tell he wanted it. And I knew you weren't the abusive type anyway."

Scott opened his eyes and stared up at Keegan, who was tonguing his lip ring like he always did when he was thinking. "How could you have known that, Keegan? Hell, how do you know that now? Maybe I'm exactly the monster he wanted you to think I was."

I sure as fuck feel like one. It didn't matter that Logan had some twisted need for pain inflicted in anger. It didn't even matter that Scott had always known Logan enjoyed it more than he did. The fact remained that Scott had done those things, and he'd gotten off on them. Worse, it had never even occurred to him that Logan might need help. And he clearly did, if he felt the need to hurt and manipulate his lover in order to get what he wanted.

The feel of fingertips on his cheek brought Scott out of his thoughts. Keegan stood between his knees, close enough that a breath could push them together, stroking Scott's jaw. His eyes brimmed with painful memories, underscored by a longing Scott could feel in his bones. He realized with a shock that it was the first time he'd seen past the lighthearted, teasing wall Keegan kept between himself and the world.

"You're no monster, Scott," Keegan said, so softly Scott barely heard him. "Believe me, I've known my share and you're nothing like that. Nothing at all." Keegan's callused fingertips traced the outline of Scott's mouth, making his pulse race. "You're kind. And compassionate. And gentle. You'd never hurt m...anyone, I mean, you never would've gotten rough with Logan if he didn't want you to, but you knew he liked it, even if you didn't know he was manipulating you into doing it."

It was a quick save, and Keegan's subsequent babbling almost distracted him from the slip. But not quite. He'd heard what Keegan almost said, seen the man's eyes widen just slightly. He reached up and buried his hands in Keegan's shining curls like he'd been dying to do since the moment they met.

"You're right," Scott heard himself say, as if from a distance. "I'd never hurt you. Keegan..."

He didn't have to say anything else. Keegan bent down, cradling Scott's face between his palms, and pressed his mouth to Scott's.

Everything went still and silent for a heartbeat. Then Keegan's lips parted, his tongue traced Scott's lower lip in a feathery touch, and Scott's world turned inside-out. He tilted his head and opened to Keegan, kissing him with a hunger he hadn't felt in years.

Keegan let out a sound that was almost a sob. He straddled Scott's lap, skirt hitching up as his thighs spread. His erection dug into Scott's belly, barely contained by the black satin G-string he wore under the dress. Scott moaned and thrust up, rubbing his own achingly hard cock against Keegan's ass. The functioning part of his brain wished mightily that his jeans weren't in the way.

"Oh God," Keegan breathed against Scott's mouth. "God, I want you so bad."

Scott pulled back enough to see Keegan's face. Those strange, beautiful eyes were heavy-lidded and hot with need. "I've wanted you since the second I first saw you," Scott whispered.

Keegan smiled fiercely and took Scott's mouth in another deep kiss. His hair fell around them like a golden curtain, tickling Scott's neck and tangling into their joined mouths. Scott slid his hands down Keegan's body, caressing the smooth pale skin of his hips and thighs, the firm swell of his buttocks. Whimpering, Keegan pushed his groin against Scott's belly.

"Oh, ooo, whoopsie!"

They broke apart, Keegan scrambling off Scott's lap and tugging his dress back down as Scott sat staring at the young man who'd just barged in. It was one of the other strippers. Scott hadn't even heard the door open.

"Tommy," Keegan growled, "how many times do I have to tell you to knock?"

Tommy pouted, pale green eyes flashing. "It's my dressing room too. What do you want me to do, change in the hall? I'm on in twenty minutes."

Keegan sighed, one hand raking through his hair. "Yeah, okay. We're clearing out."

"Don't hurry on my account." Tommy grinned. "I don't mind watching."

"No way, Tommy." Keegan took Scott's hand and pulled him to his feet. "C'mon, we can talk in Earl's office. He'll be out mingling by now."

Scott followed on Keegan's heels. Keegan dragged him down the hall with long, determined strides, ignoring the stares from the other staff members. Inside Earl's office, Keegan locked the door and shoved Scott against it. Smiling, he rubbed his crotch against Scott's thigh.

"Now," Keegan said, leaning close to nuzzle Scott's neck. "Where were we?"

Scott's mind shrieked at him to stop, even as he yanked Keegan to him for a passionate kiss. *You're no better than Logan, doing this.* Growling, he grabbed Keegan's ass in both hands and squeezed, drowning what was left of his good sense in a wash of desire.

It was Keegan who finally broke the kiss. He pushed away and took a step back, breathing hard. "Wait, Scott, stop. We can't."

Scott wanted to argue. Keegan looked gorgeous standing there in that tiny black dress, hair wildly mussed and lips swollen from kissing. Scott wanted to take him, right there on the floor of Earl's artfully decorated office. But he knew Keegan was right. Leaning against the door, he shoved his hands in his pockets, not trusting himself to keep from touching Keegan the way he wanted to.

"You're right," Scott said, his voice rough with the lust still thumping through him. "Christ, what are we thinking?"

"I don't regret it. But if we take this any further, you will." Keegan gazed up at Scott with a serious expression. "You're a good person, Scott. I know you want me, but you're not the type of guy who screws around. You'd never forgive yourself if you cheated on Logan like he does to you."

"I know." Scott bit his lip, fighting the urge to touch Keegan again. "Sorry."

"Don't be." The corner of Keegan's mouth turned up in a bitter half-smile. "If all I can have from you is friendship, I sure as hell don't want to fuck it up."

"Nothing's fucking that up," Scott promised.

"Good."

Gazing into Keegan's eyes, Scott saw the walls go back up, and in that moment he made up his mind. "I'm going to break it off with Logan. It's the best thing to do, for both of us."

"For all three of us." Keegan smiled. "Let me know when you're unattached. I'd sure love to pick up where we left off."

"Me too." Scott grinned, seeing the light at the end of the tunnel for the first time in ages. "I need to do this right now, tonight. You don't mind if I miss your show, do you?"

"For a cause this good? I'll deal." Keegan flicked at his lip ring with his tongue. "Hell, maybe it's a good thing you won't be here. I'd be hard as a fucking rock if I knew you were watching me tonight."

Scott bit back a groan. "God, Keegan."

Laughing, Keegan pulled Scott to him. Scott's arms went around him like they were meant to be there. They kissed, the contact light and quick.

"Hurry," Keegan whispered.

"Yeah." Scott brushed a soft kiss across Keegan's temple and forced himself to let go. "It may not be tonight. I won't leave him alone if I don't think it's safe."

Keegan nodded. "Do what you need to. Just don't let him talk you into anything you don't want, yeah?"

"I won't." Scott stroked Keegan's hair, letting the silky strands curl around his fingers. "I'll be back."

"Just like the Terminator." Keegan grinned. "You know where to find me."

Scott returned the smile, turned and slipped out the door before he lost control of his rising desire. He didn't want to make love to Keegan until he was free to do it without guilt.

He got lots of surprised looks as he left the club. No one was used to seeing him leave so early; he always stayed for Keegan's show. He couldn't suppress a wide smile as he walked into the frigid night air. In a little while, he'd be a free man. Free of Logan's lies, free of a relationship that had dragged at him like a stone for far too long.

Part of him felt bad for having found someone else while he was still with Logan. But, he reasoned, he hadn't set out to do any such thing. It had crept up on him before he realized what was happening. The attraction between himself and Keegan had always been there, simmering under the surface, but they'd never spoken of it, never acknowledged it. Scott desperately needed the unexpected friendship he'd found with Keegan, and he didn't want to lose that. Discussion wasn't required for him to know that Keegan felt the same.

The drive back to the apartment he and Logan shared took longer than the usual ten minutes, due to the heavy Saturday night traffic. Scott parked the car in the lot out front and sat there for a minute, gathering his courage. Now that he'd made up his mind, he was absolutely certain about his decision, but that didn't make it any easier to do. Logan, he figured, was not going to take it well.

The thought of Keegan finally galvanized him into action. He locked the car and bounded up the stairs to their second-floor apartment, keeping the image of Keegan's sunny smile in the forefront of his mind.

He heard the noises as soon as he opened the door, but didn't immediately recognize them for what they were. He set his keys on the counter and started toward the bedroom, frowning at the muffled sounds coming from behind the closed door.

"Logan?" he called. "Are you okay? I heard—"

Scott opened the bedroom door just in time to see a man he didn't know pull the sheet hastily around himself. The man's eyes were so wide the whites showed all around. Sweat ran in rivers from his nude body and dripped from his hair. Logan lay on his back, both hands bound to the headboard, the strange man kneeling between his wide-flung legs. Scott's stomach lurched when he saw the bloody welts crisscrossing Logan's groin, belly and thighs. Logan's lover held a wicked-looking riding crop clutched tight in one fist.

"Wh-who are you?" the man demanded, his voice quivering. "You can't just—"

"It's my boyfriend, Darryl," Logan said, sounding tired and irritated. His eyes flashed. "What the fuck are you doing here, Scott? I figured you'd be at that damn club, jerking off while that pretty boy strips for you."

Darryl turned to gape at Logan. "Hey, you didn't tell me—"

"Darryl, was it?" Scott interrupted, never taking his eyes from Logan's angry face. "Untie Logan, then get out. I have something I need to say and I'm not doing it like this." He glanced at Darryl. "You can call him later."

Darryl gave Scott a cautious look. He was clearly curious about why Scott wasn't angry with him, but he didn't say anything. Leaning over, he whispered something that Scott couldn't quite hear, and Logan's lips curved into the ghost of a smile as Darryl started to untie him. Something about that interaction made Scott feel better about the whole sordid mess. In spite of everything that had happened, he wanted Logan to be happy. If Logan could find what he needed in a healthier way with Darryl, so much the better.

Logan didn't look at Scott until Darryl had dressed and left. He sat up, pulled his knees to his chest and wrapped his arms around them, fixing Scott with a sullen stare. "Well?" he snapped. "What did you want?"

Scott sat next to the man he'd lived with for over six years, not knowing quite how to start now that it came to it. He decided on the direct approach. Logan might not like it, but it would be easier in the end.

"This isn't working anymore, Logan," he said. "I think it's time we called it quits."

Logan laughed, the sound harsh and bitter. "Oh, you think? What was your first clue, Sherlock?"

Scott ignored the dig, determined to stay calm. "Keep the apartment. I can stay in a hotel or something until I find someplace else."

"What, you can't stay with your stripper boyfriend?" Logan sneered.

Pinching the bridge of his nose, Scott silently counted to ten. "I'm not going to pretend I don't want him, not at this point. But I've never cheated on you before, and I'm not cheating on you now. Keegan and I haven't slept together."

"Yet," Logan spat. "That's why you came running back here tonight to break up with me, isn't it? So you can fuck that little slut without sullying your almighty virtue."

Scott felt the blood rising in his cheeks, along with a dangerous fury. The fact that Logan had it almost exactly right just made it worse.

"Don't sit there and act like you've done nothing wrong," Scott shot back. "Not when I just caught you in bed with another man. Christ, Logan, you're fucking *bleeding*! What the fuck is *wrong* with you?"

Logan's tongue crept out to probe the corner of his mouth. His eyes grew heavy with an expression Scott didn't want to see. "You could finish what he started." Logan leaned back, spreading his legs again. "You want to, don't you?"

Scott looked away. He really didn't want to see the blood oozing from Logan's torn skin. "That's not gonna work, Logan. You can't make me do those things to you anymore."

Logan's face flushed dark red. "Damn you, I know you want to. Just fucking do it."

"No." Scott leapt to his feet. "I don't like myself when I'm like that, and I'm not doing it anymore."

Logan moved so fast Scott didn't even have time to react. Before Scott knew what was happening, Logan was up and pushing him against the wall.

"I need it, you fucker!" Logan screamed, his shaking hand fisted in Scott's shirt. "I fucking need it! Fucking hit me already!"

Scott grabbed both of Logan's wrists, stopping the blow he figured was coming. He'd seen Logan fight. He didn't want to be on the receiving end of the man's surprisingly powerful punches.

"You need help, Logan," Scott said as calmly as he could. "If pain is what you want, there's better ways to get that. What we've been doing isn't healthy, and I won't be a part of it anymore."

For a second, Logan looked as if he couldn't decide whether to yell or cry. He snatched his hands away and turned his back on Scott. "Fine. Go on, then. Go fuck your stripper."

Scott stared at Logan's unmarked back, remembering all the times he'd left that same stretch of skin red and bruised. "Will you be all right?"

"Why would you care?"

"We were together for seven years. Of course I care."

Logan sat on the bed again and pulled his knees up under his chin. He kept his face twisted away from Scott. "I'll be fine. Just go."

Not knowing what else to do, Scott went to the closet and took out a duffle bag. He gathered some clothes and toiletries, watching Logan out of the corner of his eye all the while. Logan never moved, never once looked at Scott, and he remained silent.

When he had enough things together to last a few days, Scott stood in front of Logan, staring at his mop of tousled blond hair. He cleared his throat. "Well. I guess that's it then."

Logan nodded, but said nothing. Letting out a huff of irritation, Scott squatted in front of his former lover and laid a hand on his bare knee. "This is best for both of us," he said softly. "Call Darryl, if you want. Maybe he can give you what I couldn't."

Still no response. Scott sighed, rose to his feet and kissed the top of Logan's head. "I'll come back later for the rest of my stuff."

Turning away from Logan's huddled form, Scott walked toward the door. His hand was on the doorknob when Logan spoke.

"Scott?"

Scott stopped, shoulders tense. "Yes?"

"I'm sorry it ended like this."

The unfamiliar note of regret in Logan's voice made Scott turn around again. Logan was looking at him now, hazel eyes full of mingled sadness and relief, and Scott's worry eased a little. "So am I," Scott said. "Be happy, okay?"

The corner of Logan's mouth twitched in what might almost have been a smile. "You too."

Scott left the apartment with his bag slung over his shoulder and a chaotic whirl of emotions churning in his guts. He felt light and heavy at the same time. After so many years together, severing the ties with Logan felt like surgery to remove a diseased organ. A part of him was lost forever, but it had to be done before their dying relationship poisoned them both beyond repair.

Back in his car, driving to Ganymede's Grotto and Keegan, Scott reflected on his years with Logan. He hadn't seen it in the giddy high of falling in love all those years ago, but lately he'd come to realize that he and Logan had always been missing something vitally important.

Tenderness. Honesty. Trust. The building blocks of a solid, lasting, loving relationship. They'd never had that. Not even close.

Sometimes Scott wondered if he'd ever find that kind of love. Other times he wondered if it was right there in front of him, in a pair of laughing odd-colored eyes and a smile that made him feel ten feet tall.

"Scott," he said out loud, "I think it's time you found out."

Grinning, he drove on through the bustling winter night.

Chapter Four

Keegan took the stage that night with a rare gusto. He loved performing and it showed, but the possibility of being with Scott put an extra oomph in his movements. The crowd loved it. Keegan smiled and flirted, lapping up the whistles and applause like nectar.

Just as he wormed his fingers into the holes he'd cut in the lace dress and ripped it open, Keegan spotted Scott in the audience. Pleasantly surprised to see him back so soon, Keegan grinned and gave him a tiny nod. Scott smiled back.

Keegan couldn't see Scott's eyes past the glare of the spotlight, but he could feel the heat of the man's gaze. He let himself respond to it, running both hands suggestively up the insides of his thighs and over his groin. The black satin of his G-string did nothing to hide his excitement. Falling to his knees, he tugged at a nipple ring with one hand and cupped his balls in the other, hips rolling in a slow, sensuous motion, his head lolling back as the appreciative whoops of the audience washed over him. He loved it, loved feeling this beautiful and sexy and wanted.

The rest of his show was a blur. He let his desire take him over, moving his body in ways that whipped the crowd into a frenzy. He could smell the lust rolling off the panting men like an exotic perfume. By the time the music stopped and he took his bows to thunderous applause, his cock was fully erect and leaking a damp spot on the satin. He left the stage with a wave, intent on finding Scott as soon as possible.

He didn't have to wait long. Scott came barreling down the hallway before he'd gotten halfway to the dressing room. Those dark eyes burned with a need Keegan understood perfectly. He felt a wide, eager smile spread across his face and didn't even want to stop it.

"Hi Scott," he said. "Wow, I didn't expect you back so— mmph..."

His words were abruptly cut off by Scott's mouth on his. The kiss was hard and aggressive and exactly what Keegan wanted right then. He melted into it, running his hands over Scott's muscular shoulders.

"Where?" Scott growled between kisses. "I need you right fucking *now.*"

"Uh..." Keegan tried to think, but Scott's hands on his skin threatened to drown him in an ocean of pure sensation. "Dressing room," he gasped.

Lifting Keegan right off his feet, Scott moved toward the dressing room, which was thankfully nearby. Keegan wrapped both legs around Scott's waist, rubbing himself shamelessly against Scott's hard, flat belly. Scott flung the door open, shuffled inside and kicked it closed again, and they were alone at last. Alone and hard and wanting and finally free to act on it.

"Did you?" Keegan mumbled without taking his mouth from Scott's. "Can we?"

"Yes, and yes." Scott bit Keegan's bottom lip, tugging the silver ring between his teeth. His thumbs plucked at Keegan's G-string. "Off. Now."

Keegan laughed breathlessly. "Let me down."

Scott pulled back enough to look him in the eye. "Hang on."

Keegan didn't have time to wonder what Scott meant. Scott's hands left his hips altogether, and he clamped his legs harder around Scott's waist to keep from falling. He was about to ask Scott what he was doing, when Scott's fingers curled under the thin elastic strips at the edges of Keegan's thong and gave a sharp pull. The elastic tore loose. The satin triangle stayed, held between their pressed-together bodies.

Scott reached back and tugged the bit of fabric gently away, leaving Keegan clinging to him stark naked. One big hand wriggled between them while the other arm clutched Keegan's hips, holding him up. Keeping an arm around Scott's neck, Keegan slipped his free hand down to help undo Scott's pants. After a moment's fumbling, they got the button and zipper open. Keegan grasped Scott's thick shaft, feeling like he'd won the lottery. Scott moaned and thrust against him.

Keegan wished they could make it to the sofa in the corner, or at least the chair. But he didn't think he could stand to let go, and was pretty sure Scott wouldn't want to either. So they stayed there, Scott braced against the wall with Keegan clinging to him, humping each other like a couple of teenagers. Keegan would've laughed if he hadn't been busy kissing Scott like his life depended on it.

It didn't take long before Keegan felt the orgasm building in his belly. "Uh...S-Scott...gonna come."

"'S okay," Scott panted. "Come on."

Scott pressed a finger against Keegan's hole, probing gently, and that did it. Keegan shot so hard his vision sparkled. His hand spasmed around Scott's cock and Scott came with a hoarse cry.

"Holy fuck." Scott slid down the wall, landing sprawled on the floor with Keegan plastered against him. "I haven't shot so fast since high school."

"Yeah, me too." Keegan laid his cheek against Scott's chest.

"Sorry it was so quick," Scott said, stroking Keegan's hair. "And so upright."

Laughing, Keegan wiped his sticky hand on Scott's jeans. "We can have a real fuck later. For now? I think we both needed it like this."

Scott's chuckle rumbled against Keegan's ear. "You have no idea what you were doing to me, up there on stage. Dancing like that. Flaunting that hard-on."

"Your fault." Keegan snuggled closer and kissed Scott's throat. "I saw you in the audience, looking at me like you wanted to fuck me right there in front of everybody."

"That turned you on, huh?"

"Like you would not believe."

Scott lifted Keegan's face and smiled at him, brown eyes shining. "You were gorgeous tonight, Keegan."

"Just tonight?" Keegan smiled back, hoping his casual tone would hide the crazy thumping of his heart.

"No." Scott laughed. "You're gorgeous all the time, of course. It's just tonight was special. Because I knew what was going to happen."

Keegan kissed Scott's chin, dragging his lip ring across the stubble there. "You knew we were gonna come in here and rub off like a couple of kids?"

"Yeah. I'm psychic, didn't I tell you?"

"Guess you forgot to mention it." Keegan laid a hand on Scott's cheek, thumb caressing the corner of his mouth. "I thought the same thing. I knew we were going to be together, and that made everything different. Made it all better."

"Exactly."

Staring into Scott's eyes, Keegan felt an unwelcome stirring inside. He'd felt like that only once before, and it hadn't ended well. Mild panic clenched in his belly.

Scott's brows drew together. "Keegan? What's wrong?"

Shaking off the feeling, Keegan smiled. "Not a thing. Hey, what about we take this up to my apartment, huh?"

"You don't have to work?"

"Naw, I'm off bar duty tonight." Keegan leaned forward and sucked softly on Scott's upper lip. "Let's go, Scott. I need you to fuck me."

Scott's breathy moan was answer enough. Keegan got up, swaying a little, and went to find his clothes. He felt Scott watching him as he pulled on jeans, sneakers and a sweater.

"Where do you live?" Scott asked, scrubbing at the semen stains on his jeans with a towel. "Please tell me we don't have to go through the club when I've got come all over me."

"We don't." Keegan finished tying his left sneaker and snatched his keys out of the dressing table drawer. "My place is above the club. We can go out the employee entrance in back."

"Oh good." Scott stared at him for a moment, his eyes full of a strange tenderness underneath the lust. He crossed the room in a couple of strides, cupped Keegan's face in his hands and kissed him.

Keegan's arms went around Scott's waist, his body molding to Scott's as the kiss deepened. They fit together perfectly, like it was meant to be. Like they belonged in each other's arms. The fluttery feeling returned, swooping like a great bird in Keegan's chest. Scott's touch held the same gentle yet passionate possessiveness as his eyes, and it was delicious and terrifying.

It's just because he wants me. We've both wanted to hook up for ages, and now it's gonna happen. It's anticipation, that's all. That's why he looks at me that way. That's why he touches me like he does.

By the time Scott broke the kiss, Keegan had managed to half-convince himself. He ignored the little voice whispering the truth seductively in his ear. That their feelings for each other ran deeper than lust, that it didn't have to end the way it had the last time. That it could be wonderful between them. That maybe, just maybe, it could be permanent.

He didn't want to hear it. The one and only time he'd seen someone look at him the way Scott did now—the only time he'd felt the things he felt now—it had ended in the worst pain he'd ever endured. He was determined to never put himself through that kind of hell again.

"Take me to your place," Scott whispered, fingers raking through Keegan's tangles.

Keegan plastered a teasing smile on his face and kissed Scott again. "Come on."

He took Scott's hand and led him down the hallway to the alley door opening off the storage rooms behind the kitchen. Lights bathed the back door and the stairs to Keegan's apartment in a harsh white glow. They climbed the stairs in silence. Keegan's hand trembled as he turned the key in the lock and swung the door open. He frowned, hating that Scott could affect him that way just by his presence.

It's just sex. That's all. He doesn't want anything more than that. And neither do you.

He wished he could believe that.

"Well, here it is." Keegan flipped on the light. "Home sweet home."

"Nice," Scott said without looking. "Where's the bed?"

Keegan licked his lips as Scott stalked toward him. "Over there. In the corner."

Scott nodded, grabbed Keegan's hand and pulled him toward the bed. Sitting on the edge of the mattress, Scott leaned back on his hands. "Strip for me."

Keegan laughed. "What, you don't see me strip enough already?"

"That's for the crowd." Scott grinned. "I want my own private show."

"Okay." Keegan returned Scott's smile. "Turn on the CD player there, it's next to the bed."

Scott twisted around and hit the play button. A primitive instrumental heavy on bass and drums thumped through the air. Keegan began to move, letting the sensuality of the music guide him. He managed to toe his sneakers off without breaking his rhythm, which was an achievement. Taking off jeans, shoes and a sweater just didn't have the same innate sexiness as stripping off a costume.

Scott didn't mind, if the inferno in his eyes was anything to go by. He let out a soft, needy sound when Keegan's sweater came off, the heavy knit catching on the nipple rings. When Keegan wriggled out of his jeans, exposing his leaking erection, Scott groaned and pressed a palm to his crotch.

"Do you like this, Scott?" Keegan asked, lowering his voice to a husky near-whisper. "Do you like how hard I am for you?"

"God, yes," Scott breathed, eyes glued to Keegan's rigid prick. "I like making you hard."

Keegan slinked naked over to Scott, stroking his shaft with one hand. "Good, because you make me hard all the time. I get it up just talking to you." Keegan stroked faster, pressing his thumb firmly into his slit. "Sometimes I have to go to the bathroom and jerk off during work so I won't come in my pants, because I've been thinking of you or talking to you and it makes me so fucking horny I can't control myself."

Scott's throat worked, as if he was trying to speak and couldn't. "Keegan...I...fuck..."

Keegan was unprepared for Scott's sudden grab. He let out a little yip of surprise when Scott's hands clamped onto his hips and pulled him close. Not that he was complaining. Especially when Scott bent and swallowed his cock to the root.

"Ooooh, oh fuck," Keegan whispered, hands fisting in Scott's hair. He fought to stay upright as Scott's strong, sure suction threatened to vacuum his brains out through his cock. Scott was very, very good, deep-throating him with ease and tongue fucking the slit on every backstroke. Keegan bit his lip and hung on, trying to keep from going off as quickly as he had in the dressing room.

It wasn't easy. Keegan was no blushing virgin; he'd had more sexual partners than he could easily remember. But he'd never had anyone suck him quite like this. It wasn't just Scott's obvious skill that made it so amazing. It was, Keegan mused with the few brain cells still working, Scott's attention to detail. He picked up on Keegan's every response, no matter how small, unerringly sorted out what Keegan liked the most, and used it to stunning effect.

When Keegan felt his orgasm start to ripple through him, he remembered he wasn't wearing a condom. "Coming," he gasped, tugging on Scott's hair. "Scott, c-coming, Scott..."

Scott pulled off him with an audible pop and began stroking his prick. "Come on me," he growled. "Come on my face."

"Oh shit," Keegan groaned, and did exactly that. Closing his eyes, Scott smiled as Keegan's semen spattered his cheeks and chin. Keegan thought it might be the sexiest thing he'd ever seen.

"Jesus, Scott," Keegan said, collapsing onto the bed beside Scott. "Horny bastard."

"Still horny." Scott fell onto his back, reached over and dragged Keegan on top of him. "Do you have condoms?"

"Yep." Keegan snatched a T-shirt from where it hung on the headboard and wiped the spunk off Scott's face. He moaned as Scott thrust up, driving his trapped erection against Keegan's still-sensitive cock. "Fuck. Gotta have you inside me."

"Soon as you're hard again," Scott promised, eyes twinkling.

Keegan let his head fall down onto Scott's chest. "That might take a few minutes. I just got done coming for the second time tonight."

"I can wait." Scott dug his fingers into Keegan's buttocks and spread him open, tearing a sharp cry from Keegan's throat. "But I can help you along. If you want."

"I want," Keegan said with some difficulty, pressing his rear against Scott's probing finger. "Oh my God, you're aggressive."

To Keegan's disappointment, Scott's finger stopped moving "Tell me if you want me to back off."

"No!" Keegan blushed at the desperation in his own voice. "I mean, I like you being aggressive. Taking me like this, you know? Taking what you want."

Scott went still, brown eyes penetrating Keegan every bit as much as the big fingers inside him. "I never want to take anything unless you want to give it. Nobody has a right to do that."

Keegan's chest went tight. Scott had just plunged directly to the heart of his fear and difficulty with intimacy in a way no other lover had ever done. Not even the one who'd sworn to love him forever and never hurt him, before cutting his heart out and stomping on it.

"I'll give you anything," Keegan whispered, hoping he would still mean it when he found out exactly how much Scott wanted. "Anything you need. Take it. Take me."

Scott's intense gaze made Keegan feel far more naked than his lack of clothes. "You tell me if I do anything you don't like, or if there's something you want me to do, okay?" Scott said, one hand petting his back while the other probed his hole. "Promise?"

Keegan swallowed. "Promise," he answered shakily. He let his eyes drift half-closed, a seductive smile curling his lips. "Make me hard, then fuck me."

Scott stared at him for a moment longer, as if sensing he was hiding something, then smiled. "Get on your knees and elbows. Let's see that pretty little ass."

Keegan scrambled to obey. With his chest flat on the mattress and his ass in the air, Keegan felt vulnerable and wanton. Scott's gaze burned into him, as physical as any touch. Turning his head to the side, he watched Scott undress. God, but the man had an amazing body, all sculpted muscle, not an ounce of fat on him. Keegan had a second to wonder vaguely what kind of workout routine Scott followed. Then Scott's hands pushed his thighs apart and all the blood in his brain headed south.

"Mmmm," Scott purred, circling Keegan's hole with a fingertip. "Bet you'd like my tongue in here."

Oh Christ, yes. Keegan couldn't make his mouth work. He moaned and wriggled his ass, hoping Scott would understand.

"Oh, yeah, you do, don't you?" Scott swiped his tongue the full length of Keegan's crease, making him whimper in a terribly undignified way. "Say it, Keegan. Tell me what you want."

Keegan took a couple of shallow breaths and tried to remember how to talk. "Lick me. Lick my asshole. God, please."

Scott laughed, the sound low and seductive, rubbing across Keegan's skin like fur. Keegan felt himself spread, then Scott's tongue flickered over his hole, the touch light and teasing and not enough.

"More," Keegan begged. "Fuck, do it."

Behind him, Scott let out a hoarse sound of pure lust that set a fire in Keegan's brain. Scott's tongue probed at him, harder this time, pressing right inside him. He moaned and arched his ass higher, thighs spreading, trying to get as much of that slick wet touch as he could.

"God, you taste good," Scott murmured, the words broken and muffled. "I could eat you...mm...forever." Another stab of Scott's tongue, urging his muscles to loosen. "Makes me hard."

Keegan grinned into the mattress. *Hallelujah,* his sex drive whooped, *a man who likes rimming!* Very few of his lovers had complained when he did it to them, but fewer still had ever been willing to return the favor. And none had gotten off on it like Scott apparently did. It was about time he found someone besides himself who loved the giving as much as the getting.

Scott's tongue abruptly withdrew. Keegan whimpered at the loss. Chuckling, Scott leaned over Keegan's back. "You're opening right up," Scott whispered, his lips brushing Keegan's ear as two of his fingers penetrated Keegan's ass. "So hot, how easily you open for me."

"Oh fuck," Keegan moaned, writhing helplessly at the sensation of Scott's cock sliding between his parted thighs, brushing his balls. "God, fuck me!"

Scott's hand slid down to grasp Keegan's rapidly swelling prick. "Where's your condoms? And lube?"

"Uh..." Keegan squeezed his eyes shut, frantically trying to remember where the necessary items were. "Condoms are...ummmm...in the drawer. There." He gestured toward the bedside table. "Lube is...shit, I just had it the other day, let's see..."

Scott's warmth went away as he reached for the drawer with the condoms in it. "Not fucking somebody else, I hope?"

The possessive note underlying Scott's teasing tone sent a quick thrill through Keegan's body. "No. Had to use my dildo the other night after work." *Right here, I was right here in the bed, I slicked Babe and shoved it in me, and I threw the lube...* "On the floor," he crowed, remembering how he'd tossed the lube unceremoniously aside so he could close his eyes and pretend the toy buried deep inside him was Scott. "Lube's on the floor."

Scott leaned over the side of the bed, laughing. "You mean this dildo?"

Keegan pushed up on one elbow to look. Scott lay on the edge of the mattress, grinning ear to ear, a half-empty tube of lubricant in one hand and an enormous bright blue dildo in the other.

"That's Babe," Keegan said, though talking was becoming more of an effort with every passing moment.

Scott's eyebrows went up. "Babe?"

"Yeah. Like the big blue ox." Losing patience, Keegan reached back and spread himself wide. "In me, now."

Scott rolled onto his back and waved the dildo around, that infuriating grin still in place. "What, me or Babe?"

Keegan glared at Scott. "You. Fucking tease."

Scott laughed. Keegan let out an honest-to-God whine. Any other time, he probably would've found Scott's playfulness endearing. Right then, however, his cock was painfully hard (again) and his anus pulsed with the need to be penetrated. He was in no mood to be teased.

"Scott!" he pleaded. "C'mon!"

Scott scooted closer, laid his head next to Keegan's and kissed his lips. "I'm not sure I can measure up to Babe."

Keegan arched an eyebrow. "Yeah you do. More than, actually."

"I want to fuck you, Keegan," Scott breathed, brushing a fingertip across Keegan's lip ring.

"Then stop teasing and do it." Keegan bit Scott's lip. "I want your cock in my ass, and I want it right. Fucking. *Now.*"

Smiling, Scott kissed him again and sat up. Keegan felt the mattress move, felt Scott's thighs pressing against his own. He could have cried with relief when he heard the unmistakable sound of a condom packet being torn open. *Finally.*

"Would you rather we did it like this, or you want to be on your back?" Scott asked, slick fingers sliding into Keegan's hole.

Keegan felt himself tense. He fought it, willing himself to stay relaxed. After all, Scott couldn't be expected to know how uncomfortable it made him to look into a lover's eyes while they fucked.

"Like this," he said. "I like it from behind."

"Anything you want." Scott's voice was soft and husky, full of a tenderness Keegan wasn't sure he was ready to hear.

Keegan was on the verge of demanding Scott take him hard and fast and rough. Anything to replace what he heard in Scott's voice with raw lust. Then Scott slammed into him, impaling him completely in one swift, hard stroke, and it was exactly what he needed. He wailed, fingers bunching the bedclothes, letting his mind float away on a tide of sensation.

Scott fucked him deep and slow, his movements smooth and controlled, big hands holding Keegan's hips in a firm but gentle grip. Keegan gladly surrendered himself to Scott, letting the sheer pleasure of being taken wash through him like a tide. No thought, no worry, no control. Only the blissful burn of a thick cock stretching his ass wide.

It seemed to go on for hours. Keegan figured he'd compliment Scott's stamina later, when his brain switched back on. At the moment, he could only voice his pleasure in jumbled and disjointed phrases, *yes, so good, don't stop, don't ever stop,* while Scott moaned and gasped and waxed rapturous about Keegan's tightness and heat. Keegan thought they probably sounded like a porno flick. He let out a breathless little giggle.

"Oh Christ," Scott groaned, his shaft swelling inside Keegan's ass. "God, I feel it, feel your insides move when you laugh. Fuck, it's good."

Keegan's sudden urge to see Scott's face at that moment was as overwhelming as it was surprising. He turned and looked over his shoulder. Scott's eyes met his, and it was almost too intense. He pushed up on his hands, following the instinct to get closer. Wrapping an arm around Keegan's middle, Scott pulled him up the rest of the way, and then they were pressed together, back to chest, and Scott's mouth took his and it was wonderful.

Scott gave a brutal thrust that nailed Keegan's gland and made him see stars. His body arched and shook as he came, his hole clenching in rhythmic waves around Scott's cock.

"Oh..." Scott whispered against Keegan's mouth, sounding almost startled. He went still, drew a sharp breath, and buried his face in Keegan's neck. Keegan felt the telltale pulsing of Scott's prick and had a flash of fierce triumph knowing that Scott had come because of him.

All the strength ran out of Keegan's body and he collapsed to the bed, taking Scott with him. They lay in a tangled, panting heap. Keegan felt limp as a rag, his hole throbbing around Scott's softening cock still buried inside him.

Scott rolled onto his side, spooning Keegan against him. "That," he sighed, "was goddamned amazing."

"Mmmm-hmmm," Keegan agreed, snuggling into Scott's arms. "I seriously needed a good fuck."

"Me too." Scott managed to withdraw from Keegan's ass, remove the condom and tie it off with one arm around Keegan's waist. "I needed one that didn't involve me whipping anybody, for once."

Not knowing what to say, Keegan laced his fingers through Scott's and squeezed, trying to communicate his sympathy through touch. Scott pulled him closer and nuzzled his cheek.

When Keegan drifted to sleep a few minutes later, still cocooned in Scott's embrace, he wasn't sure which surprised him more—that Scott hadn't left, or that he hadn't wanted him to.

Chapter Five

Scott woke to the scent of sex and skin, and Keegan's bare body in his arms. He smiled with his eyes still closed, buried his face in Keegan's hair and just breathed. They'd shifted during the night. Keegan lay practically on top of Scott, head tucked under his chin and an arm around his chest. One of Keegan's legs was lodged between Scott's, firm thigh brushing Scott's balls.

Scott opened his eyes and lay staring at the ceiling, stroking Keegan's back and thinking. He didn't doubt for a second that Keegan had enjoyed the previous night's activities every bit as much as he had. But something was off. Even in the heat of sex, Keegan's eyes had a guarded, wary look that set off alarms in Scott's head.

At least that's what Scott thought he'd seen. He couldn't help noticing that Keegan had taken great pains to avoid looking him in the eye during sex. It reminded him uneasily of how Logan had been in the last few bitter months of their relationship. Back turned, eyes closed, face buried in Scott's crotch. Anything to prevent the intense intimacy of eye contact in the midst of lovemaking.

It disturbed Scott on a fundamental level that Keegan, who'd become increasingly important to him over the past several weeks, would keep him at arm's length the way Logan had. Scott wanted much, much more than a good lay, and he suspected Keegan knew that quite well.

Keegan let out a soft whimper and began squirming in Scott's embrace. "Stop it," Keegan mumbled, still asleep. "Don't... You promised..."

He trailed off and kicked Scott abruptly in the shin. Scott sat up, holding Keegan's flailing wrists in one hand. "Keegan!" he called, becoming alarmed by Keegan's silent but furious struggling. "Keegan, wake up."

Keegan wrenched out of Scott's grip. His eyes flew open, staring blindly at the wall over Scott's shoulder.

"Keegan?" Scott said, reaching a tentative hand to touch Keegan's face.

Keegan flinched away and scrambled into a crouch. Huddled naked against the headboard, eyes fevered and red-gold curls falling in wild tangles around his shoulders, he looked feral and dangerous.

"Bastard," Keegan hissed. "You *promised.*"

"Promised what? Keegan, you're scaring me."

For a heartbeat, Keegan just stared, though he didn't seem to see anything but whatever was happening in his head. Then he blinked, and his eyes focused on Scott. "Scott? What happened?"

"I don't know," Scott said, watching Keegan warily. "You were having a nightmare, I think. I tried to wake you up, and your eyes opened but I don't think you could see me. You kind of freaked out."

Keegan went deathly pale. "What'd I say? Did I say anything?"

"You said 'stop it', and 'don't'," Scott told him. "Then you said that I promised something. You sounded angry."

"Fuck." Keegan leaned against the headboard and closed his eyes.

Scott waited, but Keegan didn't say anything else. "What happened?" Scott asked finally.

Keegan drew his knees up under his chin and opened his eyes, shooting Scott a panicky glance before staring at his toes. "Nothing. It was just a bad dream."

Keegan's tension radiated from him, and Scott knew he was lying. Whatever haunted Keegan's dreams, it wasn't the product of an overactive imagination. Somewhere in Keegan's past was an event that had damaged him badly. Scott was sure of it.

"Whatever it was that happened to you, you can tell me," Scott said before he thought about what he was doing. "I hope you know that."

Keegan met Scott's gaze. A heartbreaking fear and loneliness shone in his eyes for a second before the sexy, teasing mask slid back into place. Keegan smiled.

"Can I tell you how much I want you right now?" Keegan crawled toward Scott, lithe and graceful as a cat. "Can I tell you that I'm dying to suck your cock?"

A part of Scott wanted to refuse Keegan's advances, sit him down and have an honest talk with him. Drag the skeletons out of his closet and into the light of day. But Keegan's hands were sliding up his chest, pushing him backward onto the bed, and Scott decided that maybe it could wait another hour. *Or two,* he amended as Keegan squeezed his balls. He buried his hands in Keegan's hair and pulled him down into a rough, hungry kiss.

"Let me suck you," Keegan whispered hoarsely. "I've been dreaming about doing that."

Scott ran his fingertips along Keegan's lips, marveling at their softness. Their deep rose color emphasized the brightness of the silver ring. Scott traced the curve of metal with one finger. It felt warm against his skin.

"Your mouth is so beautiful," Scott murmured. "So damn sexy."

Keegan looked startled for a second, but quickly got it under control and gave Scott a wicked grin. "It'd look even better with your dick in it. Oh, that reminds me," he added, sliding the hand on Scott's balls up to stroke his shaft, "you are the fucking master of deep-throating. That was hands down the best blowjob I've ever had."

Scott smiled, knowing he looked as goofy and sappy as he felt and not caring. "Liked that, did you?"

"Mm-hm." Keegan leaned close and pressed a light kiss to Scott's lips, his curls brushing Scott's nipples in the most wonderful way. "Loved it. Loved you rimming me too. God, I could come just from your tongue in my ass."

"I always liked doing that." Scott arched his neck when Keegan nuzzled him. Keegan latched on just below Scott's ear and started sucking up what was sure to be a spectacular mark. "Oh God, Keegan, your mouth..."

Keegan chuckled against Scott's neck. "You want my mouth on your cock, don't you?"

"Yes," Scott moaned, arching into Keegan's touch.

"I want that too." Keegan slithered down Scott's body, peppering him with tiny kisses and sharp little nibbles on the way. "Want your cock to fill up my throat like it filled my ass last night."

Keegan's tongue flicked feather-light across the weeping head of Scott's prick, tearing a sharp gasp from Scott's throat. "God yes, do it."

Keegan smiled, his eyes bright with a predatory light. He bent and slid his luscious mouth down over Scott's cock, and the feel of it ballooned to fill Scott's world. He spread his legs, drawing his knees up to give Keegan's questing fingers room to play. Keegan's hair swept across the insides of his thighs and tickled his balls. It was quite possibly the best thing Scott had ever felt.

Scott soon discovered that Keegan had a real talent for keeping a man on the edge without letting him come. Keegan licked and sucked and fingered Scott's ass until Scott's insides began to shake, then backed off just long enough to let him regain a measure of control before doing it all over again. Scott figured it might kill him, but he didn't care. Not as long as Keegan let him come before he died.

When Scott felt the sweet pressure building in his belly again, he was surprised to find that Keegan didn't stop sucking him. He didn't want it to stop. He wanted more than anything to come with his cock buried deep in Keegan's throat. But he hadn't worn a condom, and he didn't think Keegan would appreciate an unexpected mouthful of semen. He swallowed a couple of times and tried to find his voice.

"Keegan," Scott gasped, tugging weakly on Keegan's hair. "Gonna come."

Keegan looked up and met Scott's eyes, and Scott realized with a shock that Keegan wanted him to come in his mouth. Keegan hummed around Scott's prick and slid a second finger into his ass, and it was enough to push Scott over the edge. He came with a shout, shudders wracking his body as he shot down Keegan's throat.

He lay staring at the ceiling, twitching with aftershocks as the orgasm ebbed away. Keegan's smiling face appeared above him, and he smiled back.

"I think you shorted out my brain," Scott mumbled, gathering Keegan into his arms. "Damn, you're good."

"Mmmm," Keegan purred, sucking on Scott's bottom lip. "I like your dick in my mouth."

Scott remembered Keegan's lips around his cock, Keegan's throat working as he swallowed. "Hey, why'd you swallow?" he asked. "We haven't talked about tests or anything yet."

Keegan tensed for a moment, then relaxed again. "Yeah, but we've known each other a while now," he said, moving down to kiss Scott's neck. "I figured you were safe." He raised his head and grinned. "You are, right?"

"Yes, but that's not the point," Scott answered. "The point is, no matter what you wanted to think, you didn't *know* I was safe. Hell, you don't know now. I could be lying."

"Are you?" Keegan plucked at one of Scott's nipples.

"No." Scott squirmed under Keegan's increasingly demanding touch. "Christ, how can I already be getting turned on again?"

"I'm just that good." Keegan bit Scott's chin. "Get me off now."

Scott ran a hand down Keegan's back to cup one firm butt cheek. "How do you want me to do it?"

Keegan's expression turned thoughtful, then his eyes lit up. "Wanna use Babe on me?"

"Babe the Big Blue Dildo?" Scott had to admit that the mental image of the gigantic toy sliding in and out of Keegan's ass was a huge turn-on. "Hand it to me."

Keegan's eyes went hot. Sitting up, he leaned over and grabbed Babe off the floor. Scott took it and started stroking it, holding Keegan's gaze the whole time.

"Now lube up and get yourself ready," Scott ordered. He ignored the twinge of uneasiness he felt. So Keegan liked to be ordered around in bed, so what? *Lots of people do. It doesn't make him like Logan.*

Keegan started to roll onto his stomach, but Scott stopped him with a hand on his arm. "Lie on your back."

"It's easier the other way," Keegan answered, looking uncomfortable. "You can get at my ass better."

"Maybe, but I can't get at your cock as well. And I definitely want to play with your cock." Scott didn't mention that above all else, he wanted to see Keegan's face. He had a feeling Keegan wouldn't like that.

Keegan stared at him for a minute, as if trying to decide if he were sincere. "Okay," he said finally, and smiled. "You're the boss."

Keegan eased down onto his back and spread his legs wide. Scott's prick twitched. Much as he hated to admit it, the knowledge that Keegan would do whatever Scott said turned him on nearly as much as the sight of Keegan splayed and hard and flushed with desire.

"Pull your knees up," Scott whispered. "Let me see your hole."

Keegan did as he was told, curling his open legs up against his shoulders. He reached down and spread himself. Scott gulped at the sight of that sweet little pucker. His mouth watered, wanting to taste.

"You want to eat my ass again, don't you?" Keegan licked his lips, the movement slow and suggestive. "You can, if you want."

"I do want to," Scott agreed, grinning. "But it'll have to wait." Glancing around, he found the lube and tossed it onto Keegan's stomach. "Get yourself ready. I want to watch."

Keegan obediently flipped up the cap on the lube and slicked the fingers of one hand. His eyes held Scott's, and Scott was glad. This was the kind of intimacy he'd wanted all along with Keegan.

"When I'm ready, will you fuck me with my toy?" Keegan circled his hole with one slippery finger, then slipped it inside, pumping slowly. He bit his lip. "God, thinking of you sticking Babe up my ass turns me on so much."

"Me too." Scott scooted closer and gave one of Keegan's nipple rings a sharp tug. "Put another finger in."

Keegan did it, his breath running out in a soft sigh. "Oh, oh Scott. God."

Scott sat back on his heels and drank in the picture Keegan made. Naked on a bed of his own silky hair, erect cock flushed and dripping against his belly, sleekly muscled legs up and apart, two fingers buried deep in his ass. He added a third as Scott watched. His hole pulsed visibly, stretching to accommodate the increasing girth, and it was almost more than Scott could take.

Scott ran the tip of the dildo down the inside of Keegan's thigh. "You have no idea how hot you look right now."

Keegan moaned, balls drawing up as Scott rubbed Babe against them. "Fuck. In. Now."

Monosyllables, Scott figured, were a good thing at this point. "Take your fingers out," he ordered, snatching up the lube to coat the length of the large toy.

Keegan obeyed. He dug his fingers into his buttocks and held them apart, displaying his stretched hole. "Scott, Scott please..."

The whispered plea nearly destroyed Scott's control. He loved seeing Keegan like this, shameless in his lust, open and vulnerable. He watched Keegan's face as he slid the dildo inside him, watched Keegan's features go slack with pleasure, pale cheeks flushing pink.

"You're so beautiful," Scott murmured, pushing the toy in all the way to the base. "So fucking beautiful."

Keegan blinked up at him, panting through parted lips. "Scott...fuck..."

Scott pulled Babe all the way out, watching Keegan's hole twitch, then slammed it back in to the root, making sure to nail Keegan's gland. Keegan let out a wail. "Yes! Yes, God, please."

Scott did it again, and again and again, until Keegan was shaking from head to foot. When he heard Keegan's breathing quicken, he shoved the toy in and held it there with his knee. Leaning over, he kissed the tip of Keegan's cock. Keegan whimpered.

Taking Keegan's shaft in one hand, Scott pressed a lube-slick finger against the slit and pushed gently inside, the way he'd seen Keegan do to himself the night before. The second he drew it out again, Keegan gasped, shuddered and came.

By that time, Scott was hard again and so close he didn't think he could wait long enough to get out a condom. Sitting up on his knees between Keegan's legs, he began jerking his cock as hard as he could. Keegan grinned, propped himself up on one elbow and reached out to roll Scott's balls between his fingers. Scott came with a groan, adding his semen to the puddle on Keegan's belly.

"Oh my God," Scott gasped. He managed to pull Babe out and toss it aside before collapsing on top of Keegan. "You're gonna kill me."

Keegan chuckled, arms coming up to hold Scott against him. "But what a way to go, huh?"

"Mm-hm." Scott slipped an arm under Keegan's neck. "You're so gorgeous when you come, Keegan. I love watching you."

Keegan stared up at him. His odd-colored eyes shone with something Scott was almost afraid to identify, because being wrong would hurt too much. Keegan laid a hand on Scott's cheek.

"Kiss me," Keegan whispered, brushing Scott's lips with his thumb.

Scott smiled and pressed his mouth to Keegan's. Those soft lips opened right up for him, Keegan tilting his head to take the kiss deep. Their tongues slid lazily together, exploring each other without hurry. There was no urgency to it now, and Scott loved that, loved being able to learn the feel and flavor of Keegan's mouth without his libido—or Keegan's—distracting him.

As the kiss went on, Scott reflected that he loved everything about Keegan. His unusual good looks, his twisted sense of humor, the way he could cut a person to ribbons with a few well-placed words when he was angry. It all melded into an imperfectly wonderful package, one he never wanted to let go.

Oh my God, I'm in love with him.

The sudden realization hit Scott out of left field. He broke the kiss and pushed back enough to look into Keegan's eyes, searching for that tender shine he'd seen a few minutes before.

"No, don't stop," Keegan pleaded, trying to pull Scott back down.

Scott captured Keegan's grasping hands in his and held them gently against the mattress. "I need to ask you something."

Keegan blinked. "Ask me what?"

Scott took a deep breath. "What're we doing, Keegan? What is this?"

"Huh?" Keegan's brows drew together, concern replacing the lust in his eyes. "Scott, what the hell are you talking about?"

Scott let go of one of Keegan's hands to touch his cheek. "Is this just sex?" Scott asked, very quietly. "Or is it something more?"

For a brief second, Keegan's guard dropped and his eyes blazed with a need so intense it stole Scott's breath. Then Keegan smiled, and Scott knew he wasn't getting any confessions of love today.

"What, sex isn't enough?" Keegan pulled his other hand free and slid both palms down Scott's back to squeeze his ass. "I must be doing something wrong."

Scott refused to be distracted. He stroked the tangled hair away from Keegan's face and kissed his nose. "The sex is absolutely mind-blowing, and you know it. But I want to know if that's all there is, or if we could have something more solid."

Keegan's body went tense under Scott's. "It's, um, a little soon, don't you think?"

"Not really. We've been friends for weeks now." Scott followed the curve of Keegan's cheek with his fingers. Keegan leaned into the caress, eyelids fluttering half-closed, and Scott decided he had to tell him. "This is way more than just sex for me, Keegan. I love you."

Keegan went still. "What?"

Bending down, Scott kissed Keegan's lips. "I'm in love with you. I think I've loved you for a long time."

Keegan's reaction shocked him to the core. Shoving Scott off, he leapt out of bed and stood staring at Scott with fiery eyes. "Don't you fucking say that to me," he hissed. "You don't mean it."

Stunned, Scott rose to his feet and walked toward Keegan, keeping his pace slow and measured. "Yes, I do."

Keegan backed away, shaking his head. "Don't touch me! Just stay away."

Keegan's entire body trembled violently and his eyes glazed with panic. It was all Scott could do to resist the urge to sweep Keegan into his arms and hold him tight. He stopped, his gaze never leaving Keegan's face.

"I'd never hurt you," Scott said softly. "Tell me why you're so afraid."

Keegan's back hit the wall. His teeth chattered together and his eyes darted like flies around the room, refusing to settle on anything. He looked utterly terrified, and suddenly Scott saw the connection.

"This has something to do with your nightmare, doesn't it?"

Keegan shot a wide-eyed look at Scott. Their eyes only met for a second, but it was enough for Scott to know he was right.

"Keegan, please," Scott said, taking a step forward. "Whatever it is, let me help. You were there for me these last few weeks, when I wanted to leave Logan but didn't know it yet. Let me be there for you now. Tell me what happened to make you like this."

To Scott's surprise, Keegan's eyes filled with tears. He slid down the wall and sat huddled on the floor, shoulders hunched and knees bent up to his chest. "Go away," he whispered. "Leave me alone."

Wanting to comfort Keegan, Scott reached out and touched his shoulder. Keegan flinched and curled up tighter, squeezing his eyes shut. Tears leaked down his cheeks. Scott had never seen Keegan lose control like that and it scared him.

"Keegan…"

"Leave me alone!" Keegan shouted. He covered his face with his hands.

Scott ached with the need to fix whatever was wrong. But Keegan obviously wouldn't accept his help now.

"Okay," Scott said reluctantly. "But I'm not letting this go. I'll be at the club tonight, and every night. When you're ready to talk, you know where to find me."

Keegan didn't answer. Scott sighed, stood and started looking for his clothes. While he dressed, Keegan sat there on the floor, face still buried in his hands. Clothes on and hand on the doorknob, Scott turned to look at Keegan again. He hadn't moved.

"I really did mean it, you know," Scott told him. "When you're ready, I'll be here."

No response. He hadn't expected one. Taking a deep breath, Scott opened the door and left Keegan's apartment. It was the hardest thing he'd ever done.

Scott didn't see Keegan at the club that night. By the time he left Ganymede's Grotto the next night, Keegan still hadn't shown up and Scott was frantic with worry. The only thing that kept him from busting down Keegan's door to make sure he was all right was Earl, who was concerned but not overly worried.

"Keegan's a very private person, believe it or not," Earl said when Scott finally approached him Tuesday evening and told him a heavily edited version of events. "He just needs some time on his own, to think things over."

They were sitting at a small table in the corner, talking over Irish coffee. Earl was easy to talk to, Scott found. Though clearly curious about what precisely Scott had said to upset Keegan, he didn't push, and he seemed confident that Keegan would get over it in time.

"But he hasn't even left his apartment." Scott thought about it and realized he didn't actually know that. "Or at least he hasn't come to work the last two nights that I've seen. I just want to know if he's okay."

Earl patted his hand. "He'll be fine, honey, never fear. I went to check on him Sunday night when he called in sick, since he's never done that before. He was terribly upset still, but he's working through it."

Scott nodded unhappily. "Did he tell you anything about what happened?"

"Nothing at all." Earl sighed. "I've gotten much more from you, actually."

Scott stared at the tabletop, tracing a swirl of purple paint with one fingertip. "I told him I'm in love with him. He, um...wasn't happy about it."

Silence. Scott glanced up again. Earl was studying him with a keen eye, one hand stroking his lavender tie. He gave Scott a reassuring smile.

"That explains a lot," Earl said.

"Why?" Scott leaned forward across the table. "Why would that upset him so much? Even if he doesn't feel the same..." He stopped. The thought that he may have lost Keegan already hurt something deep and vital inside him.

Earl took his hand and squeezed. "It's not my story to tell, Scott. Suffice to say, our boy has had a rough life, with far too little love in it. Eight years ago, when I first met him, he probably would've kicked your ass and thrown you down the stairs. He handles it better these days, but it's still difficult for him to accept real affection from others. He hasn't let anyone close enough to love him in a long, long time."

Scott's throat went tight. "What can I do?"

Earl regarded him with a keen blue gaze. "How late can you stay out on a work night?"

"Actually, I already took tomorrow off. I was kind of hoping, you know…" He trailed off, feeling foolish. He'd asked off for Valentine's Day and the day after a couple of weeks previously, telling himself it was for Logan. He knew now even then he'd harbored a vague hope of spending that time in Keegan's bed.

"Say no more." Earl grinned. "Do you know where Café Noctem is?"

"That all-night coffee shop? Sure."

"Be there at one a.m. Keegan will meet you there, and you can talk."

Scott's eyebrows shot up. "How do you know he'll agree to meet me?"

"He will," Earl promised, looking smug. He stood. "Now if you'll excuse me, I have work to do."

"Okay." Scott gave Earl a wan smile. "Thanks."

"Any time, hon."

Earl patted Scott's shoulder and waltzed off into the crowd, already calling to one of the waitstaff. Scott sat there, sipping his coffee and gathering his courage. By the time he left to go back to his hotel room and get ready to meet Keegan, he thought he was ready to hear whatever Keegan would tell him.

Chapter Six

Earl was back, knocking on his door. Keegan pulled the pillow over his head.

"I'm fine, Earl, go away!" he shouted.

"I'm sure you are," Earl called back, the sarcasm coming through loud and clear, "but Scott is not."

Scott. A bubble of misery rose in Keegan's chest. "I'm sorry," he said, almost to himself.

"Keegan Matthew Rourke," Earl growled, "let me in right this *minute*."

Keegan threw the pillow on the floor and glared toward the sound of Earl's voice. He knew how stubborn Earl could be when he was on a mission. The man would stand there yelling all night if he had to. Sighing, Keegan got up, stomped over to the door and threw it open.

"What?" he barked.

Earl arched an elegant eyebrow at him. "You have company, love, you could at least put on clothes."

"I didn't ask you to come here," Keegan snapped, slamming the door shut and shuffling back to the bed. "If it bugs you to see me naked, don't fucking look."

"My goodness, aren't we in a nasty mood," Earl commented mildly, taking a seat in one of the wobbly plastic chairs in Keegan's tiny kitchenette. "Fine, lie there in your birthday suit and sulk if you must, but you"—he pointed a stern finger at Keegan—"are going to damn well listen to me."

"Whatever," Keegan muttered. He knew he was acting childish, but he couldn't seem to stop. It helped to know that Earl would understand why he was being so sulky, and not hold it against him.

"Scott came to talk to me tonight," Earl said. "He told me what happened."

"Well that's just fucking great," Keegan grumbled, blushing in spite of himself.

Earl leaned forward, elbows resting on his knees, his expression earnest. "Honey, I know how difficult it is for you to accept what he wants to give you. But don't you think it's time to try?"

"What if it happens again?" Keegan asked, eyes fixed on the ceiling. "I couldn't handle it, Earl. I just couldn't."

Walking over to Keegan's bed, Earl sat on the edge and took Keegan's hand in both of his. "Scott isn't Tony. Most men aren't, thank God."

"I know," Keegan whispered. "It's just hard, you know?"

Hard not to see Tony's face when he'd held Keegan close and told him he'd love him forever, that he'd take care of him and never hurt him. Hard not to see the contempt twisting that same face a few short weeks later, when he'd left Keegan nude on a street corner, confused and sobbing and too weak to walk. So fucking hard to ever believe in love again after that.

"It's been eight years, sweetheart," Earl said gently. "Let it go. Let Scott give you the kind of love you deserve. And let yourself give it in return."

Keegan didn't bother to tell Earl he didn't love Scott. Earl could always smell a lie a mile away.

Keegan laced his fingers through Earl's. "I was awful to him. He won't want me anymore."

Earl chuckled. "You're dreadfully mistaken about that. He's beside himself with worry, and he definitely still wants you."

"So what now?" Keegan turned to meet Earl's gaze. "I've never done this before. I don't know what to do."

Earl smiled, leaned down and planted a kiss on Keegan's forehead. "I told Scott you'd meet him at one a.m. at Café Noctem. Go tell him the whole story, right from the beginning. He'll understand. And what's more, I believe he can help you learn to let the past go."

Cold fear churned in Keegan's guts. Starting his first real romantic relationship at age twenty-nine-and-a-half was one thing. Telling Scott the sordid story of his life—which he'd never told anyone other than Earl—was another thing entirely.

Scott loves you, a hopeful little voice whispered in his head. *You're safe with him.*

Deep inside, he knew it was true.

"Okay," Keegan said, his voice only wavering a little. "I'll go. I'll tell him."

Earl smiled. "You're doing the right thing, hon."

"I know." Moved by a sudden surge of affection for the first human being to ever care for him, Keegan sat up and flung his arms around Earl's neck. "Thanks for being so good to me, Earl. I love you."

"Love you too, son," Earl answered in a choked voice, rubbing Keegan's back. His eyes glittered wetly when he pulled away. "Now go get cleaned up, you smell. And for God's sake, put on clothes."

Keegan laughed. "Yeah, yeah. Go on back downstairs, before somebody misses you."

"Yes, I know, the place is in danger of falling apart if I'm gone for five minutes." Earl patted Keegan's knee, stood and started toward the door. He turned and gave Keegan a wide grin. "Good luck. I'll expect full details tomorrow, of course."

"Of course," Keegan agreed. "Bye."

Earl blew him a kiss and breezed out the door.

Keegan lay there for a while longer, trying to gather enough nerve to actually do what he'd promised Earl he'd do. He'd never laid himself bare the way he was about to tonight, and it terrified him.

"Scott loves you," he repeated aloud. "You're safe with him. He won't hurt you like Tony did."

Keegan kept saying it, over and over again until he believed strongly enough to overcome the fear that blazed through his mind and made his body shake. He hauled himself out of bed and into the shower, hoping he could hold himself together long enough to apologize to Scott, and to make him understand.

He refused to consider what might happen if Scott didn't understand after all. One hurdle at a time.

Keegan walked into Café Noctem at five after one. The place was packed with the usual up-all-night crowd, huddled around the little round tables singly or in groups, talking or reading or writing over lattes and double espressos. A Billie Holliday tune played in the background. Something more raucous and bass-heavy thumped up through the floor from the basement below, punctuated by bursts of laughter.

A group of college-age kids in togas came running up the stairs from the basement, made their way across the room and disappeared through the door into the night. *Oh yeah, it's their Celebration de la Vie party. I'd forgotten.* Keegan smiled, thinking that explained the hordes of costumed revelers in the streets.

Walking a little further into the room, Keegan scanned the faces around him. Scott was nowhere to be seen. Keegan's stomach dropped into his feet.

A hand on his shoulder made him jump. He whirled around, startled, and came face-to-chest with Scott, who had evidently been sitting at a table in the corner near the door.

"Fuck, you scared me," Keegan said weakly. He looked up into Scott's eyes. "Um. Hi."

Scott stared at him with worry written all over his face. "Are you all right?"

"I am now." Keegan twisted his hands together, wishing his heart would settle down and stop galloping like a prize thoroughbred. "I, uh, I'm gonna go get a coffee, you want anything?"

"I've got mine already."

"'Kay. Um, I'll be right back."

Keegan turned and headed for the counter to place his order. A couple of minutes later he started back toward the table carrying a huge mug of the featured dark roast. He made it the whole way without sloshing coffee on himself, in spite of his trembling hands.

Keegan set the mug on the table, avoiding Scott's eyes. Now that he was actually here, he had no idea how to begin. Scott saved him by speaking first.

"I'm sorry, Keegan." Scott reached a hand across the table, bit his lip and pulled it back. "I didn't mean to upset you like I did."

Surprised, Keegan looked up at Scott. His dark eyes were sorrowful. Keegan took Scott's hand in his. "We both know that I'm the one who ought to be apologizing here, not you."

"Don't apologize to me," Scott said, weaving his fingers through Keegan's. "Just tell me I haven't fucked it all up."

Keegan dropped his gaze to the tabletop. "*You* haven't. I just hope *I* haven't."

Scott's chair scraped across the floor as he moved closer. "I'm here, aren't I?" Scott brushed a light kiss across Keegan's forehead. "And I still... Well, you know."

It killed Keegan to hear the hesitancy in Scott's voice. He hooked a hand around the back of Scott's neck, pulled him close and kissed his lips. Scott made a soft, desperate sound in the back of his throat. Keegan fought the urge to open his mouth and take the kiss deeper. It could wait. They had talking to do.

"Earl said I should tell you about my past," Keegan said as they drew apart. "I want to. I want you to understand why I reacted like I did."

"I'd like that." Lifting Keegan's hand, Scott kissed his knuckles. "But not unless you're ready to tell me."

Keegan gave a hollow laugh. "Scott, if I wait until I'm ready, it'll never happen. I have to do this now, before I lose my nerve."

Scott smiled reassuringly. "Tell me."

Here goes. Keegan took a deep breath.

"I grew up in Charleston. My parents kicked me out when I was fifteen. Don't ask why. I was a wild kid, always in trouble, and they never wanted me to start with. I was happy enough to leave. I felt safer on the street than I ever felt at home."

"Jesus. What did you do?"

Keegan shrugged. "I tried getting a regular job, but I found out pretty quick that no one'll hire a homeless high-school dropout. I was living in an abandoned building and they wouldn't let me back in school, not that I tried all that hard."

"Shit, Keegan," Scott said, brows drawing together. "Please tell me you didn't have to—"

"I never whored myself," Keegan interrupted hotly. "Not once. I found out about the peep shows from a girl I knew who worked at one. She said there was a big demand for boys. So I went down to the place she worked and talked to the owner, Ray. He hired me on the spot."

Scott frowned, his expression thunderous. "He hired a fifteen-year-old kid?"

"I told him I was eighteen."

"There's no way he believed you," Scott declared with an impatient gesture. "You barely look eighteen now, I can only imagine how young you must've looked then."

Keegan smiled grimly. "The regulars there liked 'em young, and Ray wasn't about to ask questions that might cost him money. There wasn't a performer there over nineteen. Most were seventeen or eighteen. A couple of them were even younger than me."

Scott growled, dark eyes flashing. "Those fucking perverts that went there didn't lay hands on you, did they? Tell me they didn't."

"Customers were supposed to stay in their booths and not touch the performers, but they never paid attention to the rules. The booths didn't have glass in front, so there was nothing to stop them doing what they wanted." Keegan stared at the table. "I knew there were worse things I could've done to survive, but I hated it when they touched me. I kept telling them they weren't supposed to, but they always ignored me."

Scott cupped Keegan's cheek in one big hand. Keegan raised his eyes reluctantly to Scott's face, half-afraid he'd see disgust there. Leaning forward, Scott kissed him, light and quick, and the fear inside him eased a little.

"I'm sorry," Scott said softly. "I'd beat them all bloody for doing that to you, if I could. How long did you work there?"

"Three years, five months and sixteen days," Keegan answered. He smiled grimly at the realization that he still remembered. "I left and went to work at a gay strip club not long after I turned eighteen. I'd been working out and practicing my act, and of course at that point I was legal. They hired me right away. It was my first legitimate job."

"I hope it was better than the peep show." Scott looked like he'd gladly murder all the people who'd used and abused Keegan all his life, if given half a chance. It made Keegan feel warm right to his toes.

Keegan took a sip of his coffee. It was hot and almost lethally strong, just the way he liked it. "The strip club was way better than the peep show." He stroked the back of Scott's hand with his thumb. "I actually enjoyed it, when the crowd was good and gave me tips instead of trying to grope me. At least security was better there. Anyone who came on stage or tried to grab me got thrown out. And all I had to do was take my clothes off."

Scott gave him a puzzled look. "Isn't that what you did at the peep show?"

"Um, not exactly." Heat rose in Keegan's cheeks. Scott clearly had no experience with such places, and Keegan wished he wasn't the one who had to explain it. "I jerked off, mostly. Sometimes I had to use toys on myself."

Scott's hand tightened around his. "You never had to...you know. Have sex?"

Keegan couldn't help smiling at the half-pleading, half-angry tone of Scott's voice. "No, I didn't."

"Good."

There was something wonderfully thrilling about Scott's possessiveness. On impulse, Keegan set his coffee down, hooked his hand around the back of Scott's neck and pulled him close for a kiss. Scott's mouth opened under his, warm and tasting of espresso. It felt incredible. Not just the silky heat of Scott's mouth, but the knowledge that he was loved. Caring about a lover, and having him return the feeling, was something he'd never experienced before. It made him feel light and giddy.

"I love you," Scott whispered, twirling a strand of Keegan's hair around his finger.

Keegan felt himself tense, even though he tried to fight it. "Scott—"

Scott cut him off before he could get any further. "You don't have to tell me why that scares you so much," he said, his breath warm against Keegan's cheek. "But I'd like to hear it, when you're ready."

A hard lump of dread formed in Keegan's guts. He swallowed the bile rising in his throat and made himself meet Scott's eyes. This was going to be rough.

"I met Tony just over eight years ago, at the club where I worked," he began, keeping his voice deliberately calm. "He was a lot older than me, about fifty, really fit and handsome, and he treated me like I was special. Like I was more than just a stripper. Suckered me right in."

Scott's eyes never left Keegan's face. "What happened?"

Here we go. Keegan took a couple of shallow breaths. "We'd been dating for about six months when he told me he loved me. Nobody had ever said that to me before, not even my parents."

Scott made a soft, surprised sound. "Christ, Keegan."

Keegan plowed on, wanting only to finish his story and never have to think of it again. "I was so happy. I was crazy in love with him. Would've done anything for him. So when he asked me to live with him, I said yes. We celebrated with a bottle of wine at his place. I went to sleep in his bed. I woke up the next morning in a cage, with a collar around my neck that was chained to the wall."

"Oh my God," Scott exclaimed, eyes wide.

"It was several days before I saw him again," Keegan continued. "When he finally showed up I screamed at him, called him the worst things I could think of. Told him to let me go or I'd kill him. I meant it, too. But he just laughed at me and told me I'd get used to being his slave."

Scott swore under his breath. Keegan rocked in his seat, eyes fixed on the far wall. "I don't know how long he kept me there. Several weeks, I think. He drugged me to keep me weak, but he wanted me to be submissive and I would rather have died than submit to him after what he'd done. Finally he said I wasn't worth the trouble. He shot me full of narcotics, drove me all the way here to Asheville and dumped me on a street corner."

"That fucking piece of shit," Scott growled, eyes flashing. He wound a protective arm around Keegan's shoulders.

"He'd promised he'd take care of me. That he'd never let anything hurt me again. And then he...did that to me." Keegan closed his eyes and leaned into Scott's embrace. "When he had me in that cage, he kept telling me that love was nothing but slavery and I should be glad I had someone like him willing to look after me. When he threw me out and told me nobody else would ever love me, I believed him."

"His sick version of love was the only one you'd ever known. No wonder you panicked when I said that to you." Scott kissed his hair. "That's what your nightmare was about the other day, wasn't it? He promised never to hurt you, and he hurt you worse than you could've imagined."

"I'm sorry I'm so fucked up," Keegan said.

"Actually, I think you're a whole lot less fucked up than most people would be after going through what you did." Scott raised Keegan's face and kissed his lips. "So what happens now?"

"I...I'd like to try," Keegan told him, heart fluttering madly. "Us, I mean. Being together. If that's still okay."

Scott's smile melted away the last of Keegan's fear. "You know it is."

Keegan laughed for sheer happiness, and Scott laughed with him. When they kissed, it swiftly escalated from tender to heated. Desire coursed like lava through Keegan's veins, sweet and hot. He broke the kiss and grinned when he saw his need mirrored in Scott's eyes.

"Come home with me," Keegan whispered, running a hand up Scott's thigh. "I need you right now."

Scott stood, pulling Keegan with him, his expression hungry. "Come on."

❤ ❤ ❤

Café Noctem was only a couple of blocks from Ganymede's Grotto. Keegan figured that was a good thing, because if they'd had any further to go they may very well have ended up screwing in the street. They stumbled up the stairs to Keegan's apartment, mouths locked together. The second Scott kicked the door shut behind them, Keegan fell to his knees, hands working open Scott's jeans.

"Oh fuck." Scott groaned as Keegan yanked his pants down and wrapped a hand around his cock.

Keegan swiped his tongue over the head of Scott's prick. The taste of pre-come sent a shudder of pleasure through him. "Fuck my mouth, Scott."

Scott blinked down at him, a question in his eyes. Keegan let his lust shine through, showing Scott it was okay. Scott growled, buried both hands in Keegan's hair and shoved his cock down Keegan's throat. Keegan relaxed his muscles and let Scott in all the way, humming happily as Scott pounded into him. He loved the feel of Scott in his mouth, the smell and taste of his lover's need, the moans and gasps that spoke Scott's pleasure more eloquently than words ever could. It was a powerful feeling to know he could make Scott lose himself like this.

Within minutes, Scott's body began to tremble, his thrusts losing their rhythm. Smiling inwardly, Keegan slid his mouth down Scott's cock until his chin hit Scott's balls, and swallowed. Scott hissed, his prick pulsed and he came in a salty-bitter flood down Keegan's throat. Keegan dug both hands into Scott's ass and held him in place so he wouldn't miss a drop.

He was forced to let go when Scott's knees buckled and he slid gracelessly to the ground. "Oh, man," Scott sighed. "That was amazing."

Keegan grinned, feeling light and free and happier than he could ever remember. He climbed up to straddle Scott's lap.

"Let's go to bed," he murmured, rubbing his cheek against Scott's. "I want you to fuck me as soon as you get it up again."

Scott laughed, arms coming up to hold Keegan close. "Hell, it's *still* up."

"Hm." Keegan ground his ass experimentally against Scott's lap, which got him a heartfelt groan. Scott was indeed still hard, his unflagging erection pressed against Keegan's balls. "Oh yeah, that's what I want." Keegan bounced up and down a couple of times, snickering when Scott's eyes crossed. "Can you stand up?"

Scott gave him an evil grin. "To get inside that hot little ass? Fuck yeah."

Keegan squeaked in surprise when Scott surged to his feet, strong arms clutching Keegan close to his body. Grinning, Keegan wound his legs around Scott's waist.

"Caveman," he teased, biting Scott's bottom lip.

"Ugh," Scott grunted. He shuffled across the room with his pants around his ankles and Keegan clinging to him like a monkey. "Me fuck Keegan through mattress."

Keegan laughed as Scott tossed him onto the bed and started stripping. He squirmed out of his own clothes, tossing them in an untidy heap on the floor, and spread his legs wide. "Come get it, big boy."

Scott crawled up between his legs, dark eyes dancing. He leaned down and kissed Keegan's lips. "Where's the lube?"

"Uhhh..." Keegan scrunched his face up, thinking hard. "Oh yeah. Here." He dug around under the pile of pillows, drew out the little tube and handed it to Scott. "Hurry."

Scott coated his fingers in lube and pushed two into Keegan's ass. Keegan moaned, feeling his body opening right up. "Scott, please, I can't wait," he begged, pulling his legs up to his chest. "There's rubbers in the drawer, just do it."

Scott shook his head, adding a third and fourth finger at the same time. Keegan gasped, shaking with the pleasure of it. "I want you bare, Keegan," Scott whispered. "Is that okay?"

Keegan blinked at him. "I...I could show you my test results. You're the only one I've been with since my last test."

"Are you clean?" Scott twisted his wrist, sliding his fingers deeper into Keegan's body, thumb stroking the stretched ring of muscle.

"Uh...y-yes. *Fuck*, Scott..." Keegan pushed up on his elbows, straining to see between his legs. Scott practically had his entire not-at-all-small hand up Keegan's ass, and Keegan wanted very much to see that.

"Okay. Bare, then." Scott tugged on one of Keegan's nipple rings with his teeth. "Ready?"

In answer, Keegan grabbed Scott's cock and pulled it toward him. Scott smiled. Taking his fingers out of Keegan's hole, he laid his hand over Keegan's on his prick and guided himself inside.

"Oooooooh," Keegan breathed as Scott filled him up. "Yeah, that's it. God."

Scott studied Keegan's face with an unnerving directness. "Don't close your eyes," Scott said in a lust-rough voice when Keegan's eyelids fluttered. "Look at me."

Keegan bit his lip and fought the urge to shut his eyes with everything he had. If Scott wanted that intimacy, Keegan was determined to give it to him.

It surprised him more than a little to discover how good it felt to stare into Scott's eyes while they made love. It was incredibly intense, making him feel bare and raw and vulnerable. But at the same time, he felt a sense of completion and peace like he'd never known. He cupped Scott's face in his hands, panting through parted lips as Scott fucked him deep and slow.

"You feel so good," Scott whispered. "So hot. So fucking alive inside."

"Want you inside me forever." Keegan ran both thumbs over Scott's soft lips. "So good, Scott."

"Yeah. Good." Scott's eyes went unfocused for a second. "Close. Oh God..."

"Fuck, yeah." Keegan wriggled until he could sling his legs over Scott's shoulders. The new angle sent Scott's next thrust slamming into his prostate and he cried out. "God, now, now, hard, baby, come on!"

Growling, Scott planted his hands on the mattress at Keegan's sides and pounded him in short, sharp jabs. Keegan's world shrank until all he could see was Scott's face hovering over his, all he could feel was Scott's cock filling him up.

Keegan came with his eyes wide open and locked with Scott's, watching Scott's orgasm take him. It was the best thing he'd ever felt.

Scott pulled out, rolled over and folded Keegan against his chest before Keegan recovered enough to move on his own. Keegan cuddled right up, one arm snug around Scott's middle. Scott's heartbeat thudded under his ear, strong and fast and steady. He sighed in perfect contentment.

"Wow," Keegan mumbled when he could talk again. "That was unbelievable. I've never kept my eyes open during sex before."

Scott's hand came up to stroke Keegan's sweaty hair. "Was it good?"

"Incredible. I always thought it would be too much, you know? Maybe with someone else, it would've been." Keegan lifted his head enough to see Scott's face. "With you, it was perfect. I'm glad we did it that way."

Scott smiled, his hand sliding down to cup Keegan's cheek. "Me too. Come here."

Keegan moved to meet Scott's kiss, opening his mouth to Scott's probing tongue. There was something wonderfully different, he thought, about kissing someone who truly knew you and loved you anyway. He knew he'd never be able to live without that feeling, now that he'd tasted it. With any luck, he'd never have to.

Now if only he could work up the courage to tell Scott how he felt. Scott had helped him rise above the past that had dragged him down for so long, and Keegan wanted him to know that.

Tomorrow, Keegan thought as he snuggled back into Scott's embrace. *Tomorrow, I'll tell him I love him. It's Valentine's Day, after all.*

His mind made up, Keegan closed his eyes and slept.

Chapter Seven

Ganymede's Grotto was packed to the rafters when Scott arrived the next night. Leaning against the bar, he signaled the bartender, Jordan.

"Keegan said you spent the night with him," Jordan said without preamble.

Scott grinned. Jordan was always shockingly direct. "Yeah, I did. He kicked me out this afternoon at three, when he had to come to work. Could I get a whiskey and soda, please?"

"Coming up." Jordan poured the drink and handed it to Scott. "I'd give good money to watch you guys going at it. You ever considered doing it in one of the viewing rooms?"

Chuckling, Scott shook his head. "No."

"You should." Jordan gave him a cheerful leer. "That'd be hot."

"Not happening. Sorry." Scott glanced toward the stage. Keegan's show wasn't supposed to start for another five minutes. "So tell me about this Lupercalia thing."

Earlier that day, Keegan had explained that every February fourteenth, Ganymede's Grotto observed the ancient Roman holiday of Lupercalia. According to Keegan, the sexual nature of the festival was frowned on by the newly powerful church when Christian rule began in Rome. The church replaced the centuries-old celebrations with its own, tamer activities. A romantic story of a rebel priest was invented and whispered among the people. It took hold, and Valentine's Day was born.

Keegan had hinted that the club observed some of the Romans' traditional sexual games, but hadn't said what they were. Scott was horribly curious, even though he had no plans to participate.

Jordan shrugged as he drew a draft beer for another customer. "Not much to tell. It's basically an excuse for a big party with lots of sex. The group sex rooms and the viewing rooms'll be packed later, after the drawing."

Scott raised his eyebrows. "Drawing?"

"For partners. Anyone who wants to participate puts their name in a bowl. Earl draws names in pairs, and the couples go fuck. They can use a private room, or join a group, or put on a show, whatever they want. It's about the most popular night of the year for the Dungeons too, other than Halloween."

Scott cleared his throat. He knew that Ganymede's Grotto had "dungeons" for the use of their members who were into the BDSM lifestyle, but he didn't want to think about it. It reminded him of Logan.

Just then, the primitive throb of Keegan's music started. Scott turned toward the stage. Earl stood in front of the mic, grinning at the cheering crowd.

"Good evening, gentlemen," Earl said. "Welcome one and all to the eleventh annual Lupercalia Festival here at Ganymede's Grotto."

Wild cheers and lewd suggestions rang out from the audience. Earl laughed. "Remember, if you'd like to participate in our sex-partner drawing, please see any of our wonderful waitstaff. They'll make sure that your name is entered. We'll draw names after the show. And now, without further ado, I give you the God of Love himself, the one, the only, Eros!"

The curtain swung open as Earl exited the stage, and Scott's breath caught. Keegan stood there under a red spotlight, poured into the skintight white pants and sheer shirt he'd been wearing the first time Scott watched him strip. He had his back to the audience, the feathered wings framing his ass in shining white, his red-gold curls tumbling in a wild cascade down his back. Scott thought, as he did every time, that he'd never seen anyone so hot in his life.

The show was more or less Keegan's usual Eros act, but it seemed different to Scott. Keegan's body moved with a feral grace, his features lit by the most beautiful smile Scott had ever seen. Fierce and free and joyful. Keegan was always sexy when he stripped, but this unguarded delight made Scott want to jump him right there on stage.

By the time Keegan took his bows and left the stage, Scott was painfully hard and squirming on the barstool he'd managed to snag. A big, annoyingly handsome man who'd been eyeing Keegan earlier had gotten a phone call and left halfway through the show, much to Scott's relief. It disturbed him how much he wanted to grab the guy by the throat and tell him to lay off, that Keegan was *his* and no one else's. After all, how else was the guy supposed to look at a stripper? Scott shook his head at his own irrationality.

Scott fidgeted through the drawing of names for Lupercalia partners, trying to resist the urge to glance at his watch every few seconds. His mind wandered, thinking of all the things he'd rather be doing right then. Like kissing Keegan. Running his hands over Keegan's smooth bare skin. Feeling Keegan's breath in his ear while they fucked. He reached between his legs and adjusted himself as discreetly as possible.

Scott nearly jumped out of his skin with surprise when he heard Earl call the names Logan Pitts and Darryl Rogers, followed by the name of a man clearly meant to be their third for the night. Squinting through the crowd around the stage, Scott picked out Logan's tousled blond head. A man who Scott recognized as Darryl stood behind him, arms around his waist. Logan laughed as he reached a hand toward the blushing sandy-haired young man Earl sent his way. He looked happy. Smiling, Scott raised his glass in a silent toast.

Hands slid around his waist from behind, startling him. "Hi Scott," a voice breathed in his ear.

Scott turned with a smile, pulling Keegan into his arms and kissing him. "Hi, gorgeous."

"Mmmm." Keegan nipped lightly at Scott's upper lip, one hand slipping between his legs to cup his half-hard cock. "Enjoy the show?"

"Always." Scott ran a hand through Keegan's hair. "You're definitely the sexiest stripper I've been in bed with lately."

Keegan laughed, then sobered so quickly Scott blinked in surprise. "Keegan? What's wrong?"

"Nothing," Keegan said, his expression screaming the exact opposite. "I just...I need to tell you something and I want to do it right now."

"What is it?" Scott laid a hand on Keegan's cheek. "You can tell me anything. There's no need to be afraid."

"I'm not." Keegan flushed and gave a sheepish grin. "Okay, so I am. But not because it's anything bad, just because it's something I've never said before. Well, except to Earl and that's different. And Tony." Keegan shuddered. "That was *really* different. But this time it's real, you know, and it feels like it's gonna last, and, and I...I just..."

Keegan trailed off, tongue toying with his lip ring, but by then Scott had figured it out for himself. He cupped Keegan's face in his hands and pressed a tender kiss to his lips. "Are you trying to say you love me?"

Keegan's relief was palpable. "Yes. I love you."

Scott smiled. "I know."

Keegan's eyes glinted with a mixture of eagerness and fear, but his smile was bright enough to light the whole city. He opened his mouth as if to say something, then closed it again and shook his head. "What do you think of Lupercalia? Great, huh?"

Scott looked around at the roomful of groups and couples kissing and touching one another. The atmosphere was relaxed and happy. He spotted Logan, Darryl and the sandy-haired stranger heading for one of the dungeons, and he smiled. It made him happy to see Logan had evidently found what he'd been looking for.

"Looks like everyone's having fun," Scott observed.

"Hey, isn't that Logan?" Keegan nodded toward the threesome disappearing through the dungeon door. "What's he doing here?"

Scott had to laugh at Keegan's thunderous expression. "Don't worry. He's found somebody else, and it looks like they're happy together."

Keegan frowned at the doorway, then turned back to Scott with a smile. "Good. He's not allowed to fuck with us."

"In any sense of the word," Scott agreed. "But I'm glad he got his happy ending."

Keegan pressed himself between Scott's legs. "I'm more glad that we got ours. I'm so happy, Scott. I've never been this happy before."

A lump rose in Scott's throat. He pulled Keegan close and they kissed for a long time.

"Let's go somewhere private," Scott whispered, breaking the kiss. "Before I lose it and fuck you right here in the middle of all these people."

Keegan laughed. "Most of this bunch would like that."

"Too bad. I'm not sharing you, even if they're just looking."

Keegan's cheeks went pink. He grinned. "Just a second. I want to—"

His words were cut off by Earl's voice rising above the growing din of voices. "Your pardon, gentlemen. I thought I was finished calling names, but it seems I have two more." Pulling a slip of paper out of the large bowl in his hands, Earl squinted at it. "Oh my. Keegan Rourke, our very own Eros! Come on up here, sweetheart."

Oh my God. Shocked to the core, Scott stood frozen while Keegan kissed his chin, slipped out of his embrace and bounded up to the stage. Scott's chest felt tight, his body numb. *I can't believe Keegan did this.*

Giving Keegan a quick hug, Earl drew another piece of paper from the bowl. "Keegan's partner for the evening—and, I suspect, for a very long time afterward—is Scott Jasper!"

For a second, Scott was too stunned to react. Jordan leaned across the bar and gave him a shove. "Get up there, Scott."

It was enough to snap Scott out of his paralysis. Feeling a little surreal, Scott made his way through the crowd to the stage, climbed the steps and swept Keegan into his arms. They kissed to a soundtrack of catcalls, whistles and applause. Scott didn't care about the audience. All that mattered was Keegan's body pressed to his, Keegan's hands in his hair as the kiss went deep.

"Congratulations to all our couples tonight," Earl said as Scott and Keegan drew apart. "Now go get a room, you two. This is a family establishment."

As the roomful of men roared with laughter, Keegan took Scott's hand and led him off the stage. They set off through the crowd with their arms around each other. On all sides of them, the party was in full force. The room rang with talk and laughter and music.

Keegan glanced around. "You didn't mind me setting that up, did you? I figured it would be kind of fun."

Scott laughed. "I'll admit, you scared me for a minute there. But you're right, it *was* fun." Sliding a hand down Keegan's back, Scott gave his ass a squeeze. "How long can you get away for?"

"I have a twenty minute break. I don't think Earl would mind if we take a few extra minutes, though." Keegan gazed up at him with a strangely shy look. "Maybe next year, I can ask off for part of the night. We could hang out, do some dancing."

Next year. The thought made Scott feel warm through and through. He kissed the top of Keegan's head.

"Babe, it's a date."

About the Author

Ally Blue used to be a good girl. Really. Married for twenty years, two lovely children, house, dogs, picket fence, the whole deal. Then one day she discovered slash fan fiction. She wrote her first fan fiction story a couple of months later and has since slid merrily into the abyss. She has had several short stories published in the erotic e-zine Ruthie's Club, and is a regular contributor to the original slash e-zine Forbidden Fruit.

To learn more about Ally Blue, please visit http://www.allyblue.com/. Send an email to Ally Blue at mailto:ally@allyblue.com or join her Yahoo! group to join in the fun with other readers as well as Ally Blue, http://groups.yahoo.com/group/loveisblue/

Café Noctem

Willa Okati

Dedication

For the people of Asheville, and the Cherokee nation.

Prologue

Once upon a time Brother Deer came across Sint Holo, who was sitting with his legs crossed, industriously working on a frame of stretched hide resting in his lap.

"Greetings to you, Sint Holo," Deer saluted the Snake Man. "What mischief are you making now?"

"No mischief," Sint Holo replied, "but a blessing to all mankind."

Deer peered at the thing Snake Man was making. It did not appear to him to be anything good or beneficent to the People. Instead, it looked grotesquely like a human face stitched onto a—"Is that a deer skin?" he asked in horror. "Only the People are allowed to take the skins of my kind, and they give up thanks for our offerings. Where did you get this?"

Sint Holo showed his sharp teeth to Deer. "Wouldn't you like to know?" He picked up a strand of blue thread, stolen from the song of a robin as she flew to her nest, and began to stitch a design into the cheek of the face he was creating.

Deer hid his eyes from the sight of the evil thing Snake Man was devising. "Whatever this is, I believe you mean it for evil, not good. Put it away at once. Better yet, burn the thing."

"Burn it?" Sint Holo hooted. "After I have spent so many hours of work on my art? I would never burn this. Besides, the symbols I have stitched into the skin ensure that it cannot be destroyed, not even by my own hands."

"Then this is an object with great medicine," Deer said, peeking out from behind his hooves. "I still believe it to be evil, though."

"Oh, evil, evil." Sint Holo made another stitch. "Evil is an idea that lives in men's heads, Brother Deer. You should know that as well as I do. They venerate me as a god, but they also think I am malicious, and so they never keep any totems of my kind, and they kill my little siblings if they so much as crawl through the corn. Why should I not, then, return their charity in kind?"

"Have pity," Brother Deer pleaded. "Give the Cherokee, the People, another chance before you visit something terrible upon them."

"Now, when did I say what I was making would be terrible? And did I *say* this would be an evil thing?" Sint Holo checked his work. "Yes, yes," he murmured, "just a few more colors and a bit of banding around the eye holes, and I shall be done. Brother Deer, would you hand me the orange thread?"

"Where did you get this?" Deer asked suspiciously, pawing at the small hank of yarn. "It looks like the fruit that the Spaniards brought when they tried to trade with our People."

"I stole it from a memory of one of their cast-aside rinds."

"Sint Holo, for shame."

"What?" Snake Man showed all his sharp teeth. "They took from the Cherokee without asking permission or offering anything besides beads or baubles. So, I stole myself a bit of their rubbish."

"And you have kept it by your side all this time?"

"I am a thrifty creature." Sint Holo hissed. "Go away, now. You hinder me in my work. I should have been done by now."

Deer dragged one of his hooves across the forest floor. "I will not," he said, raising his antlers. "I believe you *are* concocting something that will bring harm to the People, and I will not leave until I have stopped you or I am made to believe otherwise."

Sint Holo flickered his forked tongue in annoyance. "Oh, very well. I suppose I can't force you to go away, now can I? And if it's proof you want, well, as soon as I have finished with these last few stitches, you'll have all the evidence you need." His grin was a fearsome thing, especially to such a creature as Deer, who backed up a few steps. "I have guests coming. Invited company, unlike yourself."

He threaded his bone needle with a strand of purple, and made quick work of the remainder of his sewing, creating whorls and knots around two cut-out holes that would serve for eyes in the face he was making. Deer watched in anxious indecision, half-wondering if he should try to dash the skin out of Sint Holo's hands and trample it into the rich red dirt. But to defile one of his little brothers in such a fashion...

And so he watched, and he waited.

"There! I am finished," Snake Man said with pride, whipping the sewn-on face free of its frame. He cast the pine frame aside, as if it were trash, no longer needed. Deer knew better, though. Sint Holo was far too canny to discard anything he might find of use later. This was a bit of show for his benefit.

"So," a new voice purred from above their heads. Now Deer did rear in fright, for Bobcat was crawling out on a thick branch, crouching on the edge as if ready to pounce. "This is what you have called me here for, Snake Man?"

"This, and this alone." Sint Holo displayed his sewn face proudly, as he would a prize. "What do you think of my handiwork?"

Bobcat yawned, his mouth wide and pink, his teeth sharp and yellow. "It's well enough," he allowed. "But it isn't complete, yet, even though you told Deer otherwise. You need my own help to make the face live."

"A little favor between friends," Sint Holo agreed amiably enough. "Jump down and smell the deerskin. Taste the magic in the stitching."

"Do you think to catch me out so easily?" Bobcat demanded. "That would give you my magic, and I will not do so until Owl has arrived and given us the benefit of his wisdom on this matter."

"I am here," yet another voice answered. Deer stared as Owl, huge and snowy white, settled down on a branch opposite Bobcat. Bobcat licked his chops at the sight of the bird, but said nothing—although he did knead his claws in and out of the limb he lay on. "What mischief is this, Sint Holo?"

"I have created a face for Man to wear," Sint Holo said with pride, holding up his handiwork. "It needs a touch of foresight from you, Bobcat, and a taste of wisdom from you, Owl. It will need to know who it can work for, and who it cannot. See, Deer?" He flashed Deer a mocking smile. "I am not such an evil creature as you would make me out to be."

"No?" Deer asked, wary of Sint Holo's tricks.

"Oh, no. This mask is a gift for the Cherokee people, for their children, and for their grandchildren, and for anyone with a drop of our blood in their veins. Look, here—see?" Sint Holo fit the skin face over his own snaky features, where they molded and hardened into a mask with round holes for eyes and one for a mouth. He chuckled out hissing laughter at Deer's fright before he took the thing away from his face.

"What possible good could this do the People?" Deer asked suspiciously, a little angry, to cover his fright.

"Yes, what good?" Owl echoed. Bobcat merely yawned.

Sint Holo neatly trimmed away the excess deerskin, much to Deer's consternation, and held up his prize. "Why with this they will be able to summon one of the Dead. They will be able to bring him back, and he will live among them once again so long as he keeps this fastened to his head."

"How is this a good thing?" Owl wanted to know.

"And you are the one with the wisdom." Sint Holo tsked. "Think of all the possibility. A medicine man, dead before his time, unable to pass all his secrets along to his student? A chief, whose knowledge of the enemy is needed before a battle. A hunter, whose strong right arm would be needed to keep winter's hungers at bay."

Owl chattered his beak, a sign that he was thinking. "I can see how this would be good," he allowed. "But how will you convince the People to accept any gift from you, Sint Holo? I am willing enough to help, but they will never take anything from you."

Sint Holo turned on Deer, his diamond-shaped eyes glittering. "Why, that is where our friend Deer comes in," he said prettily, holding out the mask. "Are you convinced now that this is for the good? Will you take this as my gift to the People?"

Deer hovered, caught in confusion. Surely Sint Holo meant nothing but trouble, and such a powerfully magical object would not be good for the Cherokee. They might fall to fighting over the mask, and then what would become of them?

But to be able to call back the dead for their knowledge and strength, to have the ability to touch the spirit world at their fingertips during a time when the bridge between one world and another was growing dangerously thin...

Did he trust Sint Holo, or not?

Deer hesitated for a long time, but eventually, faced down by the staring of Bobcat, Owl and Snake Man, he made his choice...

And he forever changed the course of Mankind—albeit in a small, but powerfully significant way...

Chapter One

The small black sedan slid into place on the shoulder of the road, coming to a stop with hardly a sound from the engine. The same stillness that hung thickly in the air, like smoke, seemed to blanket the car and muffle any noises it might make.

"It's as if even voices wouldn't carry," the slender man in the passenger seat murmured to the driver, easily half again his size and weight. "So empty. So quiet." When the driver made no response, he reached over and gripped one of his hands where it rested on the steering wheel and squeezed. "Are you all right, Grey?"

The driver, Grey, shook his head once—a short, chopped-off motion. He kept his face forward, not turning to look at the man who'd ridden with him to this place. "I'm fine," he said, his voice a deep, rich rumble that would normally charm the birds from the trees but was now void of any emotion. "I promised myself—him—that I'd do this. Every year. So I'm here."

"It's causing you pain, though." The passenger carefully rubbed the hand he held. "Surely he wouldn't have wanted you to suffer on his account."

That earned him an angry stare. "Don't presume to tell me what *he* would want and what *he* wouldn't want. You didn't know us, Nicholas."

"I did know you. Both of you," Nicholas replied, stung. "We were all three of us friends until—"

"Don't you finish saying those words." Grey's hands tightened on the wheel. "We were friends, sure, but you weren't with us like Jimmy and I were together. He and I shared everything, Nicholas. Hell, we'd use each other's toothbrushes by mistake." He shrugged his thick shoulders angrily. "Jimmy knew me like no one else ever did, and no one ever will."

"I see." Nicholas withdrew his hand, watching Grey with wary eyes. "Even me, then?"

Grey started to move forward, then stopped, sliding back, eyes closed. "You know me too, Nicholas," he responded wearily. "Almost as well as he did."

"I'm not him, though. I never have been and I never will be. That's the unforgivable sin in your book, isn't it?" Nicholas felt stung by Grey's words, but he wasn't surprised. From the moment Grey had announced he'd be taking this journey, he'd known this could end in nothing but a clash and fray.

It had always been like this, ever since Nicholas had replaced Jimmy in Grey's life. Not by Grey's choice, not at first. Nicholas certainly wouldn't have ousted Jimmy on purpose, but he'd thought—hoped—that as time passed by, he'd been settling in. Things had gone well enough with being a bigger part of Grey's life, the two even reaching the point of moving into the apartment over Grey's coffee shop. Café Noctem, a perfect place to live. Gently, piece by piece, they'd eased the old out to make way for the new. Nicholas had made a home for his things and his own space in Grey's life. But still, in some small ways, he'd always felt like an intruder, though, and he suspected he knew why.

No one would ever replace Jimmy in Grey's heart.

Grey turned the car off and pulled the keys from the ignition. He jingled them briefly in one hand before tossing them into the half-empty ashtray. Luckily, he'd already stubbed out one of the cigarettes he kept burning but never smoked, which he'd lit as they drove to where they were now. "I'm sorry," he said quietly. "I really am. I'm taking this out on you. Again. You never asked for any of this, and you don't deserve it."

"Grey..." Nicholas reached for his lover's hand again and took it in his own. "He was my friend, too. You're not the only one grieving today. And that is why I understand, why I've always understood, and why I'm not upset with you for being in a mood right now. This is hard enough on the both of us."

Grey raised Nicholas' hand to his mouth and kissed the back, full lips to pale-brown skin. "You're good to me," he ventured after a moment, still holding on. "You're too good to me, and I don't deserve you."

"Whoever said we deserved anything good in our lives? We're only human, and we know what humans are like." Nicholas gently withdrew his hand. "Come on, love. Let's take care of what we've come to do, and then perhaps you'll find a little peace."

"Maybe." Grey's attention had wandered again. He stared out the driver's side window at the low-hanging mist and fog swirling around their car. "Almost seems like ghosts, doesn't it?" he asked, as if questioning no one in particular. "Makes me wonder if..."

"Don't. He isn't out there. You shouldn't torture yourself." Nicholas leaned his head back against his seat, still gazing at Grey. His heart ached with love for the man, and seeing him in so much pain made his insides twist. His great-grandmother, one of the Cherokee, would have said there was bad medicine in the air, and he half-suspected she would have been right. And while there might not be ghosts in the fog, there was definitely something sinister to the way the curls of mist twined and writhed along the ground.

Almost snakelike.

Nicholas shivered. He undid his seatbelt, then reached over to release Grey's from its clasp. Grey turned to him, seeming vaguely startled. "Come on," Nicholas prompted. "Let's move. You can do this. Out of the car, and a short walk."

"What? Oh. Yeah. Yes. Let's go." Grey shook his head. "Did you feel that?"

"Feel what?"

"Nothing, I guess. Just...this strange feeling of cold air. Like the wind outside was blowing right through the car."

Nicholas eyed Grey carefully. "I felt nothing," he said, wondering if his lover were all right. Perhaps this was too much too soon. Should they turn around and go back home instead?

But no, too late, for Grey was already opening his car door and stepping out. Nicholas followed suit, wanting to be by his partner's side. As he walked around the car, he couldn't help but admire the man.

Anyone, gay or straight, would be proud to have Grey at their side. Tall as a reasonably sized basketball player and bulky through the shoulders from lifting weights, he tapered down into a toned waist and trim hips before bulging out again with rocklike muscles in his thighs and calves. He had a bit more Cherokee in him than Nicholas, and it showed in the hawk-like shape of his features, his beaky nose and the stern cast of his mouth. His hair, too, was definitely of the People— long, the tips brushing his shoulders, and a deeply hued shade of black—although there was far more gray threading through it now than there had recently been.

He was a man of such size he made Nicholas feel small, and such a brave that next to him Nicholas felt every inch one of the white men, no matter how he had been raised. As a teacher, his great-grandmother had kept him firmly in line and made sure he knew the ways of the People and how to honor the spirits, but as a caregiver she'd loved him with all the heart in her wrinkled old body.

When he came to the dinner table one night, watching her cook, and he'd told her that he thought he was gay, she had simply smiled and continued to stir the soup she was making. He'd been trembling with fear at her possible reaction, but she'd only shaken her head and said, "Well, make sure to find a good man, strong in the arm and clever in the head, eh? Don't fall for someone pretty, with no sense. That's been the downfall of many a hunter." Then she'd offered him a taste from her pot, and, well, that had been the end of that.

He had learned many things from his great-grandmother, but simple acceptance that what would be, would be, was one of her most powerful lessons.

If she were still around, he felt sure she would approve of Grey. A strapping big man with the smarts to own and operate his own business, a small café in the heart of downtown Asheville. Café Noctem. Nicholas could remember the fun they'd all had in naming Grey's new enterprise, and finally deciding on Noctem in honor of all the night owls the artsy city teemed with.

As Nicholas recalled, though, it had been Jimmy's idea to stay open all night, almost up to the breakfast rush, and it'd been his schedule which made Café Noctem a success. At any hour of the night, you could find at least a half-dozen people hunched over laptops or textbooks, a feverish look of inspiration in their eyes and a mug by their sides.

At first, it had been Jimmy who handled the night crowd, but now that was Nicholas' job. Grey took the morning through mid-afternoon, and here, in the between-time, was when they normally caught up with one another. Grey had closed a little early today, around one instead of two, as if sensing this task might take longer than anticipated. Nicholas felt the weariness of not-enough-sleep catching up to him, but he manfully held back a yawn as he walked up to Grey's side.

Grey didn't offer to take his hand, so Nicholas did it instead. In Asheville, two men strolling so close together wasn't so odd a sight that it would turn heads, and even if it had been, he wouldn't have cared. He'd never believed Grey would be his, and he scarcely believed it now.

Although he'd never have chosen this way to... Nicholas shook his head. His thoughts were going around in circles, and that was never good. He'd end up buried in a sea of what-ifs and if-I-had-onlys. Lightly squeezing Grey's hand he asked instead, "Are you ready?"

Dark eyes narrowing, Grey nodded. "Let's go."

They set off side by side, Nicholas having to hurry a little to keep up with Grey's long stride. Shorter by a head, he was size-proportionate and looked far more white than Native, with his curling brown hair and his blue eyes. There had been legends about Natives with blue eyes, but his great-grandmother had laughed, told him his history wasn't so grand, and pointed out that his father had come from Nordic stock.

He didn't think he was half so handsome as Grey, being instead a boy-next-door type with a friendly face and a wide grin, but then you could have described Jimmy the same way...yet he transcended, somehow, and became more than the sum of his parts.

Nicholas conjured up a mental image of Jimmy as he preferred to remember the man. Snapping green eyes, the devil's own grin and rakish chocolate-colored hair that stuck up in a hundred different directions; smaller than Nicholas but equally trim, his build reflecting his habit of running five miles every morning. For his own part, Nicholas swam in a local pool when he could or canoed down the French Broad River.

He tried, for the thousandth time, to stop comparing himself to Jimmy. He knew he wasn't Jimmy, knew he never would be, and he should stop trying. But all the same, he couldn't help thinking that if it were him they were coming to visit, Jimmy would know exactly what to tell Grey to take that storm-cloud look off his face.

So it was in silence that Nicholas and Grey walked up a small, grassy embankment bare of anything but February's dead grass. "You'd think they'd keep things up better," Grey remarked, toeing a few stalks. "We don't pay them enough for maintenance?"

Nicholas bit his lip and kept quiet. To distract himself, he reached out and laid a hand on the first thing they had come to—a tombstone, one of the old breed, built like an obelisk. The O'Connor family—husband, wife and six children. They had died at different times, but he'd no idea where any husbands or grandchildren might lie at rest. He always touched this stone for luck when they visited the cemetery.

When they came to see Jimmy.

Grey knew about Nicholas' superstition, but chose to view the obelisk as a directional sign rather than a totem. He pointed, even though he didn't have to, and jerked his head forward. "This way."

Nicholas knew the path, but kept silent. It was important to Grey to maintain the illusion of staying in control. He knew, having held the man after previous visits, that keeping his cool in public was all Grey could cling to from time to time.

"I should have brought flowers," Grey muttered. "That poinsettia was nice at Christmas. But it seems kind of girly, bringing roses and such, doesn't it?"

Nicholas gave a careful shrug. "Jimmy was a gardener. I think it would be appropriate. He liked tulips the best."

"I remember. He used to beg me for a trip to Biltmore every spring so he could see their gardens. We'd go to that fancy restaurant they have and split a bottle of the most expensive wine they had."

"Then leave the glitz behind you, go to a pub, and come home rip-roaring drunk," Nicholas joked.

There, that earned him a grin from Grey's handsome lips. "Jimmy had a lot of sterling qualities, but the ability to hold his liquor was definitely not one of them." He put a hand over his heart. "I, myself, was never in need of any assistance after one of those little trips."

"Of course not." Nicholas bumped hips with Grey. "I've completely forgotten the time I had to come over and nurse the both of you through the most spectacular set of hangovers I've ever seen."

Grey chuckled. "Oh, don't worry—I remember. God, I forget just how many pints of beer we did get through that night..." His voice faded off. He coughed. "We had good times. If I had a mug, I'd drink to them."

"To good times," Nicholas replied quietly, rubbing his thumb along Grey's. Grey gave him a fond look and rubbed back, the look and gesture sending a bolt of warmth to Nicholas' heart. His proud Native man didn't often display affection in public, and to touch him tenderly here and now made Nicholas feel almost weak with pleasure.

The feeling didn't last for long, though. As they turned around a mausoleum with a marble angel at every corner, their destination was in sight. Nicholas held back, tugging at Grey to get his attention. "Here's Annie," he commented, petting the marble foot of one seraphim. "She looks to have weathered the winter well. Not a chip off her."

"Nicholas?"

Nicholas grew still, except for stroking Annie Angel's foot. "Yes?"

"Stop trying to distract me."

Nicholas looked up to see Grey with a half-smile on his face. He pulled at their joined hands. "Come with me," he asked politely. "I need you."

"Yes. Of course." Nicholas gave Annie a final pat and pushed his free hand into his pocket. Asheville had terribly chilly Februarys, and this year was proving to be no exception. Grey had worn gloves, the sensible thing to do. Nicholas shook his head at himself. He could manage his life up to a point, could even run a café with a waitstaff of half a dozen, but could he remember to keep his hands warm?

Well, to give himself credit, he did have to admit he was somewhat distracted by the thought of where they were headed.

Grey kept Nicholas close by his side until he pulled up short in front of a flat stone just at the rise of another hill. Still new enough that the polished marble shone, it read:

```
JAMESON NEIL KELLY
     1975-2006
  BELOVED FRIEND
```

"They wouldn't let me put anything else on there," Grey said quietly, although Nicholas had heard all this before—at length—even before they had come together as a couple. "His family insisted he lie here all alone, not even in the family plot. No kin around to keep him company."

Grey fumbled in his jeans pocket and brought out a handful of three round, river-washed stones, the size of small clay discs, green and gray and red. Nicholas gave a start at the sight of them. "Where did you get those?"

"From the creek that runs down through the campus. He and I went wading there one time." Grey turned the stones over and over in his palm, their soft clinking almost musical as the water that would have flowed over them. "I thought he'd like a reminder of the good times. He must be lonely as hell out here by himself."

He squared his shoulders. "Well, as long as I'm able to, I'll still come visit."

"As will I." Nicholas slowly let go of Grey's hand to go down on one knee next to the stone. He traced the deeply carved letters with two cold fingers, feeling their grooves like comfortable old friends. Above him, he could almost feel Grey struggling to stop himself from saying *no* and *don't*. But Jimmy had been his friend, too. "Hope you're resting well," he whispered. "We've still got to watch each other's backs."

He felt Grey touch his shoulder, the leather of his gloves tangible through the light jacket he wore. Nicholas shivered. "Should have worn something heavier," he explained when Grey gave him a puzzled look. Carefully, as if he were an old man, he stood. "I'll let you take your time."

Grey acknowledged him with a nod. One by one, he put the stones on Jimmy's grave. "It's a Jewish custom, I know," he said, "and I don't follow that path, but it's a sign of respect." He paused. "I miss you. More than I can—well. I do. You probably know I have Nicholas taking care of me now. But he's not—ah, Jimmy." He caressed the stone. "Every Valentine's Day, right? Not the fourteenth, though, the thirteenth. Your lucky number. You always said you'd scoop up all the good luck leftover from everyone else having bad luck. Pretty clever of you." Grey gave a shuddering sigh. "Happy hearts and flowers day, lover. Wish you were here."

Nicholas exhaled softly and huddled deeper into his coat. He'd been by alone the night before to pay his respects. This moment was solely for Grey. To occupy his mind, he raised his head to gaze out across the rows of stones and crypts, some so old their lettering had long since worn off, and let his gaze go unfocused. He knew Grey didn't mean to hurt him by anything he said.

It was just, once you'd known Jimmy, you found it very hard to say goodbye to the man. And if you'd been as close as Grey and Jimmy—Nicholas could hardly believe Grey had ever turned to him at all.

He might not have if Nicholas hadn't been there for him every moment up to and after the funeral, keeping an eye out for his friend the way Jimmy would have wanted. It'd become something of a habit, dropping in every day or so, and then things had just happened naturally.

He'd started bringing over groceries, and staying to cool a meal. They'd watched the game together, Grey coming out of his gloom long enough to root for his favorite team. Then Nicholas had taken over for an incompetent night-shift manager at Café Noctem, napped upstairs in Grey's bed instead of commuting home on a busy day, and woken that afternoon to find Grey lying on the sheets next to him, a strange, wondering look in his eyes as he reached for Nicholas, and Nicholas, amazed at himself as he went...

No, Grey didn't mean any harm. He just hadn't said his farewells yet, no matter how many times he spoke the word "goodbye". Perhaps he would, someday. Nicholas didn't mind. For a man like Grey, he'd be willing to wait. The love of his life, who'd taken him by surprise, was worth being patient with.

"There's so much I don't remember, even though my mother and father claim to have raised me right," Grey said with a sharp, aborted laugh. "Walk the spirit roads in peace, my love. That sounds about right. So long, Jimmy."

He stepped back from the grave and reached out for Nicholas, his face set in lines that clearly stated he wasn't going to talk about anything. Nicholas didn't protest. As a rule, men didn't share their feelings all that openly, himself included—mostly—and he understood Grey wanting to keep his grief private at the moment, even if he didn't think it was too healthy.

Nicholas allowed himself to be gathered in, knowing Grey wanted something to protect as they walked out of the graveyard. He did, however, look backwards once over his shoulder and mouth the words, "Watch our backs, my friend." Then he turned his face forward, able to walk at his own pace as Grey was going slowly.

"The festival starts tonight," Nicholas ventured after a moment. "The masqueraders will be out. Do we have enough trimming for the café cellar?"

Grey tilted his head in thought. "Probably. And if we don't have everything we need, we'll go and get it. How does that sound?"

"Like a plan." *Like you'll be too busy with carnival plans to sink into any deep fits of gloom tonight.* "We've got plenty of time left to get things ready."

"Don't look at me. You're the one in charge." Grey chafed one of Nicholas' cold hands between his leather gloves. "This is your night shift, and it's your show."

Nicholas gave his lover a playful nudge. "Do you think you can stay awake through all the festivities?"

"I'm almost positive."

"I could be persuaded to reward you after the morning rush tomorrow..."

As Nicholas had hoped, that earned him a genuine laugh. "Oh, could you now? Well, what about me rewarding you before the morning crowd comes in? We should have a couple of hours to kill if we don't waste them in cleaning up the cellar..."

Nicholas reached up and seized Grey by the lapels, kissing him hard. His move took the other man by surprise, but after a moment Grey kissed back, his arms coming around Nicholas' back. When their lips parted they stood swaying lightly for a moment, foreheads cradled together, their breath misty white in the cold air. They kissed again, soft and gentle, heads tilting to allow each other access to their mouths. Not a kiss full of passion, but one filled with promise. Grey pulled Nicholas tight, holding him close as the moment washed over them and passed, leaving them feeling somehow more at peace.

The mist on the ground began to fade away in curls.

Neither man noticed.

They stood in silence for a long moment before Nicholas cleared his throat. "Are we ready?" he asked in a quiet voice, showing respect for the dead on whose land they stood.

"Let's go," Grey said, much to Nicholas' relief. "The car will be warm. And we have a night of celebrations to prepare for. Celebration de la Vie in Asheville; it's not to be missed, or so I hear." He grinned and tweaked Nicholas' nose. "Or so I've been hearing since I was old enough to attend. Let's get out of here."

Nicholas nodded, relieved that this trip out, at least, had ended well enough. "I'm right behind you."

"No. You're at my side. Always at my side. First my friend and now my partner." Grey gave Nicholas a rough hug. "I don't know what I'd do without you."

"Then just be glad you have me and that I'm not going anywhere," Nicholas said softly, too softly for Grey to hear. "Not if I can help it."

And with those being his final words, the two of them left the cemetery behind them. Grey drove them away, still all but silent on the smoothly paved roads, through the gated entry and out onto the Blue Ridge Parkway. All the way back to their home, Nicholas occasionally placed his hand on Grey's thigh, subtly reminding him of who he was with now, anchoring him to the present instead of the past.

He found himself wary of what might be coming next. But then again, no one would suspect. Or should not have.

But if Nicholas' great-grandmother had been alive, she'd have seen the snaky smoke and warned the son of her daughter's son about what would be coming their way.

Nicholas might, or might not, have even believed her...

Chapter Two

The curling mists seemed to follow Grey and Nicholas home, twining around their wheels and distorting the road in front of them until Grey cursed and put on the brakes, going at a crawl. Mountain roads could be treacherous, and Nicholas knew he wouldn't put either of them at risk.

He also knew better than to try and talk to Grey when the man was driving. He didn't have passion for many things these days, but the café, Nicholas and his car were in the top three. Just an ordinary black sedan, but he kept it polished to a gleaming shine and looked after the thing as carefully as a baby.

He and Jimmy had picked the car out together, and it had belonged to both of them. Sitting in the passenger's seat, Nicholas felt uncomfortably as if he were sharing it with a ghost. If it'd been Jimmy there instead of him, he'd have lightened the atmosphere with a few jokes and his irrepressible good humor. Nicholas? All he could do was sit back and keep one eye on Grey, one eye on the road. Waiting. Watching.

When they finally reached Asheville proper, the fog let up a bit. Nicholas eased out a sigh of relief in time with Grey's explosion of, "It's about damn time!" and his step on the gas. Nicholas gripped the seat as Grey began to drive a little too fast, taking curves with an almost reckless abandon.

"Ease up," he said, trying to keep it light. "The café will still be there if we go by the speed limit."

Grey flashed him a half-annoyed, half-amused look. "Yeah, but we only have so many hours to put up the decorations. Party time in Asheville tonight!"

"Celebration de la Vie," Nicholas agreed. The town, small and full of artistically inclined folk—plus a healthy student population—loved a good excuse to get out and shake their groove thing. He'd been to Carnival once, during the height of Mardi Gras, and Asheville's street party reminded him somewhat of the Louisiana festivities.

This would be the first year he and Grey celebrated it alone, without Jimmy along to tease them into drinking just one more beer while he smoked just one more cigarette. Nicholas resisted the urge to look over his shoulder, as if the ghost of Jimmy were sitting in the backseat. He could almost feel his old friend's presence leaning up between Grey and himself, one hand on either of their shoulders, his grin broad, ready to cut loose with something that would have both of them reduced to helpless giggles.

Last year, he'd been hoping women would walk down the street decorated in feathers, with beads on their butts. He'd rolled down the car window—of course, they'd only been on a supply run then, and he'd been in the front—and yelled at a likely pair of pretty ladies, "Hey, show me a little something!"

Only Jimmy could have gotten away with it. The ladies had whooped with laughter, and the bolder of the pair had shouted, "Hey, mister, throw me a little something!"

Nicholas shifted uncomfortably in his seat. His great-grandmother would have said he was thinking too much of the dead and that it would be bad luck. He wanted to wish Jimmy nothing but peace now that the pain had passed.

God, the days when Jimmy was sick had been hard. The cancer had hit Jimmy out of the blue, one day healthy and within a week, on a respirator. *Nothing we can do,* the doctors said, one by one turning up their hands in a helpless gesture. *Too large...inoperable...pressing on the brain stem.*

Inside of one month, Jimmy had gone from being a vital, vivid personality to a shell it had been a mercy to let go. Nicholas had stuck by Grey almost every second that the man spent by his lover's bed, letting the café be run by waitstaff and not caring if it went under.

The rest of the time, Nicholas had been at Café Noctem, doing his best even though Grey had never known about it.

It'd been odd, he'd thought as he'd worked. Ever since college, the three of them—the gay men who signed up for an art class that was otherwise all women—had been inseparable. Nicholas hadn't minded when Grey and Jimmy had partnered off, since they'd continued to spend most of their time together. It'd seemed strange not to have that grinning face around, up to his old pranks.

Stranger still, after he'd passed, to realize what a gap the man left in his wake. A hole Nicholas felt like he was forever trying to fill.

Even though he and Grey were a couple now, he couldn't shake the sensation that he was merely standing in shoes made far too large to fit, as if, should Jimmy appear one day out of the blue, Grey would leave him behind in a heartbeat to follow his one true love. His great-grandmother would have told him he was dwelling too much—actually, she'd have smacked him with a wooden cooking spoon and told him to get over himself—but the niggling uncertainty coiled in his heart like a snake, and he didn't know how to get rid of his doubts.

Not really. Did he?

Nicholas dared one look behind himself to find the backseat empty as Grey pulled around to the side of Café Noctem, into one of the employee parking spaces. He didn't have one reserved especially for himself, figuring that they should be open to anyone who worked there. If he found a car that didn't belong, though...look out.

Grey turned to Nicholas with a smile. If he'd been thinking his own thoughts during the ride home, his face and eyes both hid any traces of them. "Let's get inside," he said with a friendly nudge to Nicholas' shoulder. "The cellar awaits us."

Nicholas nodded, undoing his seatbelt. "You start the coffees brewing. I'll see to putting up the decorations."

"We can't share and share alike?"

A reluctant grin tugged at Nicholas' mouth. "That'll cut our time in half."

"So? I want you by my side." Grey's hand slid from Nicholas' shoulder down to his thigh. He let it rest there, warm even through his leather glove. "You're my better half, after all. This is our first Celebration together. We should have an equal share in all things."

Nicholas' smile brightened. "We'll have to hurry, then."

"Worry, worry." Grey brushed Nicholas' doubts aside with a gesture. "We have a couple of hours. How long does it take to hang a few garlands?"

"Longer than you'd think," Nicholas warned.

"We can still do it. Watch us and see."

The two men got out of Grey's car, Nicholas having to hurry again to keep up as Grey headed for the staff entrance on the lower level and sorted through his ring of keys for the right one. They'd had an old-fashioned lock on this door until not long ago, and a long, iron key, but Grey had finally given in to the times and installed a deadbolt. Right about the time he'd given in to the expensive German-steel espresso makers and brewing urns.

They'd kept the same old door, though. Good, solid wood set into the red-painted brick of the walls. Nicholas followed Grey through into the cellar of Café Noctem, stopped in the middle, and put his hands on his hips to survey what he'd already done.

Students in particular liked the cellar of the place. Mostly underground, with only a few tiny windows near the ceiling to let in the day, it was a quiet place where they could tap away on their laptops or spread out textbooks, highlighters and spiral-bound notebooks.

Nicholas liked it for the memory of the time Grey had taken him on the floor. Pounced him from behind just as he was about to start bussing the tables—the signs said to clear up after yourself, but did anyone ever listen?—yes, pounced Nicholas and brought him down to earth, the two of them laughing and rolling around until Grey had ended up on top, his dark eyes hungry.

And then they had kissed...

And then, the cold floor be damned, they had done so much more...

Nicholas glanced down to realize he was standing in the exact same spot where they had lain together, panting in the afterglow of a truly stupendous orgasm. Where Grey had stroked the damp strands of Nicholas' over-long bangs out of his forehead and eyes, and kissed the skin beneath.

Where he had said, "You're all I have now, Nicholas. You and the café. Don't ever leave me. Promise?"

Nicholas had given his word. He'd never had cause to regret it. He loved Grey with his whole heart, no matter how the situation had come upon them both all unaware. Memories of the time they'd made love down here only reinforced his pleasure in the bond they shared.

He was about to point it out to Grey when he realized his lover had taken off his gloves, stuffed them in his coat pockets and taken off the garment. Nicholas followed suit. Then, Grey went on to the stack of boxes sitting by the near wall. He opened one and muttered to himself in dismay.

Nicholas laughed. "I told you it would take a while."

Grey turned to him with a sheepish look. "Well, I still can't start the coffees now. They'll scorch. And God knows, burned coffee is not love. I can at least give you a hand."

You already gave me your heart, didn't you? "I'd appreciate the help," Nicholas said softly. "All right, look in the second box. That one's got the coffee-cup garlands I made a few years ago."

"Oh, I remember those." Grey made a dive for the cardboard and all but tore it open, pulling out the cups strung on and glued to strings of Christmas lights. "These were a great idea. Did I ever tell you that?"

"A few times." Nicholas came over to his partner's side to check out the decorations, standing a little closer than was strictly necessary. "Did they get hopelessly tangled up?"

"You know Christmas lights." Grey looked rueful. "Shouldn't be too hard to untangle them, though. You take one end, and I'll take the other."

They worked in silence for a few minutes, Grey making small noises of pleasure as he unsnarled one loop and then another, Nicholas flashing him little grins every time he had a success. Like the cartoon dogs with their spaghetti, they worked their way closer and closer, until their hands touched over the last cup.

Nicholas couldn't help himself. He raised up on his toes, wrapped one arm around Grey's neck, and kissed his lover. Not sweetly, but hungrily, demanding that his mouth open and that he let Nicholas inside. A fire burned in his belly, brought on by seeing Grey so deeply immersed in his work, and his cock had begun to swell inside his jeans. He rubbed against Grey, letting him feel the evidence of his desire.

Grey gave a small groan, carefully putting the cup decorations aside before grasping Nicholas' ass, kneading the twin globes. "You have the most perfect..." he said between kisses, his own passion seeming to grow. "And your... Not to mention your..."

"Hush," Nicholas whispered, touching his tongue to Grey's. He traced it along Grey's lips, imagining that he could taste the remnants of a sugary latte the man had drunk earlier, before going to the cemetery. "If we have time to decorate, and time to make the coffees, do we have time for me to go down on my knees in front of you?"

Grey looked stunned. "You—you would—right here?"

"Location didn't stop us once upon a time." Nicholas cast a glance at the floor, then back up at Grey, delighted to see the faint blush on his cheeks. "Think about it," he crooned. "Me down below you, this magnificent cock in my mouth...an early start to the Celebration."

Grey ran a hand over Nicholas' hair, the heat from his fingers tingling against Nicholas' scalp. "You would do this for me?" he asked softly. "Is the Celebration the only occasion?"

Nicholas frowned at Grey, puzzled. "What else would I—oh." A lead weight sank in his heart. He understood. "You think I'm trying to do what Jimmy would, don't you?"

Grey blinked. "What? I—no. Of course not, Nicholas."

"Of course not." Nicholas drew back, folding his arms over his chest to protect himself. "You would never think of such a thing." The words were hurtful, he knew, but he couldn't seem to help himself. "All day long I've been competing with the spirit of a dead man, and you never even thought to realize what you were doing."

"Nicholas, it isn't like that, I swear."

"No? Maybe not consciously." Nicholas picked up the strand of coffee-cup garlands. "Go upstairs, Grey," he said quietly. "I'd like to finish this myself, if you don't mind. I can work quickly alone, and you need to get the whole café, not just the coffees, in order."

"Upstairs has already been decorated," Grey replied—but he didn't reach for Nicholas. A frown creased his forehead. "I want to help. Let me."

"Because Jimmy would have wanted you to?" Nicholas pressed a hand to his forehead. "Grey, I'm sorry. There must be a bad spirit in me to make me say these things."

Grey's mouth turned down at the corners. "Do you think they're true?"

Nicholas shook his head in thought. "Answer me this, and I'll know—what would you do if Jimmy were here now, instead of me?" One glance at Grey's face, expression startled but eyes alight with a sudden shine, was all the answer he needed. "You do it all yourself," he said in a rush, shoving the garland into Grey's hands. "I've got a costume to put on. It's intricate and it'll take time to get myself into. I'll clean the upstairs on my way, and then I'll be up in the studio apartment, getting ready."

He hesitated, then leaned forward to kiss Grey one more time. "I'm not angry," he whispered. "But time apart cools anger in the heart. Forgive me, Grey. It's just been one of those days." He traced one finger down Grey's solid chest. "It's hard to compete with a man who was always better and will always be the best, and I'm not up to the challenge right now."

"Nicholas," Grey replied just as quietly, putting the decorations aside to comb both his hands through Nicholas' wavy hair. "I'm with you now, do you understand? I made my choice. You're not in competition with anyone."

"Then why does it feel like I am?" Nicholas bit back further angry words. "We need to be apart for a few minutes, Grey. Let me go and work the poison out my way, and you take care of these things." He reached up to kiss Grey one last time, as if he could put his mark on the man. "Let me go in peace, Grey."

"Grey." The man came back, catching and grasping Nicholas' fingers. "Not love? Not lover? Just Grey?"

"Please," Nicholas whispered, eyes downcast. "There are emotions swirling around in here like the fog outside. And time is passing by, minute by minute, with nothing done. Let me go. We'll get this place ready more quickly apart than together. If I stay, we'll be dancing in this circle until the revelers are approaching." He pressed back against Grey's hand. *"Please."*

Grey let him go, seeming reluctant. "We'll talk about this later," he replied, voice flat. "I think there are more than a few things we need to discuss."

Nicholas nodded, meeting Grey's gaze straight on. "We do." He let out a sigh. "But now isn't the time. We have the Celebration. Go on, then. Get things ready. I'll take care of my end. Keeping the Café a roaring success is part of my end of our bargain." He smiled a little tentatively. "Things aren't bad...love. We just need a moment or two for me to compose myself."

After a pause, Grey inclined his head to signify agreement, and Nicholas exhaled in relief. He'd tidy up the main café, set out the coffees all ready to be ground and brewed, and put on his costume. Hopefully the work would exorcise the bad spirits coiling inside his heart. Jealousy, anger, bitterness...all of those needed to be purged.

He needed to be a better man, for Grey's sake.

"No blow job?" Grey asked with a half-smile. "I would have loved that, you know."

Nicholas, already heading for the spiral staircase that would lead him upstairs, paused to look back. "I would have, too. But we need to work now. I'll be in the apartment when you need me."

With those parting words, Nicholas left his partner behind, his mind troubled and his heart a mass of confused love and anger. If he couldn't replace Jimmy, perhaps he could become the dead man's equal in Grey's affections. He would work at this. He *would*. And he'd succeed. He *would*.

Grey belonged to him now, and he wouldn't share the man's affections with a ghost. Even if he'd loved that ghost like a brother when Jimmy had still been alive.

Time to get to work.

Grey watched Nicholas go, admiring as ever the way his perfectly shaped ass flexed in the jeans he wore, always just a little too tight. He'd good-naturedly complain about needing to buy some new ones, but never seemed to get around to it. Grey half-suspected he liked knowing he was being watched and appreciated.

And yes, he was definitely that. Grey sighed, running a hand through his hair. He hadn't been looking for love, or a new partner, after Jimmy had gone so suddenly, but things had just happened. Nicholas hadn't filled the void, but he'd made a space for himself and they'd been happy together.

Perhaps he shouldn't have taken Nicholas along to the cemetery.

Exhaling a noisy gust of air, Grey turned back to the decorations. He checked, and the nails were still in place from where things had been hung for years upon years of Celebrations. Tall enough to reach, he began twining the garland around the room. It'd been clever as hell of Nicholas to cut these cups in half and install a small light bulb in each one. His lover had the magic touch, all right—and when he plugged the string in and all the lights came on, not a single one blown out, he grinned wide in approval. Oh, yes, the magic touch!

He'd never seen Nicholas get so upset before, but he felt as if the man would get over his mood pretty soon. He'd always been laid back and easygoing, even when they were in school together. When plans had been laid for the Café's renovation from a hardware store to a coffee house, Nicholas had been in the thick of things, helping to move old boxes and shift ancient paint cans, laughing all the while.

Grey adored his partner's laugh. The sound always made him think of rich gold, burnished and polished up to a shine, just like the man's voice. Nicholas made little of himself, saying he was short and not anywhere near as handsome as Grey himself or...Jimmy...but he didn't know his own looks very well. Nicholas was a man anyone would be proud to show themselves with.

All he had to do, it seemed, was convince Nicholas of the fact. He hadn't known this was a problem, but if it was, he'd overcome it, and they'd be happy as they had been before.

Grey continued on with his work, humming to himself again as he went around the room, even murmuring snatches of old legends underneath his breath—"And then Brother Deer spoke with Sister Sky, asking her why his People were not allowed to fly, and she said to him, because you have no wings; he asked her why they had not been granted to him, and she said, because some things must run on four feet, for why else would there be a ground to tread on and why would the Great Spirits have created a forest that suits you perfectly?"

A sudden knock startled him into nearly dropping a wreath of dusty green leaves. He whirled around to the cellar door, which he realized he'd left open. "Hello!" he said in surprise to the figure standing there, a small, wiry man wearing a deerskin mask that covered his face and his hair. He'd dressed himself in plain black clothes, a turtleneck and soft trousers, and although he was committed to Nicholas, Grey couldn't help but admire the line and length of the man. "I'm sorry, but we're not open yet."

His guest made a gesture, as if to suggest he should leave and come back—but he didn't speak. Grey frowned. "I'm sorry, I don't understand," he said, wanting to be sure. "It doesn't matter that you're early. You might have to wait a while for a cup of coffee, though. I guess the partiers are out earlier than usual tonight, eh?"

The man, whose mouth was visible through his mask, grinned and swept a low bow. Grey laughed despite himself at the old-fashioned gesture. "Come on in, if you want. Take any table that you like. All I have to do is hang this and I'll be done here."

Nodding, as if relieved and pleased, the man came inside. His shoes must have been padded or made of something like soft suede, for he made as little noise as a cat when he walked. Pointing to a nearby table, he pulled out the chair and sat down, smiling at Grey. Green eyes twinkled through the holes in his mask.

Grey took a moment to admire the handiwork on the thing. Definitely Native in origin, and old. It should have been a museum piece, but this odd visitor wore the face covering like a second skin. "That's a fine mask," he said, tacking the last bit of decoration into place and flipping the wall switch that would turn on the ambient lighting in addition to the coffee-cup trimmings. "Where did you get it?"

The man held a finger to his lips. Grey grinned despite himself. "So you're like a monk, eh? Taken a vow of silence for the Celebration?"

His visitor nodded. Grey chuckled. "That's a switch. Most of the folk out there will be whooping and carrying on as if this were an old-time pow-wow, never mind that almost none of them have the People in their bloodline. I'm guessing you do...?"

Again, a nod. The green eyes looked friendly and so did the smile, but something about the man sent an odd shiver of sensations Grey didn't understand through him. He felt peculiarly attracted to his guest, and with Nicholas waiting for him upstairs, that wouldn't do. Especially not now. He sternly scolded his libido and told it to behave, that he belonged to someone else and wasn't free to go flirting wherever he felt like.

"Well, just wait down here." He waved one hand at the empty room. "Plain coffee is free tonight, but specialty drinks are still for sale—half-price, though. When you smell the brewing, feel free to come upstairs and grab a cup."

The guest nodded, not taking his eyes off Grey. Grey felt a little bit more uncomfortable, and along with the feeling came the need to get up to Nicholas as quickly as possible. "Take it easy, now," he said, loping toward the staircase. "We'll see you around the Celebration!"

Taking the stairs easily, he hurried up to the top. The main café gleamed, and everything had been set up in readiness for brewing. Grey grinned, well-pleased with Nicholas' capable handling of things. He'd reward his partner with a kiss when they met in the studio. He'd seen Nicholas' costume. Maybe the man would even let him help lace a thing or two in place...or let him unlace them...

All but forgetting his early arrival in the cellar, Grey ducked back into the staff room and opened the door to his private staircase. "Nicholas, I'm coming up!" he called. "Ready or not..."

"Ready," Nicholas' warm voice came back at him, kindling a fire in Grey's belly. "Still getting dressed though."

Good. He was right on time, then. Grey took the stairs two at a time, set on double courses—to make up to Nicholas in whatever way it took, and to see if they couldn't steal a few intensely private moments together before coming back down to open the café proper.

And with that, he *did* forget about their early guest.

Down in the cellar, the man in the mask drummed his fingers on the table. *Who would ever have thought the legend of Sint Holo was true? It was Nicholas' great-grandmother who told me the story, I remember that now.*

He doesn't recognize me. I'd have thought he would.

Perhaps there's more magic in this mask than even I had thought.

Jimmy sighed and shifted in his seat. *I don't know why I'm back, why Sint Holo chose me, or what I'm supposed to be doing here. But I have all the time in the world to think, and in a few minutes, I'll get a cup of coffee to start the brain moving.*

God. It's been months since my last cup.

He laughed without humor, and leaned back in his chair. One thing was for certain, this would definitely be an interesting night.

Chapter Three

"Are you dressed? Damn, it's dark up here. What are you...? Oh."

Nicholas heard Grey pull up short as he entered their apartment above the café. *Their* apartment. Nicholas had added his own touches to the place.

But Jimmy still remained, didn't he? He was there in a dream catcher hung above their beds, in an arrangement of dried flowers on the kitchen table and in a stack of CDs Grey still occasionally flipped through. What were Nicholas' clothes, books and collection of mugs compared to those?

"Nicholas," Grey breathed, as if startled and confused. Nicholas looked down at the taper he'd lit, which sat on a table close by his side. Another unlit candle stood next to the first, tall and white, waxy and solid. He wasn't surprised by Grey's reaction. He would have felt the same way if he'd come across Grey stripped down to his skin, clad only in a warm glow and moonlight.

"You said you were getting ready for the Celebration," Grey said slowly, not sounding as if he minded that Nicholas wasn't finished putting on his costume.

"I changed my mind." Nicholas raised one shoulder in a half-shrug. "Are you angry?"

"Angry? God, no. Not when you... Nicholas, do you know how you look?"

Nicholas thought he did. He'd seen himself in mirrors enough times to know he had a tight, trim ass and a shapely line to his body from head to toe, the line of his back elegantly curved. He stood nude by one window, holding an edge of the pale brown curtains in one hand, looking out at the sky above. He had deliberately positioned himself to face away from their entrance so Grey could get a good look at him when he entered.

And, as he'd hoped, the sight had stopped Grey in his tracks.

"You're naked," the man said, sounding dumbfounded. "Nicholas, my God, you're fucking edible framed only by one candle and the moonlight from outside."

"Once upon a time," Nicholas began quietly, "Father Sun and Mother Moon looked down upon two of their stars, who danced together so merrily that the People liked to watch them at night and say they must have been in love, the way they twinkled and shone."

"Nicholas..." Grey started. Nicholas heard him begin to move, probably toward himself.

He kept talking, speaking in a low voice, as if he were sitting by a campfire with half a dozen children from the reservation. "These two stars were called after the animal spirits Rabbit and Mouse, to humble them. Lowly names hardly stopped them, though, from glittering and glimmering each night, paying one another homage and doing courtesy. Their love grew day by day, but as is the way with stars, one night Mouse lost his grip on the heavens and fell to earth, streaking from the sky in a cascade of light that made the People gasp to see it."

"Nicholas..."

He held up a hand. "Rabbit was disconsolate, for he had loved Mouse with all his heart. With his friend and lover gone, who would he turn to?"

"To the Deer star," Grey said, close enough now to lay his hands on Nicholas' shoulders. Despite himself, Nicholas shuddered and leaned into the touch. "I've heard this story myself, and you tell it very well for someone who looks like an outsider."

"Not like you," Nicholas agreed. "Not like Jimmy."

"I didn't love Jimmy because he looked like one of the Cherokee."

"I know." Nicholas turned his head to the side, looking down at where Grey touched him. "The Deer star courted Rabbit, hoping to comfort him in his time of troubles. But Rabbit, all unknowing, began to fall in love with Deer. And once he had, and realized it, he was aghast with horror. How could he betray Mouse's memory by loving again? By dancing in the cool glow of Mother Moon?"

"Nicholas, don't."

Nicholas ignored him. "The People watched this show with great interest. Rabbit would first approach, and then retreat. Deer waited patiently, glowing brighter when Rabbit came close, and dimming when he turned back. They waited to see what would happen."

"Then one night, the two stars glowed with the same white-hotness, and the People knew they had decided to let Mouse's memory rest in peace." Grey began to slowly massage Nicholas' arms. "I know that isn't how the real story ends, but it's how my version does."

Nicholas bent his head, leaning it against one of Grey's strong arms. He spoke into a cord of muscle, "Does it, really? And is Mouse resting in peace?"

146

Grey nodded. "He was a Mouse that roared, but yes, he is."

Nicholas felt a kiss on the back of his scalp. "Rabbit and Deer are happy together. If you pulled back the curtain, if you could see above the lights of the city, you could watch them glowing together in the skies above."

"It's just a story…"

"Everything is a story."

Nicholas felt Grey kiss him again, this time moving over to one of his temples. His tongue flicked out to trace a small pattern on the shell of Nicholas' ear, drawing a quiet moan out of him. "We're all part of a tale. The world we live in is our frame. Everyone else has their own stories, and we all intersect at some point. The world is full of legends and myths that come alive every day." With his mouth, Grey seized Nicholas' earlobe and caught it between his teeth, nipping sharply, then salving the bite with his tongue.

"And are we glowing together?" Nicholas asked. "Do we dance in the heavens?"

"As we do here on earth." Grey pulled Nicholas hard against him. He reached around and took Nicholas' cock in his hand. "Everything's ready downstairs," he coaxed. "We have time, if we're quick about things…"

Nicholas shook his head. "I don't want quick. Not hurried, nor rushed. I want slow."

"There's no time."

"Then when will there be time? It seems that every time we make love, you're always rushing through the act to get to something else."

"You think I don't appreciate you?"

"No…it isn't that." Nicholas shivered as Grey began to slowly stroke his prick, which clearly had a mind of its own. It

147

began to lengthen and thicken in his partner's palm, rising to the occasion for him. "It's that I think you appreciate..."

"What, Nicholas?" Grey asked, mouth tickling his ear. "What do I want more than you?" He ran his thumb around the swollen head of Nicholas's cock, circling the fat crown in slow motion, then nudged his own hard groin into the curve of Nicholas' ass. "What could I possibly want more than this?"

A ghost, Nicholas wanted to answer—but didn't.

"Come and lie down on the bed with me," Grey wheedled.

"You're still dressed."

"I can take care of that. Go and rest your head on the pillows. Watch me as I've watched you. Will you do that for me?" Warm fingers caressed his cheek. "Love me, Nicholas, as I love you."

Nicholas' eyes fluttered shut. After a moment he nodded, and pulled reluctantly away from his partner. He padded silently to the bed on his bare feet and lay down on his side, facing Grey, taking him in from head to toe.

Grey's face was unreadable as ever, but Nicholas thought he saw a heated, simmering spark in those dark eyes. Grey tugged the black shirt he wore off over his head and cast it to the side, revealing the hard muscles of his chest and stomach, bare of any hair except for a small line that disappeared beneath the band of his charcoal-colored dress pants. As Nicholas watched, Grey toed off his shoes and his hands went to his zipper.

As he jerked the fastening open, he began to speak. "I have a story of my own to tell you," he said, his voice taking on a cadence almost older than time. "This is the story of a holy man, a Berdache, one who loved his own sex more than the sweet flesh of the women in his tribe."

Nicholas shifted on his hip, watching Grey get rid of his pants and socks. When he stood gloriously naked, prick jutting out before him, he put his hands on his hips and continued. "This Berdache, named Clever Fox, had heard the story of another of his kind trapped inside a maze of thorns, asleep at the very heart."

A half-smile tipped up the corner of Nicholas' mouth. "I believe I've heard this one before."

"Hush. Let me tell it in my own way." Grey bent and crawled onto the bed, silently nudging Nicholas onto his back and pushing his legs apart. Nicholas let himself be maneuvered like a doll, waiting patiently until Grey knelt between his knees and laid his palms to rest on Nicholas' thighs.

"Clever Fox," Grey went on, "determined that he would rescue the sleeping Berdache, who he had heard was called Blue Sky for the color of his eyes. The other Berdache had fallen asleep for lack of someone to love him, and Clever Fox knew that he could be the one to wake the sleeping man."

Grey reached for a bottle of lubricant sitting on their bedside table and clicked it open, squeezing a healthy dollop of cherry-scented gel onto his fingers. "Raise your legs," he instructed. "Rest your feet upon the blanket—good." He paused, gazing intently at Nicholas. "Do you know how beautiful you are to me?"

Nicholas let his legs fall apart, baring himself to Grey's view. He reached down and began to fondle his own cock in silent challenge. "The story," he demanded softly. "Go on."

"You almost make me forget my place."

"Then let me remind you." Nicholas swiped up a drop of pre-come and brought it to his mouth, tasting his own saltiness. "Clever Fox prepared himself for battle, knowing Thorn would be a tricky opponent."

Grey swallowed. "Yes...yes. Clever Fox armed himself with bow and arrow, with spear and with knife, with magic prepared for him by the medicine man, and..." Grey's fingers began to stroke the lubricant into Nicholas' hole... "Paint. He decorated himself as a warrior, even though he had no claim to that status, because he was going forth to do battle."

Nicholas arched underneath the touch, his mouth falling slightly open as Grey's clever fingers manipulated the hundreds of nerves in his opening. Fingers slid inside him, working him open, making him ready. He would have been able to take Grey if he had simply coated his own cock and slid straight inside, after having made love with this man so many times, but to be treated like a prince from a fairy tale made the encounter take on an entirely different turn. From the look on Grey's face, heavy-lidded, with lips parted, he was enjoying this as much as Nicholas.

"Finish the story," Nicholas prompted as Grey began to scissor his fingers. He writhed on them, unable to help himself. He felt so empty without Grey inside, but soon enough—soon enough. "What did Clever Fox do next?"

"He went on a long journey, through woods and plains, down valleys and up mountains, across streams and over bridges, until at last he came to the maze of thorns where Blue Sky lay imprisoned, asleep." Grey reached for the lubricant again, smiling when Nicholas moaned at the loss of the fingers inside him. "He knew then that his journey had only been the beginning. Now he was about to face the real challenge."

"And did he?" Nicholas asked breathlessly, watching as Grey applied shimmering slick to the fullness of his cock, the cinnamon-colored skin taking on a deep, rosy shine. "What happened next, Grey?"

"Part your thighs further for me—yes, just that way." Grey moved closer, lifting first one and then the other leg over his shoulders. The tip of his cock pressed against Nicholas' stretched hole, not quite entering, not yet. "Clever Fox tried to cut down the thorns with his ax, but they were too hard." He pushed slightly. "He tried to part the way with his spear, but the tangle was too thick." He pushed again. "He even lit an arrow on fire and shot it through the tangle, hoping to burn the branches, but no luck."

With a gasp, Grey pushed inside Nicholas. He drew in a ragged, lusty breath as Nicholas did, feeling himself being stuffed to bursting with Grey's cock. His head spun from the sensation of being fucked and from the story, as if someone were burning mesquite and sage, the scent filling his nose. Reaching up for Grey, he asked, "And what then? Tell me, Grey, what then?"

A mix of emotions crossed Grey's usually implacable face as he gripped Nicholas' thighs. Nicholas grinned wickedly, knowing that all of Grey's attention would be focused on his dick, pushed so far into Nicholas that there was no more he could take. His balls rested heavy and full against Nicholas' ass.

To tease him, Nicholas took hold of his own cock, beginning to pump it lazily. The muscles in his channel seized up in a series of jerks, making Grey gasp. He withdrew and said hoarsely, "Clever Fox finally called upon his magic."

"He did?"

"He did. He prayed, using the words the medicine man had taught him. Begging the Sun to give him power."

"And what happened then, Grey?" Nicholas asked as Grey pushed in again with a groan. "Tell me."

"He...he saw the thorns crumble, as if they were powder... Ah, God, Nicholas... God..."

Nicholas grasped at Grey with one damp palm. "Finish the story," he ordered in a low voice. "Finish it, and then fuck me through the mattress."

Grey shook his head hard, resting fully inside Nicholas' body. "He...he was surprised by how well the medicine worked. Magic was more...more powerful than a sharp edge or a keen point. He...aah...once the thorns were nothing but dust, he found a path inside."

Nicholas tightened his legs around Grey's back. "What then?" he asked, rolling his hips. "What then?"

"He followed the path. Nicholas, please."

"Finish the story." Nicholas gazed at Grey with eyes he knew were shining with the lust he felt. He undulated, relishing the feel of the long, thick cock buried inside him, and the way Grey's muscles trembled from holding back. "Go ahead. I want to hear the rest."

"After—"

"No," Nicholas insisted. "Now."

Grey gave a deep, ragged breath, and went on. "Clever Fox made his way to the heart of the maze and found Blue Sky there, asleep on a soft bed of furs made from the deer and the otter. He was so...so beautiful that he took Fox's breath...took Fox's breath away."

"And then?" Nicholas pushed. "What then?"

"Then he remembered the medicine again," Grey whispered hoarsely. "And instead of shaking Blue Sky awake, he bent to kiss the man..."

"And Blue Sky opened his eyes," Nicholas finished.

"He did. And the two fell in love right there on the spot, and for the love of *God,* Nicholas, please let me fuck you now."

Nicholas pulled at his own cock. "Go ahead. No one's stopping you." He let his eyelids droop. "I want you, Grey. I need you."

"Thank you," Grey murmured, and bent Nicholas almost double leaning over to press a searing-hot kiss of his own to Nicholas' mouth. In moving, he seemed to grow inside Nicholas, turning the pure pleasure into a burn, but a good one. Nicholas gasped into Grey's mouth, tasting his partner's tongue, catching the last remnants of coffee and the full flavor of desire.

He began to beg. "Now. Hard and fast and now."

Grey didn't answer in words, but in actions, wasting no time. His hips snapped backwards and forwards, driving his cock deep inside Nicholas' eager body. Nicholas found the rhythm and began to pull at his own prick in time, almost imagining he could hear the drumbeats of a tribal circle. There was magic in the air that night—he could feel the enchantment in the air.

Grey groaned and said something Nicholas couldn't understand, the words too rushed together to make sense. Nicholas nodded, rocking up with his hips, pushing Grey on. "Fuck me," he chanted in time with the beat. "Fuck me, fuck me, fuck me..."

And Grey did, filling Nicholas to bursting, leaving him empty, then filling him once again. Nicholas tugged at his cock, feeling sticky strands of pre-come trickling down the side, using them to ease his own way. He could barely think by then, and his only thought about moving was to rock with Grey, winding them both up to a climax possibly better than any that had ever come before.

Grey's eyes rolled back into his head, and he burst out with another string of nonsense syllables. Bending them both fiercely for another kiss, he gripped hard at Nicholas, and stiffened except for his hips snapping forward. Nicholas felt the jets of heated spunk filling him from the inside, so warm and wet that he gasped and felt himself burst, gouts of come running down over his hand.

On the distant edges of his hearing, the drumbeats faded to the sound of a thudding heartbeat, fainter and fainter, and then there was silence. All was quiet except for the sounds of their breathing, rough and ragged, struggling to calm themselves after such an explosive climax.

Nicholas sighed, raising his hand to his mouth to lick it clean. He loved the taste, full of passion and life. Someday, he wanted to find a willing woman who would give him a child to share with Grey. They would teach the boy or girl the old ways, all the old stories, share flatbread with them and play games that were older than the white man's time on these mountains, and—

"Jimmy," Grey hummed, stroking Nicholas' chest. "God, Jimmy, you were amazing."

Chapter Four

Nicholas was very carefully tending to the coffee bar in the cellar. He'd set up several urns of coffee, some of their best beans, roasted to perfection and freshly ground for brewing. The smell filling the room was nothing short of heavenly.

Jimmy inhaled as deeply as he could, savoring the fine smell of Café Noctem's good coffee after going so long without it. There was just something about the java they were able to make in this place. He himself had joked that there must have been good spirits in the old building, ones who liked a buzz, and that was why they had the best coffee in Asheville.

He took a sip from his mug, a sturdy ceramic model in a deep cobalt blue, and let the flavor roll over his tongue. He closed his eyes. Perfection.

Pity nothing else was going right. Jimmy watched Nicholas, his old friend, and how absolutely precise his movements were as he tended bar. He didn't look up, didn't look down, didn't look around, and specifically didn't look at Grey, who had entered a few minutes after him. Neither man was dressed in a costume, although it was customary for Celebration de la Vie.

"I can do this," a young girl insisted—well, young to his point of view. She was probably nineteen or twenty, a student at college, working to pay her tuition. Piercings ringed her ears from cartilage to lobe, and a tribal tattoo showed on one upper arm. She'd dressed herself in a skin-tight cat suit, complete with furry ears and a tail that swished behind her—and not much else. "Nicholas, go mingle. Make with the schmoozing. I can dish out coffee."

"Thank you, Belinda. I'm fine right here," Nicholas replied. Then, as if regretting his terse words, he glanced up and gave her a friendly smile. Jimmy suspected he was the only one who noticed the warm look didn't reach Nicholas' eyes. "I'm not even dressed up. Why don't you go and work the crowd?"

"You mean bus tables," Belinda groused, but with a grin. She reached for a white plastic tub set underneath the coffee bar, and hefted it onto her hip. "I'm on it. But since when does Catwoman do the dirty work?"

"Since now," Nicholas called after her. The friendly expression lingered on his face a few moments longer, and then dropped abruptly as Grey crossed the room, heading from one local businessman to a reporter for the local community paper. He turned studiously to the urns behind him, checking them and refilling one with freshly ground beans.

As Nicholas disappeared to go bring down some more clear spring water for the brewing, Jimmy tapped at the edge of his cup in deep thought. He thought he'd figured things out—it didn't take a genius, after all. He and Grey and Nicholas had always been the closest of friends. It just made sense that the two remaining after he was gone would come together.

Now, though, it looked like they were on the verge of breaking apart.

Is this what I'm here for? Did someone know this was going to happen, and is that why I rose to find the mask waiting for me on my own grave? He fingered the deerskin edges, running one thumb over its tribal stitching. *Sint Holo, Snake Man, you're a crafty fellow. What do you have in mind? Would it kill you to drop a few hints?*

"Oh—music!" Belinda said, hastily setting down her tray, half-full of emptied coffee mugs. "We've got to have some tunes. Mr. Grey?" she asked, turning in his direction. He gave her much the same look that Nicholas had and waved his hand at the enthusiastic girl, giving permission. Belinda punched the air with a fist and headed for a stereo system set up in the corner of the room.

Jimmy watched with interest. This Belinda was right; they had been missing the tunes. Café Noctem's basement always had some music going. Usually ambient stuff, or nature sounds. All of it meant to soothe, and to ease the mind and body. He'd no idea what CD Belinda might pop in. He braced himself, expecting some wild punk or clash metal to burst out of the speakers.

Instead, he heard the opening strains of Beethoven's "Moonlight Sonata". One of his favorite pieces. Jimmy hummed softly in pleasure, wondering if Sint Holo were playing games with him—but he didn't mind, if he could hear this song again.

Where he had been was—different. There was nothing in that place but peace.

Belinda turned back to Grey, looking for his approval. He seemed surprised, but then nodded and gave her a thumbs up. She looked next to Nicholas, who was standing wholly still, staring at the speakers. He'd even stopped halfway through sliding a basket into the coffee urn he was working.

Belinda's face fell. "You don't like it?"

"Bagels," Nicholas blurted abruptly. "We need some bagels and cream cheese. Muffins, croissants, buns..."

Grey crossed the room, shaking his head. "Not a good idea."

"Because it was mine?" Nicholas asked very quietly.

Grey looked frustrated. "No. Nicholas, I—look, everything that's left over from this morning is going to be stale, and we didn't order anything for the night crowd," he said in a flat voice.

"You should have thought of that," Nicholas replied, still ever so quiet. "Free coffee demands free snacks to go along with it. But as I'm night manager, I made the call, and I ordered a special delivery for tonight." Nicholas seemed to refuse to look Grey directly in the eye. "Small things. The bagels are bite-sized, and so are the muffins. The croissants, too."

"It's a waste of money," Grey snapped, thin-lipped.

"It's good business," Nicholas shot back. "I'm going to go get them. Belinda, will you help me?"

Belinda cast a glance between her two bosses, bit her lip, and then followed Nicholas up the stairs. Leaving Grey alone, without anyone to talk to at the moment, and Jimmy, sitting in his chair, watching.

The song changed to something else—apparently this was a mix. A woman's voice, pure and haunting—*and I should know*—floated out of the speakers. Jimmy realized with a start that she was singing in the Cherokee language. Someone local, perhaps? He could pick out most of the words, enough to get the gist—

Welcome back, my beating heart...for so long you've been gone...come into my arms again...let the Night Wind sing for joy...

Grey leaned against the wall, putting his hand to his face. He looked tired, as if the whole evening were too much for him. Perhaps it was the song. Tomorrow was Valentine's Day, after all, and if Jimmy knew Grey, he knew the man would be going over and over old memories of times gone by.

What the hell? he thought. *One for the road, before I find out what's happening here.*

One more chance to hold my Grey.

Standing up, his chair scooting back from the table, Jimmy abandoned his coffee cup to cross the room to Grey. This was madness, he knew. Nicholas could come down at any moment, and with the way the tension flowed between his two friends, he knew he could be the straw the broke that old camel's back.

But just to hold him, one last time...

A pair of college students dressed in the latest Goth gear—definitely not punks themselves—got up and began dancing in a small space between the tables. They caught the attention of the room, the inhabitants of which started eagerly clearing away an open spot on the floor. Couples came together to sway with the music.

The song was a long one, the Cherokee woman's voice mournful and sweet, and Grey smelled like tobacco, leather and heaven when Jimmy approached him. Grey glanced down at Jimmy, tilting his head as if curious. "Do you need something?"

You. Jimmy nodded, not trusting his voice. Something inside him, too, warned him to be quiet, as he had been before. Somehow it didn't feel right to reveal himself to Grey—not yet. So in alternate answer, he lifted one hand to Grey's hip and one to the man's shoulder, then swayed gently, indicating that he wanted to dance.

Grey went slightly pink under the dusky copper skin of his cheeks. "Oh, man. Look, I'm sorry, but I'm with someone. The gentleman with the light brown hair and the glasses. He just went upstairs."

So they're faithful to each other. This is a good thing. Lovers should watch one another's backs. Jimmy frowned. The words were ones he'd used a hundred times with Grey, but all the

159

same they struck an oddly familiar chord with him, one he couldn't place.

Grey carefully tried to remove Jimmy's hands. "I can't, I mean, I shouldn't. You're a charmer of a guy—why not go and find someone else?"

Because I want you. Jimmy refused to be budged. *It's been so long since I saw you, lover, and God, how you've changed.* He raised up to touch Grey's long, straight hair, noting all the silver threads running through the otherwise inky blackness. Small lines had appeared by the corners of his eyes, and Jimmy didn't think they were from smiling. His body, though, it was hard and tempting as ever.

He'd never do Nicholas any wrong, but he *did* want one last dance.

The crowd was egging them on, he realized, drawing back from his examination of Grey's face to focus on the rest of the room. Grey looked embarrassed, but Jimmy turned around with a grin to their audience:

"Go on, Mr. Grey!"

"One time around the floor."

"One dance won't hurt anything."

"Show us a little something!"

"Yeah, show them how it's done!"

Grey shook his head, setting his hair swinging. "Look," he said, dropping his voice, "my partner's already angry with me for really putting my foot in things earlier. He'll be coming back down those steps any minute, and I don't want to make him even angrier. You understand, don't you?"

Jimmy nodded, but placed his hands even more firmly on Grey and refused to be budged. He couldn't have explained why he did as he did. Maybe it was just being able to feel with hands of flesh again. He knew he should move away. This wasn't his life anymore, and he didn't have any right—not now—to lay hands on the man who had been his lover. He belonged to Nicholas, and Jimmy had no problems with that. He'd wanted Grey to be happy after he moved on.

The crowd continued to cheer them on. Jimmy had to admit that death hadn't changed him much, and he did love an audience. Loved the feel of warm skin beneath his hands. Remembered night after night of undoing those buttons, stroking across the hard muscles underneath, being all but crushed under the man's heavy weight and loving every second of it...

He came to himself with a start. Grey was casting a spell over him again, he knew it, and he had to pull away before it was too late. Before Nicholas—oh.

Oh, shit.

Standing above them on the spiral staircase, a tray of small and fragrant things in his hands, was Nicholas, gazing down at Jimmy and Grey, standing together as if they were embracing.

Nicholas looked down upon the sight he had always most feared he would see—Grey standing with another man, the smaller figure all but pressed up against him, face raised as if for a kiss even through his mask. A mask that covered his face from forehead to chin, and stretched back over what appeared to be dark, curly hair. The body was slim but muscular, dressed in plain black clothes, and looked as if it would be a good one to touch.

But the mask, though...despite the heart-crashing sensation of seeing Grey with someone else, the mask, all-too familiar to him, caught Nicholas' attention.

His mind went back to a time years past, when he'd still been a teenager like many of those who filled the room. He'd been sitting at his great-grandmother's feet, holding out a skein of yarn for her to wind into a ball.

"Ah, Sint Holo," she'd said, waving a wicked-looking knitting needle at him. "That one, you need to watch out for. He's a clever, cunning sort of spirit. Remember when I would not permit you to have a garter snake as a pet?"

Nicholas had made a gesture of nonchalance. "Not a big deal, Grandmother. All the same, it wouldn't have hurt anything. They're not poisonous."

"Oh, oh, not poisonous, eh? They are the representations of the Sint Holo I speak of, and yes, they are very dangerous, at least to the Cherokee. We keep no snakes in our homes, and no images of them, either." She'd nodded decisively. "He was once venerated as a god, but even then the People knew better than to invite the attention of such a trickster."

She'd paused, winding up the last of the thread. Nicholas' hands had fallen to his sides, then folded together on his knee, sensing that Great-Grandmother was about to tell him a story. They had no kin that he knew of, and they lived far away from any reservation—"On our own land!" she would say, chin upraised—and so there were no elders to tell him the ancient legends.

She'd claimed she would tell the old tales in their place, and even though part of Nicholas had squirmed, protesting that he was too old for things like helping Great-Grand with her knitting and for listening to stories, there was another part that was still like a little boy, eager to listen.

"Did I ever tell you about Sint Holo and the mask he made of Deer?" she'd asked, starting to twine yarn around her needles. She'd been making Nicholas a sweater to wear the next winter. Her first gift to him since they'd spoken about him being gay, and in her own way, it had been a token of blessing on his chosen path. "No? Then make yourself comfortable, and listen..."

Nicholas shook his head to clear it, gazing down at the man in the mask. "So," he said softly. "Friends do watch out for one another's backs. So closely that sometimes they don't even see the knives. Sint Holo is busy tonight."

It is a night of legends, after all, he thought. *And be damned if I'll stick around while the Snake Man plays his games.*

Without a word, Nicholas carefully handed his platter over to the girl who'd accompanied him, and headed back upstairs.

Grey stared at the strangely masked man who'd come up to him and had the balls to ask for a dance. He must not have been a local or a regular, or he'd have known that Grey was spoken for and his personal dance card was permanently full.

He'd been taken by surprise when the man laid his hands on him, feeling a shock of something almost like recognition. Why, he couldn't have said. There was an odd familiarity to the way the stranger touched him at shoulder and hip, and the shimmy of his narrow hips as he swayed to-and-fro to the melodic tune coming from the stereo.

This song was one of Nicholas' favorites. He'd been pleased when it came on, hoping for a dance from his partner, himself, when Nicholas came back down. He'd planned an apology, too. Nicholas had been right. Providing free snacks was just plain good business, and he'd been a good manager to think of offering the service. There must have been a bad spirit riding on his back to make him short and snappish.

Probably, it was the same one that rode him while he tried to deal with the stranger. Carefully pushing at the man's hands, he made one last effort to dissuade him. "I have a lover," he said carefully. "I don't want to make him jealous. If he saw us like this, he might get the wrong idea."

The man stopped, looking upward. Grey could make out very few details of the face beneath the mask, but he'd have sworn he read dismay in those features.

He followed the gaze of the bright green eyes and saw Belinda standing on the staircase awkwardly balancing three platters, when she should have just been carrying two. She had a look on her face that spoke volumes, as if she didn't know whether she should come downstairs and go ahead with business as usual, or go back up...maybe going after someone who'd started down, and then returned. Gone back all too suddenly.

Fuck. Nicholas.

His heart gave a wrench. No longer caring about being rough, Grey pushed his would-be dance partner away and ran for the stairs, dodging past Belinda and up into the café proper. He stood still for a moment, both legs braced wide, searching the room for any trace of his partner.

No sign. None, that was, except for the front door, swinging open on its hinges, left unlocked. The bell continued to jingle faintly in a mocking little chime, as if to say *Ha, ha, too late, Grey man, Clever Fox!*

Grey made for the entrance and stepped out into the street—right into the middle of a crowd gone wild, the sidewalks choked with men and women of all ages, dressed in elaborate costumes or almost nothing at all, and a few with more body paint than clothing. Their laughter rang loudly and the hum of a thousand voices chattering all at once drowned out everything else. With the crowd and the noise, there would be no way to track Nicholas down.

Stepping back inside, Grey sat heavily down in a chair and leaned his elbow on a table, dragging one hand through his hair. First one mistake, and now another. When would it end? Where?

Damn that man in the mask for taking a bad situation and making it even worse. If he wasn't gone by the time Grey got back down to the cellar...if he decided to go, and not head out hunting for his lover...

Jimmy watched the staircase, hoping against hope that he would see Nicholas or Grey come walking down it, separate or together, although he hoped for together, maybe even hand in hand. Hair slightly mussed and lips noticeably swollen from kissing, that would have been the best sight of all. But no matter how long he waited, no one appeared.

If he'd had the nerve, he would have torn his mask off. But even as his fingers reached for the edges of the deerskin, they began to shake with some feeling he couldn't identify. The harder he tried, the less able he was to even grasp an edge, much less peel the thing off to reveal his true face.

So. Sint Holo wanted the game to continue. *Well, fuck you, Snake Man,* Jimmy thought angrily. *I still don't know why you brought me back here or gave me your mask, but I won't play by your rules.*

I know what I have to do. Find Nicholas, find Grey, and push them back together. They belong with each other now that I'm gone, and oh, no, I'm not going to lie to myself, I'm not here to stay. I shouldn't have been brought back in the first place.

Since I was, though...

I'll find them. Either or both, I don't care, and I'll do whatever it takes to get them face-to-face and talking. They're both stubborn men, and this won't be easy, I know.

But what's the worst that could happen? They'd kill me?

Jimmy removed his hands from the neck of his mask, and ducked out the back door of Café Noctem's cellar. He had a mission, and he thought he knew just where to look.

The very place Grey would never think to start hunting.

It's showtime.

Chapter Five

Music from a set of loudspeakers filtered through every street in Asheville, even into the hidden nooks and corners that few knew about. Nicholas had hidden himself away in one of them, and the woman's whiskey-rough singing voice tickled at his ears all the same.

He could hide from everything but omens, couldn't he?

Nicholas sat hunched on an old cardboard box outside the one place he knew Grey would never look for him—the alleyway behind Ganymede's Grotto. They'd visited once, only once, but the dungeons had put Grey off and neither of them had been able to afford the membership fee. They couldn't afford such luxuries and still manage to stay current on the new car payments as well as keeping Café Noctem running. A shame, really.

All the same, Nicholas had truly enjoyed the drink that swishy old queen Earl had offered, poured by a sinfully gorgeous bartender with a long white-gold braid. They'd ordered double shots of a brand he couldn't remember, one that had gold flakes floating in the bottom. *Rich,* the bartender had said with a wink.

Powerful, too. One more drink and Nicholas would have been begging Grey to get a lip ring just like that bartender's. The thought of having a piercing to play with...perhaps he should have gotten his own.

The liquor had tasted all the sweeter for being drunk with Grey by his side. They'd laughed and joked with the owner and the bartender, not really watching the live shows, but loving the camaraderie. Nicholas had been especially interested in their habit of celebrating ancient festivals.

If he remembered right, tomorrow night, Valentine's Day, that would be Lupercalia, wouldn't it? Nicholas sighed and leaned his chin into his palm. Not his pantheon, but it would have been fun to celebrate the holiday with Grey.

Now, he wasn't sure at all what Grey's plans would be.

Sint Holo, Sint Holo, damn you, Sint Holo. I never asked for...

But no. He couldn't allow himself to think along those lines. If, after tonight, all he would have were memories, then he'd cherish them with every bit of his mind. Ignoring the curious glance he got from someone coming out the back entrance of Ganymede's and passing him by, he huddled up on his box and drew on some of his favorites.

He and Grey going swimming in a small lake, racing each other to the end of the pier and doing twin cannonballs into the water. Surfacing to find one another laughing, wiping water out of their eyes. Grey pulling Nicholas to a shallower spot where they could stand on the rocky bottom and dragging him in for a hungry kiss. "You're fun, Nicholas," he'd said, as if he were surprised. "You're really fun!"

Another time, another place, cooking a late lunch together. Something over-complicated and wasting time they could have spent making love, but enjoying every second they spent bumping hips in the apartment's tiny little kitchen. What had they been preparing...? Ah, yes, veal parmesan. The room had been rédolent of the smells of frying meat and tangy tomato sauce. Nicholas recalled opening his mouth like a bird to taste a bite, and Grey licking a smear of sauce off his skin...then turning the burners down to low while he kept on working with his tongue, finding all sorts of new places to investigate...

Watching Grey sleep, having slipped under the covers after his night shift ended. Being unable to stop himself from tracing the lines of tough muscle that came from hard work and Grey's time with the weights. Feeling wicked and slipping beneath the body-warmed sheet and comforter, down to Grey's hips—he always slept in the nude—and sucking the man's semi-hard cock into his mouth. Feeling Grey wake, startled at first, then hearing his sigh of utter contentment and pleasure as he took hold of Nicholas' head and guided him slowly, both of them taking as long as they pleased.

Good times.

Were they over now?

Nicholas pressed his hands to his forehead. He knew he hadn't made things better by running away. All he seemed to do lately, though, was make mistakes. He'd only stay where he was for just a minute longer, then. Just a minute, and then he'd move on, heading back to the café. Grey would have noticed he was gone by now. And he knew Grey. Whether they were still partners or not—and oh, but how his heart contracted at the thought of *not*—Grey would be worried about him.

He had to go back.

Any minute now...any minute now...

As Jimmy wound his way through the crowds out partying their way through the night of Celebration de la Vie, he couldn't help noticing that for the most part the crowds parted before him like water. Was it the mask? Did he frighten them in some sense they couldn't even put a name to? Or was it Sint Holo, up to his tricks again?

Clever devil, Jimmy thought in exasperation. He opened his mouth to try and call out Nicholas' name, even though he knew it was futile in this mob, and found to his dismay that his voice had no sound. He couldn't speak. Hands at his throat, suddenly desperate—and wasn't that stupid, for a dead man—Jimmy wondered frantically if this wasn't why he hadn't wanted to speak before.

I know it's you now, Snake Man. Damn you, anyway. You can't stop me, though, you hear? I defy you to stop me. Jimmy put all the force of a yell into his thoughts, knowing that if the spirit were listening and paying attention, he'd hear. And even though he knew how foolish it was to challenge one of Sint Holo's kind, he didn't feel like being careful if caution got in his way. He was dead as hell, mad as fuck, and he wasn't going to take it anymore.

As if in answer to his challenge, the crowds began to press back in. Women in the scantiest things they could get away with in February, men in everything from Captain Hook to urban punk, complete with fake piercings. He spotted a small, red-haired man who ran a flower shop, dancing with wild abandon.

Come to think of it...

A quick pantomime later and Jimmy was walking away with a bouquet of three red roses, pressed on him in celebration of the festival. They'd been stripped of their thorns, so he was able to hold them tightly to his chest as he struggled through the mob. He had plans for these flowers, and he intended to keep them whole and healthy until their time came to be used.

Once upon a time, Grey had given him a bouquet. He'd laughed at first, joking about how he spent his entire days with flowers, so why should he want to see more of them when he got home? One look at the hurt on Grey's face, though, and he'd quickly recanted, going over the blossoms like the precious tokens they were. He'd carried one of the posies with him to bed, laying it on the pillows between them while Grey rolled Jimmy up on top of him, readying him for the ride of his life...

Ah, those had been good times. But they were over. *Over.* Grey had moved on, just as he should have. Why would Sint Holo play around with their lives now, in such a dramatic way?

"Dance with us!" a young woman with long, swinging red hair demanded, snatching up Jimmy's right hand. Another woman, with wild blonde curls, took his other hand in her own. Those roses, by some mysterious means of their own, clung to his heart when otherwise he would have dropped them.

Startled, he found himself linked in a circle with a dozen wild women, each of them dressed in what looked like leaves made out of green and brown leather, garlands on their heads, and wineskins—*Christ, are those real?*—hanging at their hips.

"Dance with us," another woman hissed. "Play with us. Sing with us. Make love with us."

Jimmy tugged hard, knowing he wanted only one thing— out of there. The women held on tight. "We are of the Frenzy," a brunette warned him. "We want you to play with. You're touched by magic, old magic, and we crave the powerful tonight."

The Frenzy? Damn me! Jimmy tugged harder, desperate to get away. Seemed like Sint Holo wasn't the only spirit or god playing games that night. The Women of the Frenzy, trying to stop him from going any further, though that could only mean one thing. He was close to his goal.

But if he tried to leave before the women had had their fill, he knew enough of his mythology to realize what trouble he'd be in. He might be dead already, sure, but they could still tear him limb from limb—these women, probably ordinary wives, mothers and students during the day, possessed by the wild women of old for the night of Celebration.

Instead of pulling away, then, he pulled forward, into the middle of their circle, and began to dance. He'd been good once upon a time, had even won a handful of slam competitions, and he'd served it up a few times. The women hooted and cheered, starting to race around him hand in hand in a dizzying circle while he entertained them, listening to the drumbeat inside his head instead of the melancholy pop playing on the loudspeakers.

At the height of their frenzy, Jimmy tipped his head back in laughter, and whirled as fast as he could, breaking out of their circle. The women weren't prepared for his lunge, and they parted in shock, but before they could come after him Jimmy shoved a young punk in their direction. They seized on the distraction as if he were a new toy, pushing him into their circle.

The lad looked dazed, but not altogether unhappy to be there. *Best of luck to you, fella,* thought Jimmy, a little dizzy but still bent on his quest. With Greek and Roman folk about, what he sought couldn't be far off...and ha, yes, there it was. An ordinary-looking building on the outside, but a cave of wonders within.

Ganymede's Grotto.

And behind it, an alleyway that would be perfect for...yes. Jimmy stepped neatly around some boxes, and came almost toe-to-toe with Nicholas, sitting crouched on a cardboard box with his head in his hands. He must have sensed someone there, but he didn't look up. "Go away," he muttered through his fingers without any force or vigor in his voice. "I want to be alone."

"Well, that's too bad, isn't it?" Jimmy reeled back a little as the words came out of his mouth instead of merely being thought. His old voice, distinctively rough around the edges, like a rich rum—or so Grey had once described it. His own accent, too, touched with the deep tang of the Appalachians.

Nicholas' head came up in shock. He stared at Jimmy, his mouth working, and then blurted, "It's you, isn't it? It's Jimmy. You're back."

And Jimmy had no idea what to say at all.

Nicholas gazed at his friend and found himself at a loss for words. Jimmy's eyes stared back at him through the mask. His mouth, that wide, mobile mouth he'd seen speak a hundred thousand times was still, no more words coming out. "Can you speak?" he asked finally, not taking his eyes away.

Jimmy looked uneasy. "It would seem that now I'm with you, yes, I can." He tilted his head, eyeing Nicholas narrowly. "And why is that, I wonder?"

"Ah. Yes." Nicholas leaned against the wall of the alley, not caring if his shirt got smudged or dirty—who would care?—and folded his arms. "You know, once upon a time, my great-grandmother told me a story," he said absently, as if he weren't talking to Jimmy at all. Jimmy just happened to be an incidental listener. "I had wanted to keep a garter snake as a pet, and she'd forbidden it."

He glanced up. "She told me about Sint Holo, the Snake Man, and what he could do." He kept his gaze fixed on Jimmy.

173

"She recited the story of a mask made out of deerskin, and what it could do. She warned me against keeping any snake talismans, for fear of drawing Sint Holo down to work his mischief."

Nicholas reached into his shirt pocket, where a small lump had been all but burning him the whole night long. He drew out a tiny snake's head, carved from bone, mouth open to show its fangs. Letting the object rest in his hand, he turned it over and over again, rolling it like a marble. "I had wondered if this was all more of Great-Grand's wild tales, or if it were true. Somehow, I believed her. The Cherokee were a powerful People, and they drew their strength from the spirits. If the benevolent ones existed, then why not..."

Above him, Jimmy drew in a sharp gasp. "You brought me back. Didn't you?"

Nicholas nodded.

Jimmy let loose with a string of curses that should have colored the air blue, finishing with a hearty, "Fuck me!"

"Thank you, but I think Grey has already taken care of that," Nicholas said dryly. He squeezed his fist around the bone snake's head, feeling the sharp fangs prick his palm. "Are there thorns on those roses?"

"What? No." Jimmy looked baffled through his mask.

"Hmm. And why did you put the mask on, when you rose out of your grave? Curiosity? I would have thought as much. You never could resist anything that piqued your interest, Jimmy." Nicholas rose, a bit taller than his friend, but not having to look down far. He reached out and pressed the snake's head into the bloom of one rose, where it rested like a beetle. "There. I don't have any power over you. I might have called you, but you answer to Sint Holo, and what he has planned, I have no idea."

Jimmy shook his head, clearly baffled. "But why, man, why?" he asked, voice desperate. "I was resting in peace. There was no need for me to come back. You and Grey look to have been happy together. Why summon up someone you'd long since said goodbye to?"

Nicholas bit his lip and was silent. Jimmy apparently refused to take that for an answer and grabbed him by the forearm with his free hand, giving him a hard shake. "I asked a question, damn you. Answer me."

"I had to know," Nicholas murmured softly. "When I was with him, I always felt like you were there, as if you were a real ghost watching over our shoulders. I had to know if he would really choose me over you, or go back to you any way he could have you, if it came down to the line." He raised his face, proud as any warrior of old. "That is why I dared Sint Holo's wrath. But outside of that, the magic's not being made in my hands. Believe me or believe me not. I don't care."

Jimmy plucked the bone snake's head out of his rose—or tried to. It stuck there, leering up at him with fangs sharp as needles, hissing. Nicholas almost imagined that he could hear snaky laughter at the edge of the alley. Jimmy tried again, prying a fingernail beneath the edge of the carving.

"I don't think that's going anywhere," Nicholas said, reaching out to touch the small carving with one finger. "Three roses. One for Grey, one for you—this one—but who gets the third?"

Jimmy glared at him. "You're a deep one, aren't you? Have all your plans in a row and everything lined up. Well, I've a few secrets of my own, Nicholas, and I'll be kind enough to tell them, unlike yourself."

Nicholas rested his shoulder against the wall and indicated that Jimmy should go on. His heart ached to see his old friend in such a fury, but at the same time it was pounding with excitement at having the man back again. God, but he'd *missed* Jimmy, had grieved for him terribly, and to see him standing here—he didn't know whether to venerate Sint Holo or curse the Snake Man.

Because Jimmy couldn't stay, of course. Nothing good lasted forever. Unless Grey laid a claim to him, the moment his mask came off he would go back to his grave, to lie sleeping throughout the ages, polished river rocks resting on his headstone.

If Grey found out this was Jimmy, that was.

If, and if, and if.

"Come on," he said abruptly, reaching out to nudge Jimmy's shoulder. "If you want answers, I'll take you to go find them."

Jimmy frowned at him. "What answers? What do you mean? Answers where?"

"Just follow me." Nicholas felt suddenly very weary. "We're going back to Café Noctem, to find Grey."

"Oh, now, don't—" Jimmy swore again. "Don't tell me this is all about having him choose between the two of us!"

Nicholas gave him a slanted look. "Why else do you think I would call you back? I missed you, of course I missed you, but I respect the dead and their need to lie quiet in their graves. That was the heart of Sint Holo's mischief, you know. Bringing back the ones who had already passed over to the other side. But I had to know. I *had* to, Jimmy. And now we're going."

"You don't have to," a familiar voice said, stopping them both cold where they stood. Nicholas looked up to see Grey standing in the mouth of the alley, arms loose at his side but back stiffened with tension and eyes so wide Nicholas could see the whites of them. "Jimmy?" he asked, his voice careful. "Jimmy, is that you?"

Nicholas watched Jimmy's throat work, unsure if the magic would stretch so far, but then the young man nodded. "Yeah. It's me."

"Nicholas?"

"I'm here, too." Nicholas stepped out of the shadows. "And so is the Snake Man, so watch what you say."

"Snake Man?" Grey frowned. "What do you mean—*Sint Holo?* Nicholas, that's a fairy story, meant for kids."

"Not so much," Jimmy answered. He stood in front of Nicholas, hands on his hips. "He's brought me back, Grey. The Snake Man is working his mischief double-time tonight. It was me in the basement at Café Noctem, and it's me who's come to find your new lover. What do you say to that, then?"

Grey walked forward slowly, as if he couldn't believe his own eyes. His hand came out, ever so carefully, and touched Jimmy's cheek through his mask. Nicholas closed his eyes, feeling a stab of hurt spike in his heart, still pounding with the rhythms of a long-ago fire and the sound of men crying out as they danced around and around the flames.

"Jimmy," Grey said, his voice choked as if with tears. "I'm sorry."

What? Nicholas' eyes flew open, just in time to see Grey coming at him, arms open wide. He was enfolded into a hug warm as toast, solid and hard. Lips pressed against his temple. "I heard what you were saying," Grey confessed. "I heard most of it, but it struck me dumb, Nicholas. I wasn't able to move."

He pulled back a little, thumbing Nicholas' cheek. His eyes shone with something Nicholas couldn't put a name to, but which warmed him clear through. "You need to know something, lover," he said, his breath making plumes in the cold night air. "It was never a choice between you and Jimmy. *Never a choice.* You're the one in my life now, and while I'll always miss him, you're the one who's here to stay. And don't you ever leave me too, do you understand?"

He leaned forward to kiss Nicholas, his lips warm and comforting and arousing. As his tongue played with Nicholas' own, Nicholas couldn't help but moan softly and grind against him, raising his leg just a little for a better angle. God, but he loved this man. Loved him so much. And if it wasn't a choice...

Where did that leave them?

"Here," Jimmy said, breaking between Nicholas and Grey. "This is for you," he insisted, pressing one red rose on Grey, "and crimson stands for passion, don't you forget it. This is in memory of what we've shared in the past."

He pushed another flower at Nicholas. "This is for the passion that lies ahead, in your future, with the man I loved. You two had better take care of each other, do you hear me? If you don't, Sint Holo or not, I'm coming back to knock some sense into both of your heads."

Jimmy clutched the last flower, the one with the carved bone snake head embedded in it, to his chest. He grinned, the same bright Jimmy smile that Nicholas had once adored, and reached up to the edges of his mask. He peeled it off easily and stood there as they'd last seen him when he was healthy, sparkling with life and exuberant joy in existing. He cast the deerskin aside, letting it fall wherever it might, and laughed in what sounded like sheer bliss.

"Come here," he ordered Grey, pulling up close to the man and pressing a kiss to his cheek. "Don't forget me, but don't take your eye off the ball either, eh? Nicholas needs some reassurance, or he'll get lost again and pull another trick, and then where will we all be?"

"Nicholas," Grey replied softly, reaching out to touch him. "You took a terrible chance. I thought these were all just stories, but..."

Nicholas arched into Grey's caress. "I had to know," he said simply.

"And do you now?"

"I think I do."

"You'd better be sure," Grey replied firmly, and then he was kissing Nicholas again, lips hot against Nicholas' own, plundering his mouth with a lusty abandon that made Nicholas gasp into Grey's mouth. Somehow managing to keep hold of his rose, he sank into his lover's embrace, holding him tightly as he could.

They both heard a low ripple of laughter, as if Jimmy were amused, and both turned around to look at him, Nicholas wanting to know what he thought was so funny.

But where Jimmy had been, there was only an empty spot and a discarded mask.

The man had disappeared.

Chapter Six

Nicholas closed the cellar door to Café Noctem, waving the last of their visitors good night. "Belinda did some amazing work when it came to handling the crowd," he said casually to the man standing behind him. "We really ought to think about making her an assistant manager."

"She did a fine job." A body nestled into Nicholas', holding it close, chin burrowing into the crook of his neck. "You think she can handle the pressure full time?"

"Belinda's a tough girl, and working hard on paying off her tuition loans as she goes. I say we give her the position. She can take the responsibility."

"And give her the raise, too?" Grey's chuckle thrummed against Nicholas' back. "I notice that you, the one who doesn't hold the wallet, is offering to up her wages by a couple of dollars per hour." He paused. "And that's something else we need to take care of, too."

Nicholas craned his head to look back at Grey. "What, now?"

Grey held him tighter. "It's another thing I've done wrong. Café Noctem was mine and Jimmy's, and then just mine when he died. You've been working your ass off for me in the meantime without a say in what, where and why. It's time to make you a partner, Nicholas, a full partner, and I should have drawn up the papers months ago."

"You—me—a partner in the café?" Nicholas felt as if someone had pounded him hard on the back, knocking the breath out of his lungs. "You would do that?"

"I would." Nicholas sighed as he felt Grey's lips kissing him, tickling the edge of his jaw. "I will. First thing tomorrow, the both of us take a trip to see the lawyer."

"This isn't because of Jimmy..."

"Well, it is, in a way. You're not replacing him, though. You're just coming into your own. You've earned the position. Besides, I don't want to be your boss anymore. We're partners, right? So let's *be* partners." Grey gave Nicholas an affectionate shake. "Deal?"

Nicholas thought he could feel himself warming from the inside out. "Deal." He paused, letting the ecstasy soak through his skin. Then, he added, "Speaking of deals, what do you say we let all these decorations stay up until tomorrow morning? The cellar isn't that busy in the early hours, and the few people who do come down here won't mind you messing around with the leftover trimmings."

"Oh, mind me, huh?" Grey dove for Nicholas' ribs and began tickling him. Nicholas giggled, then whooped with laughter as Grey hit particularly sensitive spots, and was soon begging for mercy.

He wiped tears out of his eyes and struggled for breath. "Yes, you," he affirmed very definitely. "I'm night shift. It's my job to sleep the day away."

"Just the mornings," Grey warned him in the curve of his ear. "When we're both awake, I have plans for you."

"Do you, now?"

"Oh, yeah. Definite plans. I think you can pencil in your calendar from now until, oh, the end of time. You're booked up—with me."

Nicholas sighed with contentment, then brought his hand up to caress Grey's cheek. The bones beneath were hard, but the skin was silky smooth and soft. "Except for the lawyers' meeting, I'd say I agree."

"You'll still be with me," Grey countered. "Point, set, game, match."

Nicholas laughed. Then, he sobered. "And you don't have any regrets?" he asked quietly. "I know what you said in the alley, but the chance to have Jimmy back in your life...in both our lives..."

"Hush." Grey kissed Nicholas again, this time just below his ear. Nicholas felt Grey move, then the hard pressure of a cock against the crease of his ass. "Does this feel like I want Jimmy instead of you? I was too slow to let go of him, maybe, but I have. It's you I want now. Just you."

"Here?" Nicholas asked, his voice barely above a whisper. "Now?"

"Not in the detritus of all this mess." Another kiss. "You wait for me down here. Ten minutes. Then, come upstairs to the apartment. I'll make sure the café proper is closed up tight on my way, so don't you worry about that, hear?" Sharp teeth nipped at Nicholas' earlobe. "What do you say? Will you meet me there?"

Nicholas hummed softly. "It's a date."

"Good." A warm hand lightly spanked his ass, and then Grey was moving away. Nicholas turned to watch him go, admiring the way the cloth of the man's pants emphasized one of his best features to the premium. "Ten minutes, remember!" Grey called back to Nicholas. "Not a minute less."

"I promise," Nicholas said with a grin in his voice, not taking his eyes off Grey's ass and his long, strong legs. He got a pretty good view from the front, as well, when Grey began climbing the spiral staircase. His last glimpse was of Grey peeking down at him, giving him a wink, and then Grey was gone.

Nicholas sat on one of the chairs, where he could keep an eye on the clock, and sighed to himself. "What a night," he murmured, tracing patterns in some spilled sugar with one forefinger. "Lord help us all, what a night."

"It's not over yet, you know," a familiar voice said at his ear.

Nicholas nearly jumped a foot. "Jimmy!" he yelped, pressing his hand to his chest. "What the hell?"

Jimmy leaned back, eyes sparkling and mouth laughing. He crossed his arms over his ribs. "You look like you've just seen a ghost."

Nicholas' mouth felt dry. He tried to form words, but gave up trying, as the task seemed to be hopeless. Instead he gestured helplessly—*Why? How?*

Jimmy shrugged. "Hell if I know. I think, though, this isn't Sint Holo's doing. I think something else brought me back."

"For what?" Nicholas asked, his mouth finally working again.

Jimmy paused for a bit, his "thinking" face on, until his mouth quirked in a half-smile. "I believe it's to say my goodbyes."

"Say your—"

"Grey and I, we said it long ago, when I was in that hospital bed. And tonight in the alley." Jimmy leaned forward and caught one of Nicholas' hands in his own. Sugar gritted between them, tangible and real. Jimmy's flesh was cool, but not

183

uncomfortably so, and his grip tight. "I never did give you a proper farewell, though."

Nicholas blushed. "I—I don't know what you mean, Jimmy. We had our own goodbyes in the hospital."

"Yeah, yeah, but those were just words. I need to give you a real bon voyage, and something else. My blessing." Jimmy shook his head before Nicholas could protest. "I know, I know, you don't need one. Well, you're getting it anyway, so you listen to me, hear? I want you and Grey to have a happy life together. You'll have to do it without me, which is my one big regret."

He winked. "Think of how deadly we'd have been as a threesome. Can't you just see all of us sprawled out on the bed, making the kind of daisy chain they only feature in blue magazines?"

Nicholas blushed, but had to laugh. "Jimmy, you were always..."

"Full of the devil," Jimmy agreed. His face grew thoughtful. "I wonder if that's not why the old devil Sint Holo took to me so well when you summoned him up. Like calls to like, after all."

To that, Nicholas had nothing to say. Then, he did. "I owe you some words, too," he admitted, taking off his glasses to clean them. "An apology. You were at peace and I disturbed you."

"Ah, rubbish." Jimmy waved that aside, careless as if Nicholas had been confessing to a broken mug. "I was a bit pissed at first, sure, but what's life—or death—without a little excitement?"

"Jimmy..."

"If it's forgiveness you want, you have it from me," Jimmy said, bringing Nicholas' hand to his lips for a brief kiss. "But I can't apologize for the regrets." His eyes twinkled at Nicholas.

"The more I think about it, the more tempted I am to test the waters."

Nicholas felt the beginnings of a strange eagerness grow within him. "Could you? Do you think?"

Jimmy sighed. "I don't expect so. I'm already feeling a bit pulled-after, like something's wanting me to go back to rest again. And I don't think I'll have a choice when they finally snap my chains tight. But give Grey my regards, eh? Maybe we'll meet again in another life and the three of us can give things a try."

"Are there other lives?" Nicholas asked, suddenly curious— and wistful. "Will we ever meet up again?"

Jimmy's eyes sparkled. "Hell if I know. But won't it be fun finding out?" He let go of Nicholas and stood, dusting sugar off his dark suit. He lifted one finger to his mouth and took a taste. "A taste of sweetness to go with all that is bitter, just like the best coffee. It's how I always drank mine, anyway. Black, one sugar." His grin was tip-tilted. "Your ten minutes are almost up, Nicholas. Grey's going to be waiting for you."

With those words, Jimmy began to fade, turning into a misty shape, curling away at the edges. "Wait," Nicholas cried, reaching for his friend in vain. "Is that it? Is this the end?"

"Of having me in your lives?" the ghost answered. "Yeah, I believe it is. But not for you and Grey. Ten minutes are up, my friend. Now go and blow his mind before I get someone with a harp and halo to come and spank your ass."

"There really are harps and haloes?"

"You'll soon find out if you don't hustle, won't you?" Jimmy winked one last time. "Goodbye, my friend."

Nicholas touched his heart. "Goodbye, my friend," he said, and watched Jimmy dissolve into nothingness.

Saddened and somewhat wistful, he dusted off his own black shirt and headed for the staircase, flipping off light switches and unplugging the fairy lights as he went. He snagged a mini-croissant and popped it thoughtfully in his mouth.

His eyes closed in bliss. He had just happened to pick up one of the special kind with bittersweet chocolate in the center. It seemed somehow appropriate, everything else considered.

Time to go meet Grey, then.

Time to face the future with his partner.

Nicholas wasn't sure what he'd expected to see when he entered the apartment bedroom—Grey laid out naked, as he himself had been before?—but what he found wasn't at all what had been on his mind. Still fully clothed, Grey stood by the foot of the bed, turning something over and over in his hands. As colorful stitching came into view, Nicholas' heart sank. It was Sint Holo's mask, as dangerous a thing as ever.

"What would happen if I put this on?" Grey wondered aloud. "Would I turn into a ghost, myself?"

"Don't even think such a thing!" Nicholas made a grab for the mask, but Grey was too quick, and turned to the side, continuing to examine the spirit creation. "Where did you find this?"

"It was lying on the bed when I came up." Grey flashed Nicholas a half-embarrassed grin. "I'd had a few other plans in mind, as I guess you can imagine. But once I found this, I sort of lost track of the time. Look, come here." He held out his free arm, and Nicholas snuggled into it, gazing at the mask. "Did you know, really know, what you were doing when you called on the Snake Man?"

"No...and yes," Nicholas admitted. "I didn't think things would turn out like they have, but I was aware that something big might go down."

"And so it did. And now we have this to remind us." Grey held out the mask, balancing it on his palm. "So, Nicholas. You're the one who called it into being. What should we do with this dangerous thing?"

"We could try to burn it," Nicholas ventured. "Except somehow, I don't think it would catch fire."

"Bury it?" Grey suggested. "Somewhere out in the woods, where no one will find it for years and years, if ever?"

Nicholas relaxed muscles he hadn't even realized were tense and nodded. "Yes. It's a good plan. Let's do it tomorrow, after the lawyers."

"You're in that big a hurry to get rid of the mask?"

Nicholas nodded. "My great-grandmother was right about many things," he said, huddling close to Grey's side. "She said it didn't matter who I loved, as long as I truly loved them, and she told me Sint Holo was evil. I believed her about everything else, and I shouldn't have gone against her word now. Let's bury it tomorrow, Grey, and be done with everything."

"What do we do with it until then?"

Nicholas glanced around himself. "The trunk," he decided, pointing to a woven pine box in the corner. It was empty, being a recent purchase, one he had picked up at a crafts fair. He'd thought he might put some medicine items in there, and he could think of no better place. "We'll bury it in there, too, so we don't have to look at its face again."

Grey inclined his head in assent. He tilted his face down to Nicholas' for a kiss. "Agreed. Do you want to put the thing in there, or should I?"

Nicholas gave Grey a look. Grey signified his agreement. "You called it, but it's for me to put it back," he decided. "Time to end this thing."

Crossing the room, he stood briefly by the box, eyes closed, then reached out and untied the braided leather thong that held the lid shut. Carefully, with reverence, he lowered the mask into the interior, and then quickly, as if the box now held a real snake which might strike, slammed the top closed and backed away. As they watched, the box shook with an angry buzz and a rattle, but Grey refused to be intimidated. "No!" he ordered. "Your games are done, Sint Holo. No more of your tricks for us tonight. You'll be gone from our lives tomorrow, and for tonight, you sleep. Are we understood?"

The box hissed at Grey once more...then fell silent.

Nicholas relaxed again, almost too far, but Grey was there to catch and hold him up. He slid his arms around Nicholas, one hand resting on the small of his back, and one on his ass, gently kneading the mound. "It'll be all right," he crooned. "I'm not angry, Nicholas, in case you were worried."

Nicholas hadn't thought of it, and the idea brought him up short in alarm. "You're—you're not?"

"No." Grey sighed, smiling a little sadly. "I wish you had trusted me, though, when I told you that you were the only one for me."

Nicholas put his own arms around Grey. "That was my fault. I was stupid and jealous of a ghost. If you've forgiven me, then I'm glad, and thank you." He raised up the few inches he needed to kiss Grey on the lips, finding them warm and sweet. "Lover."

"What do you say we make that more of a reality and less of a statement?" Grey asked. His hand worked Nicholas' ass harder, pulling him in tight. If his erection had gone down at all when disposing of the mask, he'd come right back up again. The feel of all that desire pressing at his lower belly brought a gasp to Nicholas' lips, and an answering swell of heat to his groin.

They kissed again, bringing their tongues into play, gliding them along one another in a slow, smooth tease. Nicholas twined his around Grey's, tugging slightly, and grinning when Grey loosed a small groan.

"Your suggestion," he said, lowering his eyelids to half-mast, "sounds like the best thing I've ever heard." He nudged Grey with his own growing cock. "Less talk, less clothes as well?"

"What, you don't want to tell me a story this time?" Grey teased, but his fingers were already busy with the buttons on Nicholas' shirt.

"I think we've had enough stories for one night." Nicholas helped raise Grey's arms so he could pull the black turtleneck off him. He paused for a bit to lavish the bared, hairless bronze chest with kisses, stopping briefly over Grey's left nipple to bite, then blow cool air over the flat brown circle, which rose and hardened into a nub. "A little less talk, and a little more action."

"Your pants, then," Grey replied, tugging at their fastening. "Damn the man who invented button-flies, anyway."

Nicholas began to laugh, and together they managed to free him of his dark jeans. Grey's charcoal pants, a much nicer sort of garment, came next, and then their boxers, both black, Grey's satin and Nicholas' fitted cotton.

As Nicholas bent over to kick them off his feet, he stopped, for Grey had darted around behind him. "There's something I've been wanting to do," he breathed. Nicholas felt the light wetness of a tongue tracing along the curve of his buttock. "What do you say, lover? You up for it?"

189

"Oh, God. Yes. God, yes," Nicholas whispered, hardly able to believe his good fortune. Grey almost never did this and Nicholas loved it. "Please, Grey. Do me."

"I plan on making you scream," Grey warned. "Grab your ankles and hold on tight."

Nicholas felt his ass cheeks being spread apart. He got a firm grasp and squeezed his eyes shut as his world exploded with pleasure when Grey's tongue began to rim in circles around his hole, quick and hot and fit to drive him insane. He moaned like a wanton, spreading his legs wider to give Grey better access, and heard a low, throaty chuckle in response. "Harder," he begged. "More."

"Shameless," Grey whispered against Nicholas's entrance, the buzz of the words sending a shock wave of tingles along Nicholas' spine. He cried out, gripping his ankles so tightly his knuckles turned white. "But then again, I love you shameless."

He applied his tongue again, this time stabbing into the small hole, fingers pressing in and out. Nicholas sobbed and rolled his hips, moving as Grey directed him, lips parting wide to pant every time Grey spoke a word against his sensitive entrance.

Unable to help himself, Nicholas let go of one ankle and reached for his cock, full and heavy, hard enough to press up against his stomach. There was a small sticky spot decorating him already where he'd leaked a bit of pre-come from Grey's attempts to drive him out of his mind.

"What if I used a toy on you right now?" Grey whispered. "One of the buzzy ones. Would that drive you crazy, lover? Would that make you go out of your mind?"

"You," Nicholas gasped. "You're...enough. Make me...crazy. For you."

"Do you want me to do this until you come?" Grey lapped again in an easy, lazy circle. "I could, you know. Just keep licking...and licking...and licking..."

"God! No." Nicholas ached with emptiness where he most needed to be filled. "Fuck me. Will you?"

"Then leave that gorgeous cock alone, because I want to play with you some more." Grey brushed Nicholas' foot. "Let go of your ankle, now, and come to the bed."

"Don't think I can make it there."

"You want me to carry you?"

"No." Reckless, Nicholas turned around and brought Grey down with him to the floor, the soft woven rugs cushioning their fall. Grey gave a loud *oof* sound all the same, and then tackled Nicholas, rolling them over and over until he was on bottom and Nicholas on top.

They gazed at each other for a long moment, both sets of eyes hot and both cocks throbbing, leaking thin streams of clear fluid on their lower stomachs. Nicholas dipped his finger into the small puddle on Grey's skin and brought it to his mouth, sucking the digit in. "Delicious," he murmured with a low hiss, fellating his own finger as if it were the next best thing to cock.

Grey growled, soft and low. Nicholas looked at him, challenging his lover to call the shots. "Make me yours," he moaned, stretching out and down to pinch Grey's nipples. "I want it this way."

Another growl, this one hungry. "The lube should be just to your left," Grey instructed, gesturing vaguely in the direction of their bed stand. "I left it lying on top last time." He stroked Nicholas' flanks. "Now you're the one on top, aren't you?"

Nicholas sighed with pleasure as he fumbled in the large container with their toys and supplies. "I'll get myself ready for you." He clicked open the lid and squeezed a vast dollop of gel onto his palm. Dipping his fingers in, he gave Grey a wicked look. "What would you say to a ride?"

Grey gripped tighter. "If you're the cowboy, then I say, saddle up."

"Bet I last longer than eight seconds," Nicholas murmured. "Let go of me so I can do this right. I'll give you a show to remember in your dreams." As Grey released him, Nicholas reached between his legs with the slick lube and began to run his fingers over his hole, already wet from Grey's mouth, and to stretch himself open. Below him, Grey watched with parted lips, his breath coming in quick, rough jerks.

Nicholas moaned in pure bliss as his own fingers penetrated his hole, scissoring himself wide enough to burn. When he had three inside he hesitated, then added the fourth, just to see if he could take that much. He could, and the feeling was beyond anything he could describe.

"Your thumb, too," Grey rasped hoarsely. "Fuck, Nicholas, I can *see* you and it's...oh, hell, it's so hot..."

Nicholas had never done this, but he would have done anything for Grey. Tucking his thumb in next to his fingers, he drove the whole of his hand up his ass. He paused for a moment to breathe in and out, riding through the searing pain that lasted only for a moment, before the absolute fullness turned to pure pleasure. Then, making sure Grey could see, he began to fuck himself on his entire hand, sliding it in and out, lube dripping down his fingers onto Grey's thighs, and even more semen bubbling from the slit of his own cock.

Grey seemed to be struggling for air. "You look—the way you look right now," he managed roughly. "Never been anything hotter."

Nicholas opened his eyes a slit. "Want me?"

"Oh, damn, yes."

"Need me?"

"Yes, and yes again."

"Then take me." Nicholas withdrew his hand and grabbed Grey's cock. He poised himself over the tip and then sank down, taking him all the way, then squeezing hard as he could with his internal muscles. Grey yelled and bucked so hard, almost like a wild bronco himself, Nicholas nearly lost his balance.

He steadied himself by grasping Grey's hands, which came up readily to hold his own when he figured out what Nicholas wanted. Using them for leverage, Nicholas slowly raised and lowered himself, breathing deeply with each stroke, applying as much pressure as he could.

"Me now," he uttered hoarsely. "Now me."

"Yes. You." Grey reached for Nicholas' cock and began to jack him off, good, rough, nasty strokes, just the way Nicholas liked it. Grey used his fist as if it were a machine; he started at top speed and he didn't slow down.

"Ah, God! Fuck, fuck, fuck!" Nicholas wailed as Grey worked him hard. "Can't last...need you too much..."

"Come on then, lover." Grey's voice was strained. "I am too...I can't..." He arched again, swearing at the top of his lungs, and Nicholas felt his insides being covered with thick sprays of jism, pulse after pulse while Grey humped and bucked beneath him. Nicholas rode him like a wave, letting out a small scream as Grey's fist tightened a little too hard and his own orgasm hit him with the force of a fist to the chest. His come spurted out in thick, ropy ribbons, decorating Grey's chest as if in war paint.

The two held still for a moment, panting harshly, joined by one hand. As he began to be able to see again, Nicholas gave Grey's fingers a weak squeeze, and felt it being answered in

193

kind. He slid off Grey and lay down by his side, throwing one arm over the man's wide chest, raising and lowering like a bellows.

"Take *that*, Sint Holo," Grey gasped, dragging Nicholas closer to him. He held on tight, saying without words all that needed to be said: *you are mine. I love you. I want you. I need you. You, and only you. No more ghosts. The future is ours.*

Nicholas kissed Grey's sweat-slicked chest and gave the yawn of a wholly satisfied man. He had been a fool to ever doubt, and now he knew for sure. He could wish the whole night had never taken place, but somehow he felt that the benevolent spirits out there, those who fought against Sint Holo, had seen this through to a better conclusion than the Snake Man would have liked.

Drowsy, he began to run his fingers over Grey's skin, and started to murmur, "Once upon a time, in the land where the spirits live, there were two men who were both Berdache, preferring the company of their own sex. They shared a single lodge together and made medicine for the rest of their tribe. They were wise men, after having learned life's lessons the hard way, and so generous with their magic that everyone came to them for help, from the tall to the small, the adult to the child, and they left with their hands full of good things for the People..."

"My storyteller," Grey said sleepily but affectionately, giving Nicholas a squeeze. "Go on. Keep on until we're both asleep."

Nicholas nuzzled against his lover. "There was nothing that could part this pair of Berdache, not even the will of angry gods, for those that meant only good for the People were looking after them, and cherished their love as a holy thing..."

And somewhere, in the wherever he was, Jimmy smiled and laid himself back down to rest. He knew he could sleep in peace now, with his friends taken care of.

They would all live happily ever after.

Epilogue

In the great and grassy plains where the spirits of the People still lived, Sint Holo sat by the hole in the ground he lived in, his arms folded around his knees, and sulked. His was a look so fearsome no one with any sense would dare come near him.

Let it never be said, though, that Deer had any sense. That, he left to creatures such as Owl and Bobcat. Picking his way through the green fields of grass, he came to Sint Holo's side and had the cheek to nudge him with one antler.

"Leave off!" Sint Holo shouted. "Annoying creature. Go find some fresh young weeds to eat, or a spirited doe, and leave me to my thoughts."

"Thoughts?" asked Deer, who knew of everything that had transpired and was not a little pleased at the Snake Man's failure at causing mischief. "It looked to me as if you were in a positive fit of rage." He prodded Sint Holo again. "Now why could that be, I wonder?"

Sint Holo hissed at Deer, who did have the native cunning to step back a few feet, but then shook his head in a display of pride. "I knew your trickery would fail," he boasted. "I have been watching. Your attempt to bring a dead man back and divide two living lovers has failed now, as it failed so many hundreds of years ago, with the People."

"I said for you to leave me alone," Sint Holo muttered, lowering his head onto his arms. "Why are you here? To rub a failure in my face? Go and lord it over Owl and Bobcat too, then, as they were the ones who helped give my mask its magic."

"Is someone planning to gloat over a thing I did?" Owl asked, fluttering down to stand on his great scaly claws between Deer and the Snake Man. "Are you planning to make a sport out of me? Me, the spirit of wisdom?"

"Wisdom, ha!" Sint Holo barked. "At least in the mortal world, the People still fear my little brothers and sisters, and even if most do not remember my name, they know of you as a foolish creature with glasses who sits on a tree limb and counts how many licks it takes to get to the center of a confection on a stick." He kicked the dirt in front of him. "Go away and leave me alone."

Owl did, highly indignant over the words the Snake Man had spoken to him. He did, however, pause in mid-air. "When they bury the basket, and it rots through, and the mask returns to you, use it wisely this time, Sint Holo!" he shouted. "We gave you our magic thinking this was to be for the good of the People. You have caused us nothing but trouble for being foolish enough to trust you. Let the mask rest, and go on about your business!"

Then, he flew away.

"Business?" Sint Holo hissed. "What business? I have no business except to sit here all day, and to take care of my brood across the world. That hardly occupies a being who should have his fingers busy with every tangle of string that can be knotted together."

"Snake Man, you are not plotting more trouble, are you?" Deer lowered his head, as if he would charge. "I was enough of a simpleton to trust you once. Your fangs may be deadly but I have strength enough to crush one of these 'cars' the People ride in, and I can take you on in a fight. I—why are you smiling?" Deer eyed the Snake Man uncertainly. "What is it you find so funny?"

"Oh, nothing," Sint Holo said innocently. "Nothing at all, Deer. You're right. What do I care about a mask? It was a game I played long ago, and a small failure now means no more to me than a child breaking a toy he has as a baby. Run along, Deer, and let me go back into my hole. I have a powerful urge to sleep."

Deer moved away, casting doubtful looks behind him, but he went—and that was the important thing. Sint Holo was as good as his word for once, slithering back into his den in the ground and coiling up in a circle to sleep. He grinned to himself, though, as he drifted off into dreams.

The mask would soon be his again. And as long as people believed in him, there would soon be someone else to discover the power that came of belief in Sint Holo...

Hisssssss.

About the Author

Willa Okati has a hundred and one different stories to tell, and she's getting there one book at a time. Permanently glued to her computer chair or parked in front of a laptop, she can be found pounding the keys from before dawn until after dusk. She's delighted to have found a home at Samhain where she can write her Appalachian-with-a-twist paranormal stories. Coffee is her best friend and her lifesaver; cats are her muses; her bookshelves are groaning under the weight of a tremendous collection.

She'd love to hear from readers, and can be contacted at willaokati@gmail.com. Drop her a line anytime or join her Yahoo! group to join in the fun with other readers as well as Willa. http://groups.yahoo.com/group/willa_okati/

With Love

J. L. Langley

Dedication

To Willa and Ally. It is a great honor to be in this anthology with you both, two of my very favorite authors. And to Sasha who made it possible.

Chapter One

Dev pulled off the isolated road, parked next to the three shiny sports cars already there and opened his door. There was a line of trees and brush directly in front of him. His meeting must be taking place on the other side of them. He had no idea what to expect. Whenever his own Alpha interviewed new members he did it at his house without other pack members around.

"Nooooo!"

He paused with one foot on the ground and one still in the truck. He sniffed the air. The scents of wolf, fear and arousal nearly knocked him off his feet. His gut clenched tight and his cock filled with blood. *What the fuck?* His eyes lost focus, shifting to their lupine counterpart; his canine teeth descended. The sudden shift of parts took his breath away. He couldn't remember ever having this sort of reaction before. It was like his body didn't know whether it wanted to kill or fuck. *Shit.*

A loud scream rent the air followed by laughter. Leaves rustled and...fabric ripped?

Shit, shit, shit. Someone was clearly in distress. What was he about to walk into? Dev closed the door quietly and took another deep breath. His stomach tightened again and his cock jerked. He managed to get his eyes to shift back to human but he didn't bother with his teeth. He differentiated six separate scents. All less powerful than he, but he wasn't walking through those trees with no defense. He flexed his fingers and concentrated on making them change to claws. Claws and fangs made for nice weapons.

"Oh no, please no. I'm sorry. I didn't mean to be insolent," gasped a soft, almost boyish voice.

"You are the fucking pack Omega. How dare you question me."

Dev recognized the last voice as the one he'd heard on the phone, the pack Alpha. *Great.*

Several barks of harsh laughter followed the Alpha's statement.

"What's the problem? You like cock. Just relax and enjoy it," a third voice mocked.

Holy shit. Not just a beating, but a rape. *Wonderful.* Dev rushed through the trees and brush. He was not about to allow them to rape the Omega.

The Omega fought a losing battle. He was a tiny little thing, maybe five foot five if he stood straight up with perfect posture. He reeked of fear, but he had determination. His dark auburn hair was disheveled and in his eyes, concealing his pale face. The goons had already managed to rip his pale blue shirt in half and partially off his slim chest. One man worked on the khaki slacks, while two others held the little spitfire's arms. Another two men watched, leering and laughing. The smaller of the observers rubbed his very evident erection. Dev didn't know why, but he was almost positive the man groping himself was the Alpha. None of them had noticed Dev yet.

Dev looked around and took everything in, trying to decide the best point of attack. The clearing was surrounded by trees. It was roughly the size of half a football field. This must be where the pack met before they hunted on a full moon.

The Omega went limp, nearly succeeding in making the two men holding him let go. It didn't work, but it surprised them all enough to allow the redhead to get a good kick in. He hit the third man who was wrestling with his pants, right in the mouth. Blood flew as the man's head jerked to the side. Crimson splatters splashed over the Alpha.

"You little son of a bitch." The man the Omega struck stepped forward, doubled up his fist and popped the Omega right in the temple.

The redhead collapsed, his head lulling forward on his neck.

Dev saw red, a growl erupted from his throat and drew the attention of the five men. They dropped the Omega and turned towards Dev.

"Who the fuck are you?" the man in the green shirt, next to the leader, demanded.

The Alpha blinked over at him and put his hand on the man who'd been tugging on the Omega's pants. "This, I imagine, is Mr. Devlin Johns. The reason we were meeting out here in the first place." The man raised a brow. "Do we have a problem, Mr. Johns?"

"We just might." Dev glanced at the Omega sprawled on his stomach in the grass. He had no idea if the man was still alive or not. A blow to the temple like that could kill a human, but the man was a wolf, even if a weaker one. "Would someone like to explain to me why the five of you are beating up on a much smaller, much weaker man?"

The largest of the men frowned. "Who do you think you are, mister? This is a pack matter."

"Since I'm considering joining your pack, I'd say I have a right to know what's going on. Where I come from we treat our fellow wolves with a little more respect than what I see here. If that boy is dead—"

"You'll what, asshole?" The big man stalked towards Dev.

Dev was ready for him. He caught the man's fist in one hand and slashed his other over the man's abdomen, raking him wide open.

The man staggered back, his eyes wide, clutching his stomach.

The two men who'd been holding the redhead charged Dev. He dispatched them as effortlessly, stabbing one in the stomach with his claws and abrading the other across the face. It was pathetically easy. Dev was quite a bit quicker than them.

He looked up at the Alpha and the man in the green shirt, while the other three writhed on the ground at Dev's feet. "Who's next?"

The man in the green started forward but the Alpha's hand landed on his shoulder, holding him back. "Not now."

"But—" the man sputtered.

The Alpha shook his head, his eyes never leaving Dev. "I said not now, Peter. Gather them up and let's go."

Dev glared back at the leader, keeping the others in his peripheral vision. They were injured, but they were wolves and healed extremely fast.

Peter managed to get the other three on their feet and headed towards the cars.

The pack leader walked past Dev, head held high.

Dev turned and watched them go, keeping his front to the five wolves.

"I do hope you know what you are doing, Mr. Johns, because you have just challenged my authority and I can't have that. Rest assured, you will be hearing from me." The Alpha followed his men through the trees to the parked cars.

Dev hesitated, torn between following them to make sure they didn't mess with his truck, and getting to the kid to see if he was all right. Dev couldn't do much for the kid if he couldn't get them out of here. So he followed the men, standing in the tree line glaring at them until they piled into the three cars. They left without incident, but Dev was certain he hadn't seen the last of them. He shook his head and hurried back to the clearing as soon as the last car drove out of sight.

Dev had been taught from an early age that Omegas were to be respected, not mistreated because they were weaker. They were the ones who held a pack together, they ran interference, they coordinated and listened to the pack's complaints and took them to the Alpha, they were the pack ambassadors, the peacekeepers. What did this little redhead do to piss off his pack leader so badly?

He knelt by the smaller man, touching his back. Only then did he realize his hands were still claws. He relaxed and willed his hands back to normal. His canine teeth remained and his vision shifted, going black and white again, probably due to the adrenaline rush. It would wear off eventually and there was no one there to see him anyway. The rise and fall of the little Omega's breathing was easily discernable. *Thank God.* He leaned down next to the redhead, meaning to gently turn him, and gasped as he caught scent of him.

The man's scent was like nothing Dev had ever smelled before. He smelled like a wolf and he was definitely a weaker, submissive wolf, but he was...enthralling? That was the only word that came to mind. Dev's cock, which was still hard, began to throb.

Come on, Dev, get a grip. He rolled the smaller man over on to his back and nearly swallowed his tongue. *Happy freakin' Valentine's Day to me.* The Omega was beautiful.

Chapter Two

"Quit laughing, asshole." Dev pinched the bridge of his nose and pulled the phone away from his ear. Cole was seriously beginning to get on his nerves.

"Okay, okay. I'm sorry. It's not funny per se, but shit, Dev, how do you get yourself into these situations? I send you to scope out Asheville and some of the surrounding towns so we can move our business and you end up challenging the local Alpha?"

Dev walked back and forth at the end of his hotel bed. He stopped, glancing down at the still unconscious redhead laid out on it. *Damn it.* There went his vision again. His teeth, even now, hadn't returned to normal and his stupid eyes kept changing. Just as soon as he thought he'd gotten them under control, they switched. He was getting a headache from the constant back and forth. *Freakin' adrenaline high.* The worst of it was the imminent case of blue balls. His cock was still so damned hard he ached. He was going to have to take care of it when he got off the phone. Dev sighed and continued his pacing.

"Look at the bright side, Dev. You like everything about the town except the pack, right? If you just go kick the man's ass, you can be Alpha and then our problem is solved."

"How does that solve our problem?" Dev looked back at the bed. A glimmer of gold caught his gaze. Nipple rings, in both nipples. Dev hadn't noticed them until he'd put the man on the bed and his tattered shirt had once again fallen open. It was surprisingly sexy. He'd never met anyone with body piercings before, his fingers were itching to touch them. *Great.* His balls drew tighter, if that was possible. Seemed like every time he thought about the small redhead, his body responded. Must be the constant reminder of the confrontation with the other men. Or maybe it was just that the kid really did have a nice chest. Slim, pale and well-defined. He wasn't muscular by any stretch of the imagination, but what he had was toned.

"Dev? Are you listening to me?"

No, I was scoping out the hot young thing on my bed, thank you very much. "Huh?"

"I said, then we know we will fit into the local pack."

"What?" What the hell had he and Cole been talking about?

"If you kicked the Alpha's ass and took over. You know we only have about two weeks. I am not waiting around and letting my mate move off without me. Caroline is supposed to report to the Asheville office for her transfer in twelve days. We have got to find a suitable location to move J&M Construction."

Dev groaned, adjusted his dick and sat on the bed, careful not to jostle the injured man. He understood where Cole was coming from. Caroline was not only his best friend's wife and mate. She was Dev's friend too and he was more than just a little protective over her. She was an absolute angel, but she had an uncanny ability to get herself into trouble.

Getting up and crossing the room, Dev pulled the curtains aside and looked out. Asheville was a nice town, with a breathtaking view of mountains in the distance. "Maybe we can move the company headquarters here and we can live in one of the surrounding towns?"

"Have you even looked at any of the neighboring towns?"

Dev let go of the heavy, burgundy, rubber-backed cloth. *Burgundy? Human eyes again.* Man, he was getting so used to the constant change he wasn't even losing focus when they shifted now. He groaned and made his way back to the bed. *Damn, the man is pretty.* Dev reached out to touch the pale cheek but caught himself. He pulled his hand back before making contact and started pacing again. "No, I was really taken with this one. I even found a great location for our offices."

"Well, fuck it then. It's a done deal. Start looking for apartments for now and land for us to build on. I'm not above a hostile takeover. If the Alpha gives us too much shit, we'll beat him to a bloody pulp and take his pack. You said you're stronger than him, right? So, we'll just take over, no big deal."

Cole could fight, but he wasn't near as strong as Dev. Any "hostile takeover" would be Dev's doing, not Cole's. "We? You got a mouse in your pocket?" Despite his large stature, Dev was no stranger to a good old-fashioned brawl. He'd been gay a long time and his size didn't deter everyone. And God knew, over the years, Cole had gotten the two of them into enough bar fights with his mouth.

Cole growled. "Don't be difficult, Devlin."

Dev ended up back at the bed, drawn to the Omega. "Cole, I don't need a pack to run on top of everything else I do. I do everything you do *and* I manage our books."

"Fine, you go kick his ass, take the pack and I'll take over the books."

Dev laid down on the bed next to the smaller man. His stomach tightened and his cock throbbed. He squeezed his temples with one hand and closed his eyes. Cole started yammering about how he'd take some of Dev's workload and how Caroline could help out. Dev took a deep breath, trying to relax.

The man next to him shifted a bit, like he was waking.

Dev dropped his hand, studying the smaller man. Nope, he was still out of it. What was it about the man that kept drawing Dev back to him? Dev couldn't stop staring. The man was beautiful, yeah, but *geez*, Dev had had his share of beautiful men.

The man sighed in his sleep and rolled onto his side. His straight, dark auburn bangs fell over one eye and the side of his nose. The kid had a great nose, not too small, not too big, and turned up at the end. He had smooth alabaster skin, not a freckle in sight. Which was pretty odd considering the red hair. Didn't most redheads have freckles? Dev didn't know, but he liked that this redhead was sans freckles.

On closer inspection Dev decided the man was probably about twenty-five. He was so fair and...delicate. Not feminine exactly, or even young, but...fragile. The man's face was almost androgynous but not quite. Devlin had the urge to hold him, protect him. This man, this Omega, needed protecting. There went his eyes again and damn if his cock didn't actually get harder. Fuck, it throbbed.

"What? Dev, are you even listening to me? Why are you sighing like that? You act like I can't manage money or something." Cole sounded exasperated.

Huh? Oh shit, Cole. Dev didn't have a clue what Cole had said. "Sorry, man, I zoned. You do just fine with money, it's not that. You know I trust you." Dev unsnapped the button on his pants, giving himself some room before his cock ripped the fabric trying to get out. He gave up on his eyes altogether. Let them stay lupine, he was tired of fighting it.

The man's nose twitched, sniffing. His face wrinkled a tad.

Dev grinned. How cute was that? He had the sudden urge to reach out and smooth the lines from the fair forehead.

The Omega's lips turned up in a smile, the tips of his fangs poking out.

That was odd. He was passed out. Why would his teeth have descended? The small upturned nose wiggled as the man sniffed again.

Dev inhaled too. The scent of arousal nearly overwhelmed him. Not that surprising, considering how hard he was. If he didn't get some relief soon, his balls were just going to fall off, or explode or heck, maybe they really would turn blue. *Wait.* That wasn't only his scent he smelled. He looked down the slim body and, sure enough, the Omega's dick was clearly outlined in the pants he was wearing.

The Omega sighed in his sleep, sounding content and dreamy. His hand reached out. It landed on Dev's arm and started stroking.

A tingle raced up Dev's spine, his gut twisted and his bottom teeth joined the top. "Holy fuck!" *Oh man.* That couldn't be due to adrenaline. Nope, now that he thought about it, the adrenaline had worn off. Way worn off.

"What?" Cole sounded bewildered.

Huh? He'd totally forgotten about Cole again. "I...Cole, I gotta let ya go. I'll start looking for land and apartments and talk to the realtor about the office building. I, yeah, gotta go, buddy."

"What? Dev what's wrong? You sound weird."

"I just...you know the man I rescued?"

"Yeah?"

"I'm pretty sure that he's my mate."

Laine blinked his eyes open to find one of the most ruggedly handsome men he'd ever seen inches from his face. The man smiled at him and Laine's stomach flip-flopped. The sense of rightness overwhelmed him. A feeling of anticipation and excitement followed. His cock was harder than a steel pipe, his canines had extended and he was seeing in black and white. "Darn eyes. I hate not seeing color. I really like being able to—" *This man is my mate.* He didn't know how he knew it but he did. "You're my mate." *Shoot.* There he went again, blurting out whatever popped into his mind. What if this man hadn't figured that out? Laine's senses told him the man was a wolf, but...

"It would seem so, yes."

Nice deep sexy voice. How had he gotten a mate and not even realized it? What had he been doing? Laine pushed himself up on one arm and looked around. *Darned eyes.* The night vision was nice, but—no color?—it sucked. He was in some sort of hotel room, a colorless hotel room. "Where am I and how did I get here? Where did you come from?"

The man sat up.

Yum. Laine felt like rubbing his hands together. The man was huge. He had nice big muscles, broad shoulders. *Wow.* He wished he could tell what color the man's hair, eyes and skin were. His hair was dark as were his eyes, but Laine couldn't make out a definite color; probably black hair and brown eyes, but were they chocolate brown or a reddish-brown? *Darn it.* This was his mate, he really wanted to know these things.

"You're in my hotel room. I was supposed to meet with your Alpha and when I showed up—"

"Oh, yeah. I got my ass kicked by Victor and his goons again." He waved his hand, but the big man's eyes flicked down to his chest before catching his gaze again. "That's par for the course. You'd think I'd learn to keep my mouth shut. But, noooo, I just had to tell them they were wrong. You saved me? You must be the guy they were going to rough up..." Laine grinned until he couldn't contain his mirth any longer, then giggles escaped. This was the man Victor was going to beat up?

His mate frowned. "What the hell is so funny?"

"I'm sorry, it's not you. It's just that Victor has screwed himself this time. You're freaking huge. And strong too, I can sense it. You are way stronger than Victor." He burst into giggles again, before slapping a hand over his mouth trying to stop.

Finally, the man started chuckling too, and he glanced down. The scent of arousal in the room increased.

Laine peered down and realized his shirt was ripped. His gold nipple rings were showing. Did the man like his rings? Laine loved his rings played with. *Wait, I saw the gold of my rings. My eyes changed.* Laine looked back to the man. His eyes were copper-colored, his hair a soft black. He was darkly tanned, with a square jaw. His whole face transformed when he laughed. This man may be big, strong and fierce, but he was gentle too. "Oh." Laine's fingers were itching to touch. He reached towards his mate's cheek, hesitantly. He bit his bottom lip, his hand trembling slightly.

The man grabbed Laine's hand and laid it against his cheek.

Damn if Laine's cock didn't jerk at the contact. "You have a lovely face when you smile. Your eyes twinkle." With his fingers, he traced the darker cheek, chin and jaw, learning his mate's face by touch. "You're very handsome."

215

The big man leaned into the caress. "Thank you. You aren't bad yourself. What's your name?"

"Laine. My friends call me Lainey. What's yours?" Laine came to his knees, both hands now tracing his mate's face. He couldn't help it, he was mesmerized. This big, handsome, masculine man was his.

"Dev. Devlin actually, but everyone calls me Dev."

Laine leaned forward ever so slightly, his breath fanning across Dev's face, his hands going to Dev's shoulders. "Dev. I like that. You look like a Devlin."

"Yeah?" Dev leaned forward too.

"Uh-huh."

They tipped their heads to the same side at the same time, then tilted their heads the other way at the precise moment. They did it once more.

Laine frowned and huffed out a breath, blowing his bangs off his forehead. "I want to kiss you," he groused.

Dev smiled and grabbed Laine's chin, tilting it opposite of Dev's.

Laine whimpered and closed his eyes. *Yes*. This was what he wanted.

Dev chuckled.

Laine's eyes popped open. "Why aren't you kissing me?"

"Because you were nodding your head."

Laine felt the heat surge up his cheeks. Geez, one of these days he was going to learn not to do and say everything on his mind. He shook his head at his own idiocy.

Dev wrapped his free hand around the back of Laine's neck. "Lainey?"

"Yes?"

"Be still." Dev pulled him close and captured his mouth.

Chapter Three

Dev's cock jerked at the complete abandon at which Laine gave himself over to the kiss.

Laine went all soft and compliant once Dev's lips settled on his. He whimpered and moaned, leaning into Dev, kissing back but following Dev's lead. Laine was sensual, such a hedonist.

Dev couldn't remember ever having a lover lose themselves so completely. He gave into what he'd been wanting to do all night, his hands going right to those little gold hoops in Laine's nipples, tugging and twisting gently.

Laine came unglued. He moaned against Dev's lips, arching his back, pushing closer. He practically panted. He'd given up trying to kiss back and just stayed where he was, letting Dev have his way with his mouth. The man was very responsive. It was a complete turn-on.

Laine pulled back, his face flushed, his lips swollen. "If you keep that up, I'll come."

Now that, Dev would love to see. "From just me messing with your nipple rings?"

Laine bit his bottom lip and nodded. "I come real easily. Maybe I should just touch you for awhile? Actually, that might not help, I might come from that too. But I'm dying to touch you."

Dev groaned. God, what a confession. The man was great for his ego. "I have a better idea. Why don't you strip. Then I'll decide what we're going to do."

Laine whimpered and the smell of arousal increased.

Yes. He likes to be told what to do. Dev groaned again. He wasn't all that surprised—Laine *was* an Omega wolf, after all—but Laine wasn't the only one turned on. Dev had always liked to call the shots. He gave Laine's nipples one last tweak. "You like that? Like me telling you what to do?"

Laine whimpered, nodding enthusiastically.

"Good, then get your clothes off and lay down and put your hands over your head."

Laine hurried off the bed and started tugging on his shoes, eager to comply.

Dev grinned and began to take his own clothes off. By the time he was finished, Laine was in the middle of the bed, hands over his head, legs spread, watching Dev's every move. Dev's eyes nearly shot out of his head. Damn, his mate was a fine specimen.

Laine was pale all over; his body toned and slim, almost lanky. For such a short man, he had surprisingly long legs. The muscles in his belly were so evident you could scrub laundry on them. Red hair, a little darker than on his head, trailed a line between his prominent hipbones. And his cock... Good Lord, the man was not small everywhere. Geez. He was actually bigger than Dev. Not a lot, but certainly wider. Nice flared head, alluring vein down the... *Wow.* Dev's mouth watered.

"You like what you see?"

"Hell yeah, Lainey, you are a beautiful man. No doubt about it."

"So are you. Can I touch you? Please?"

Dev climbed onto the bed, straddling Laine's hips. "Not yet."

Laine whimpered, but he didn't move, nice and obedient.

"Is there anything you don't like?"

Laine shook his head.

"No. That isn't acceptable. I need to know if there is anything you are dead set against doing."

"I don't like extreme pain. And I'd prefer no defecation or urination, but other than that, I'm pretty open."

Yeah, Dev would just assume not have any of those things either.

"And monogamy."

Dev's brow furrowed before he could stop it. This could be a problem. He was already feeling more possessive over Laine than he had over anyone else. "You want an open relationship?"

"No!"

The knot forming in Dev's belly gave way to relief.

"I mean, I want monogamy." Laine blushed. "I've never really cared before, but...I don't want to share you, Dev. I mean, I'd prefer...I mean, I'm not...I mean—"

Dev stuck his finger to Laine's lips. "I know what you mean. And that's fine by me. You're my mate and I don't intend on sharing you. From here on out, it's just you and me, Laine."

Laine nodded, smiling at him. "Good, can we have sex now...please." He reached up, holding his arms out to Dev.

Dev chuckled. "Put your hands back over your head."

Laine made a little whimper sound, his cock jerked and his legs moved restlessly, but he put his hands above his head. The man really did like being told what to do.

Dev smiled. This had real possibilities. He was going to enjoy this immensely. Now where to start? Oh fuck it, he'd been hard all evening, his balls were ready to explode. He was going to cut the foreplay short. He slid down, settling between Laine's legs.

Laine shifted impatiently, a little moan escaping.

Lord, the man was beautiful, all that milky white skin. Even the skin on his cock and balls was lighter than Dev's. Dev laid down on his stomach, pushing Laine's knees up as he moved. He didn't waste any more time. He bent and licked a long line up Laine's balls, feeling the soft wrinkly skin on his tongue, then trailed down past them.

When his tongue touched Laine's hole the man bucked and moaned.

Dev inhaled deeply, the scent of his mate strong here. His teeth dropped and his eyes shifted. He didn't care, apparently that was going to be the norm with Laine around. He swirled his tongue, circling the tiny opening, and moved up Laine's balls again.

Laine's hips bucked, his testicles pulling in tight, away from Dev's attention, then he let out a ragged moan.

The smell of semen flooded Dev's nose. He looked up in time to watch the first drops of cum splash on Laine's belly.

Laine's eyes, his wolf eyes, flew open, making contact with Dev's. His fangs dug into his bottom lip and he writhed.

Fuck. That was hot. Dev closed his eyes, dropping his forehead against Laine's thigh. Boy howdy, Laine hadn't been kidding when he said he peaked easily. Dev couldn't remember ever having a lover climax from something so simple. It was almost enough to make him lose it too. He took a deep breath and realized his hips were moving against the mattress. He stopped before he climaxed.

221

"Sorry." Laine panted. He reached down, running his hands through Dev's hair and over his cheek.

Dev leaned into the caress for a few seconds, kissed Laine's hand and sat up. "Hand's back over your head." He slapped Laine's thigh gently in reprimand.

Laine groaned. His eyes fluttered, then closed. He clasped his hands together over his head.

Dev dipped his head, licking the spunk off Laine's belly, enjoying the salty taste of his mate.

Laine's eyes flew open. "Oh God."

Oh God was right. Dev straddled Laine, reveling in the smooth hard ridges of Laine's belly teasing his balls and ass as he inched his way up Laine's bare body. He grabbed his cock in one hand, leading it to Laine's mouth. Laine, bless him, opened right up with an eager little moan.

"Easy, Lainey. Fangs...remember the fangs."

Laine nodded. His hands curled around Dev's hips, pulling him forward. Laine engulfed him, humming happily around his cock. He squeezed Dev's ass, nudging him closer, giving Dev no choice but to fuck his face.

Dev wasn't going to last. Good Lord, his mate could suck cock. Laine was making these soft little whimper/moany noises, sounding happy and turned on as fuck.

Laine's eyes went wide, his body stiffening for a few seconds and then Dev smelled cum again.

"Oh fuck, oh fuck, oh damn." Dev wrapped his hand around his prick and balls, squeezing hard, pulling himself out of Laine's mouth. He didn't want to come yet. He was dying to bury himself in Laine's tight little body. He wanted to come in his mate's ass, but damn if Laine's orgasm didn't almost send him over the edge. The man had not been exaggerating about spewing with barely any stimulation. Hell, Dev would have never believed it was possible to come again that quickly if he hadn't been here and witnessed it.

"Fuck me...please," Laine pleaded, his wolf eyes boring into Dev's.

"Damn, you're good for my ego." Dev chuckled. "Tell me you aren't like this with everyone."

Laine shook his head. "I don't usually stay hard. I have a pretty short recovery time, but I don't—"

Dev groaned, sliding down the slim, lithe body. He gathered the semen off Laine's stomach, using it to lube up his cock.

Laine looped his hands under his knees, opening himself up. His prick was still hard as a rock, dripping again. Or was that from the last time he came?

Dev reached out, intent on capturing the thick piece of meat.

Laine squeaked and quick as lightning, batted Dev's hand away. "Not yet. Fuck me. Please, please, please."

The begging was almost more than Dev could take. He reached down, circling Laine's hole with his index finger before pushing it in, then decided the hell with it. As turned on as Laine was, he probably didn't need much preparation. Dev added another finger then another. When Laine's only response was to whimper and push towards him, he pulled out and lined his dick up to that little pink hole.

Dev pushed in.

Laine pushed towards him.

Dev barely made it. He only just managed to get all the way inside his mate's tight, hot ass. He was actually dizzy. The breath whooshed out of him, his hands turning to claws on Laine's hips. Stars danced behind his eyes and a tingle shot up his spine as he emptied himself into his mate's body. He'd never come so fast and unexpectedly in his life.

Laine cried out beneath him, tightening around him.

Finally, when he came back to himself, he realized Laine had come too. "Jesus, you're going to kill me."

Lainey giggled and pulled him down, wrapping him in a hug.

"Uh, Lainey?"

"Yeah?"

"You are supposed to have your hands over your head."

"Oops." He didn't sound repentant in the least.

"Lainey?" Dev brushed the dark rust-colored bangs off Laine's forehead and kissed it, before he slid off Laine.

"Yes?" Laine sighed and snuggled in closer to Dev's side, his fingers lightly tangling in Dev's chest hair.

"Why would the Alpha, uh, Victor, want to beat me up? I called to make an appointment with him two days ago and he ignored me. Then tonight I was at Ganymede's Grotto enjoying a beer and watching the show when he called me out of the blue."

Laine's yellow eyes fluttered as he looked up at Dev. "Because he's a real dick. He always initiates new pack members that way. Says it keeps them in line and lets them know who's boss. So far no one has fought back. But you're going to aren't you?"

Dev didn't want to fight, he always tried to make violence a last option, but he'd be damned if he sat by and watched that tyrant beat up innocent people. He was shocked that no one had ever challenged the asshole. How many people had Victor abused? What was it Laine had said about getting his ass kicked again? "Lainey, honey? Does he try to beat you up and rape you often?" What if he'd raped Laine before tonight? He'd obviously already beaten him up. The thought made Dev's teeth grind together. But he wasn't about to lose his temper. Not with Laine around. It wasn't Laine's fault and from the sounds of it he got enough anger and hostility already.

Laine moved himself further on top of Dev, linked his fingers together on Dev's chest and rested his chin on his entwined hands. "He's never tried to rape me until tonight. Thank you for helping me, by the way." Laine shuddered. "Ick, just the thought... Yeah, just, ick. He's always tried to..." He dipped his head to the side in a sort of shrug. "I don't know, flirt? Come on to me? But he's never forced the issue. He's not gay, but..." Again Laine shrugged, this time his overlong bangs fell into his eyes. "I don't know really; he's never done anything in public. Every other time it's always been just me and him, except for tonight."

Dev nodded and brushed his mate's hair back again. He liked seeing Laine's face. Not that he didn't like the red hair, but his mate's face was spellbinding. Victor's actions made perfect sense. Of course Dev didn't agreed with them, but Laine was a beautiful man. And tonight had been about control. It had been a way for Victor to get two things at once. Laine's sweet little body and the pleasure of punishing him, in front of others, for his disobedience. "What did you do to piss him off?"

Laine grinned really big, his eyes dancing. "Same thing I always do. I opened my big mouth and told him what an ass he is. I can't seem to help myself."

Dev chuckled. Oh Lord, Laine was mischief incarnate. "Didn't anyone ever tell you that Omegas aren't supposed to talk back? Your job is to quietly support your Alpha and make sure the pack is happy. You're supposed to be an ambassador of sorts, a go-between for Alpha and pack."

Laine snorted and rolled his eyes. "Yeah, like a First Lady. I get it, but I can't support what I don't agree with. The man is a dick, plain and simple."

"I got that impression. Are you okay? I mean that was pretty scary tonight..."

Laine blinked, looking surprised, then his face lit up in a big smile showing off straight, even, white teeth. "I'm fine. I'll be even better if you tell me that you are going to stick around, I mean..." He ducked his head and started drawing circles in the hair on Dev's chest with his finger, getting shy all of a sudden. "I know you're moving here, but I mean..."

A bashful Laine? Dev hadn't thought that possible. He was actually surprised the spitfire could be shy. Laine was a bit on the submissive side in bed but the man was no introvert. In truth, he was just the opposite. Dev was pretty certain that anything Laine thought automatically flew out of those pretty lips. It was something Dev was going to have to watch. Something told him that Laine's alligator mouth was going to get his cute little tadpole ass in trouble frequently. Oh well, Dev was a sucker for firebrands. "Honey, are you trying to ask me if I'm staying with you?"

He worried his bottom lip with those attractive white teeth, as he peered up from under his lashes and gave a short crisp nod.

"Hell, yeah. I'm not going anywhere. Why would I? Wolves mate for life. Sorry, Lainey, but you're stuck with me. And furthermore, Victor is going to have to answer to me if he so much as looks at you the wrong way."

"Yay." Laine lunged forward in an attempt to kiss Dev and bonked their heads together.

"Ow." Dev rubbed his head, then Laine's.

"Sorry, I was happy that Victor is finally going to get what's coming to him. I feel like dancing around the room and singing."

Dev laughed. His life was never going to be the same. Laine was such a delight. "Only if you do it naked."

Laine giggled and shook his head. "I can't dance. In fact, maybe I should warn you that I'm a bit of a klutz."

Dev was going to have his hands full. Laine was a spitfire, klutz, and said whatever was on his mind. Watching over Laine was going to be a full-time job. Dev did his best to hide a grin, but failed completely.

"I'm glad you're smiling, because I'm totally serious." Laine kissed Dev softly. "I better go clean up." Laine sat up and headed for the bathroom. Only he didn't make it.

The bedding pulled tight across Dev and Laine landed on the floor with a muffled thud.

Dev sat upright, concerned about his mate. Before he even peered over the edge of the bed he heard giggles.

Laine was sprawled on the floor, snickering, his feet still tangled in the covers. "Oops."

Chapter Four

Dev checked out of the hotel the next morning and moved his things to Laine's condo. Laine lived close to work and the realtor's office was just down the street from Laine's job. Although it was chilly out, they decided to walk and leave Dev's truck at Laine's place. It gave Dev a chance to really see the town at a more leisurely pace, once again confirming that Asheville really was a nice place.

"Ooh, let's get a cup of coffee." Laine pointed to a coffee shop, Café Noctem, a few yards ahead of them. Laine was practically bouncing.

Dev was almost scared to see what caffeine would do to him. Laine had been bubbly all morning. Dev had contributed it to the wake-up sex, at first, but now he wasn't sure. Perhaps Laine was always this chipper. He could very well be a morning person. Dev wasn't a grump in the mornings, but he certainly wasn't as bright and cheery as Laine either. Maybe the coffee would help wake Dev up. He needed it if he was going to keep up with his mate. "Okay, sure. Do you always walk to work?"

Laine nodded, smiling. "Yep, except when the weather is bad. I like to walk. That's why I moved into my condo, it's close to the shop."

"What is it you do again?"

"I'm a florist." Laine's grin was infectious.

"A what?" Dev asked as he held the coffee shop door open, allowing the smaller man to enter first.

"You know, flowers. I own a flower shop."

A florist? It was a little surprising at first, but the more Dev thought about it, somehow it fit Laine. He was a happy, upbeat person, flowers seemed to work with his personality. "How did you get into that?"

Laine shrugged. "It was my grandmother's. When she retired, I took over. I like flowers." He slid up to the counter, ordered a double espresso then turned towards Dev. "What do you want, Dev? Do you want a bagel or something? I'm sorry I didn't have time to fix us breakfast. I will tomorrow, I promise."

"That's all right, I'm not much of a breakfast person. I'll just have a regular cup of coffee." Dev had never gotten into all the froo froo lattes and such. Plain ole black coffee for him. He tried to give Laine some money to pay for it, but Laine shook his head and waved it away. Dev didn't argue. He firmly believed in the "what's mine is yours" philosophy. They were partners now, he'd be buying Laine stuff too, it would even out.

They left Café Noctem and walked the three blocks to Laine's business, just enjoying each other's company. They talked about the town and Dev's appointments for the day.

After crossing the street, Laine tripped and espresso went flying everywhere. The cup landed with a splat several feet in front of them. Luckily they weren't splashed with the hot liquid. "Oof." He turned and studied the ground where he'd just walked.

Dev looked too. There was absolutely nothing there. When he glanced back at Laine's face it was almost as red as his hair. Dev stifled the urge to laugh. Something told him that he was going to be seeing a lot of such incidents. The man hadn't been kidding about being a little on the clumsy side.

Laine grinned sheepishly. "At least I didn't throw it on someone this time."

Dev threw back his head and laughed. "Oh, Lainey, you didn't."

"Oh, yes, I did. Twice actually. The second guy wasn't nearly as understanding as the lady and her sister from the first time. Now I try to make sure I stay pretty far behind others when I walk."

Dev bit his lip to keep from cackling. "You want a drink of my coffee?"

"Nah. There will probably be some at the shop. Assuming I remembered to buy coffee." Laine scrunched up his face in thought.

It was an adorable look, making Dev grin. Caroline was going to love Laine. *God, Cole is going to kill me.* Laine and Caroline were going to get into so much trouble together. Dev started chuckling again.

"It's really not *that* funny, Dev." Laine's cheeks were still pink.

Dev grabbed his mate's hand. "It's not that. I was just thinking you and Caroline are going to love each other. You two are going to keep Cole and I on our toes."

Laine's brow furrowed, his head tilting slightly. "Who are Caroline and Cole?"

"Cole is my best friend and business partner. Caroline is his mate." Dev took the last sip of his drink and tossed his empty cup in a nearby trash can without breaking stride.

Laine started swinging their hands. "What kind of business do you have?"

Dev halted the momentum, stopping their arms from moving. He didn't think Laine even realized that he'd started their hands swinging. "We own a construction company."

"You're a contractor?"

"Yes and no. I am, but we have our own crew that does most of the work. I don't keep air-conditioning and heating guys or plumbers in employment, we contract out for them. Cole and I oversee the job sites and on occasion, we help out and get our hands dirty too. Cole and I both started out as electricians before we decided to start our own company."

"So, you do the electric work?" Laine looked genuinely interested.

Dev couldn't help but smile. What a novelty that was. Most men he'd dated could care less about the boring details of his job. They wanted to know one thing, did Dev make a lot of money. Yes, he did and that was why he'd broken it off with the majority of them. Not that there were all that many, most were one-night stands. "No, not usually. We have electricians. Every once in awhile I'll help out. Cole actually helps out more than I do. Bookkeeping and running the job sites pretty much takes up most of my time."

"Isn't being an electrician dangerous?" Laine sounded worried.

Dev shrugged. "No more than anything else I suppose."

Laine squeezed Dev's hand and tried to start their arms swinging again. "Good. I'm not ready to lose you."

Dev stiffened his arm, keeping Laine from moving it. "Good because I'm not ready to let you go yet." And he wasn't. He'd been half afraid that he wouldn't have a mate. He wasn't giving Laine up for the world. Dev was already way past attached to him.

Laine bumped his hip against Dev's and head-butted Dev's shoulder with the side of his head. "Good." Laine stopped, turning towards him. "We're here."

Dev looked up at the sign and grinned. "Flower Lane?"

Laine chuckled. "Grammy named it after me when I was a baby. Kinda cool, huh?"

"Yeah, real cool. Are you her only grandchild or are you the oldest or something?"

"I'm the only one. Grammy raised me. My parents died when I was three months old." When he spoke about his grandmother his whole face lit up. "Actually, I just moved out. I was living with Grammy until last November. I would have moved out sooner, but then we lost my grandpa two years ago and I didn't want to leave her by herself. You know? I mean she isn't that old; it's not like she's feeble or anything, but well, yeah, she's all I have."

He kissed Laine's forehead. You had to love a man who obviously adored his grandmother. "So, when do I get to meet your grammy?"

"Tonight?" Laine's smile was almost blinding. "I can cook us all dinner."

"How about I take you and your grandmother out to eat?"

A forty-something brunette woman stuck her head out of the shop door. "Lainey? Mrs. Barker from the bed and breakfast up the street wants to place an order and she won't talk to me." She rolled her eyes. "Kookie old woman." She looked at Dev and held out a hand. "Hi, I'm Serena."

Laine waved the hand that wasn't in Dev's towards Serena. "This is Dev. He's my mate."

Serena's mouth dropped open, her eyes widened then she clapped her hands together. "Oh my God. I'm so pleased to meet you." She glanced back at Laine. "Has Grammy met him?"

Laine shook his head. "Not yet. We were just discussing that. Go tell Mrs. Barker that I'll be right in."

Serena hesitated, gave Dev a wink and hustled back into the store.

Laine sighed dramatically, but there was nothing but fondness in his expression. "That's the trouble with working with women who've known me since I was two. I bet she puts Mrs. Barker on hold and calls Grammy."

Dev laughed and kissed Laine's nose. "Go in and get to work. I'll take you and your grammy to dinner tonight. Do you still have my cell number?"

"Yup, I programmed it into mine first thing this morning."

"Good." Not that he thought Laine would need him, but he would rather play it safe. Victor was definitely the vindictive type. "If anything comes up...if you need *anything*, call me. I've got a few business meetings, but I should be in the area all day. I'll be done around three o'clock."

Laine nodded. "Okay. So, you'll meet me here around three?" he asked hopefully.

Dev winked. "Just try and stop me." He gave Laine one last kiss and walked down to the real estate office to meet the realtor, smiling the whole way.

Laine floated into Flower Lane grinning from ear to ear.

Serena kissed his cheek and held out the phone as he stepped up to the front counter. "I want details, Lainey. And Grammy is on line two, after you've talked to Mrs. Barker."

"I knew you'd call Grammy. Told Dev you would." Laine tried to snatch the phone but Serena scoffed and clutched it to her chest.

"I did not!"

Beth came from the back, the top of her blonde head peering over a huge flower arrangement that she placed on the counter. "Nope, I did. Lainey, honey, he's handsome." She turned the arrangement to face Laine and waggled her eyebrows. "Is he as good as he looks?"

Laine shook his head, chuckling. *Oh brother.* "It looks nice, I like the daisies and the tulips together. And yes he is, not that that is any of your business." Laine fluttered his eyelashes devilishly, and held out his hand for the phone.

Serena mouthed the word "details" and handed it to him.

Laine pushed the blinking button on the phone that had a number one above it, his gaze never wavering from his employees. "Hello, Mrs. Barker. Sorry to keep you waiting. What can I do for you?" Laine held up his hands, about a foot apart. Okay, it was an exaggeration—Dev was only about eight inches—but Serena and Beth were fun to tease, he couldn't help it.

Serena's eyes got comically wide.

Beth snickered and ran to the back.

Laine heard her start talking excitedly and saw the orange blinking light—the one labeled two—on the phone go steady. He slapped his hand to his forehead. *Great.* Like he really wanted Grammy to know about the size of Dev's— "Yes, Mrs. Barker. I can have that ready in two hours." He quickly said his goodbyes and hit the line two button. "Hi, Grammy."

"Twelve inches? Good Lord, Lainey," Grammy said, amusement heavy in her voice.

Beth started cackling and hung up the phone. A few seconds later she popped her head around the doorjamb and stuck her tongue out.

Laine stuck his out right back, giggling.

"Lainey, tell me all about him. Do you like him, honey? Is he handsome? Does he have a job? What's his name, dear?"

He smiled so big his face hurt, just thinking about Dev. "Grammy, he's gorgeous. Tall, dark and handsome. Real tall, he's six-foot-six. His shoulders are sooo wide." Laine shivered at the thought. "He owns his own construction company, Grammy. His name is Devlin and he's from Texas. And he's really nice. He rescued me from Victor and his goons."

Grammy groaned into the phone. "Lainey, what were you doing with Victor and those ruffians?"

Laine's excitement faded just a little. It was an old argument between he and Grammy. She couldn't understand why he had anything to do with Victor. "Grammy, I can't really avoid them. Victor is my Alpha, I sort of have to listen to him."

"Your grandfather would have never put up with that nonsense, and you shouldn't either."

Laine sighed. "Grammy, I'm not as strong as Pappy was. But Dev is. He's not going to let Victor pick on me anymore." Maybe that would help.

"Then I like him already. When do I get to meet this young man?"

"How about tonight? Dev wants to take us to dinner so he can meet you."

"He sounds like a thoughtful young man. And of course I'd love to meet him, dear. What is his last name, again? You know I used to know some wolves in Texas, maybe—"

His last name? Oh man. He had no idea what Dev's last name was. How embarrassing. "Uh, Grammy, Texas is huge. You don't know any of Dev's kin. He's from around Dallas. Everyone you know in Texas is from Beaumont."

"Well, I guess we'll find out tonight. Where should I meet you?"

"We can come pick you up around seven."

"Are you driving?" she asked hesitantly.

"Grammy, I haven't had a wreck in close to four months." She scoffed.

Laine sighed. "Dev will drive. We'll pick you up."

"In that case, I'll see you around seven. I love you, Lainey."

"Love you too, Grammy."

Laine managed to get one of Mrs. Barker's arrangements done and was about to start on the other one, but he couldn't hold out any longer. He had to call Dev. He put down his shears and floral tape and bounded to the wall phone by the door. He dialed Dev's cell number, which he'd already memorized, and leaned against the wall next to the phone.

"Hello?"

Laine shivered at the smooth, sexy drawl. He could probably get off just listening to Dev talk. *Hmmm?* "Dev?" Laine asked hesitantly.

"Yes, Lainey?" Dev sounded happy.

Laine looped the coils in the cord around his finger, undid it and coiled it again. "Uh, this is going to sound really stupid, but what's your last name?"

"It's Johns. What's yours?"

"Campbell." Lord, that voice was sultry. Laine pushed away from the wall, turning to glance around the room. Maybe he could lock the door and have Dev talk dirty to him.

"Lainey, I think I found a great place to build a house. I'll take you to see it after dinner tonight."

Oh! Dev wanted him to see where he was going to build his home. "Sure. I'd love to see it."

"If you like it, we can put a bid on it and then start talking to architects. Be thinking about what you want in a house."

Laine twirled around, barely holding in a gleeful squeal. Dev wanted his help. "You mean you want me to help design it?"

"It's going to be your house too, Lainey."

Laine turned, doing a little happy dance. He didn't even try to keep the giggle in this time.

Dev chuckled. "What about your grandmother? Is she going to have dinner with us tonight?"

"Yup. Grammy says dinner would be lovely. She's really excited to meet you. That's what got me thinking about your last name. Grammy wanted to know what it was. I felt like a real doofus not knowing. I mean it seems like something we should know, yeah? Hey, how's your meeting going? Did you like the office building on the inside as much as you did the outside?"

"I'm still looking, but so far so good. I think the office building is going to work, I just need to check out a few more things in it."

"Oh. Am I bugging you? Oof." Laine was walking—okay spinning—around and the next thing he knew, he was smashed up against the wall by the phone. "Shoot."

"Lainey?"

"Yeah, I'm here." He looked down at the cord pulled tight across his chest. How had he managed to get tangled up this bad? He turned the other way and nearly fell on his butt. "Crap. Serena!"

"Lainey, you aren't bugging me, love. I like talking to you, but if you're sure everything is fine, I should get back to the realtor."

"Yeah, yeah. I—I—yeah, I'll um...crap."

"Laine, is something wrong?"

Laine heaved a sigh. He was going to sound like a goober telling Dev what he'd done. How did he get himself into these situations?

Serena's laughter interrupted any explanation he might offer.

Laine frowned. "Stop laughing and help me, Serena." Maybe if he shimmied out... Now, how had he managed to get the darn thing in a knot?

"Lainey?"

"Uh, I sort of got hung up in the phone cord."

"You, uh, don't have a cordless?"

"No, we have one of the old wall phones with the long cord in the back of the shop. I was sort of, er, twirling." Laine flinched.

"Twirling?" Dev whispered, humor evident in his tone. To give Dev credit, he held it in as long as he could—which was about five seconds—then he started cackling.

Laine groaned. "It's really not that funny, Dev."

"Yes it is funny. I'm never going to be bored am I, babe?"

Chapter Five

After putting a bid on the office building, Dev headed back to Flower Lane. He hadn't had lunch and it was only two o'clock. Maybe he could talk Laine into leaving early and grabbing a bite to eat. Perhaps he could even take Laine to see the land, so they could make a bid on that too...if Laine liked it that was.

Halfway there Dev's phone rang. The caller ID read, *Cole's Cell.* "Hey, buddy, what's up?"

"You wouldn't believe me if I told you." Was Cole laughing?

"Try me?"

"I told Caroline that you found your mate, so we took the first flight out of DFW we could find—"

"Whoa, wait a minute. Are you telling me you're in Asheville?"

"Yup. We caught a plane into Charlotte this morning then caught a flight to Asheville. We rented a car and—"

Great. "Why?"

"Why what? So that we'd have a way to get around—"

Dev suppressed the urge to roll his eyes. He knew Cole was being obtuse on purpose. "Not that. Why are you coming to Asheville in the first place?"

"Because Caroline and I want to meet your mate."

Dev couldn't decide whether to laugh or cry. "Okay, where are you?"

"On the side of the road."

"Are you stranded? If you call the car rental, they should come and get you and give you another car." *Oh no.* "Uh, you didn't wreck did you?"

"No, no."

"Okay, why are you on the side of the road?"

Cole sighed. "Caroline was eating an ice-cream cone."

Dev couldn't even imagine where this was going. "And?"

"And she decided it was too cold to eat ice cream."

He still wasn't seeing a problem that would have Cole stranded on the side of the road. "Did she drop the ice-cream cone on the map?"

"No, she threw it out the window."

"And?" Dev asked.

"And it hit a police car."

Dev's mouth fell open, then he started laughing so hard he nearly dropped his phone. He had to stop outside Laine's shop and compose himself. *Good Lord. My life would make a great sitcom.* "Okay, listen. Once you guys get situated in a hotel or a bed and breakfast or whatever, give me a call. I'm taking Laine and his grandmother out to dinner tonight, the two of you might as well join us. Then tomorrow, I'll take you to see the office building and we can make appointments with the realtor to see the plots of land. I'm thinking about putting a bid on a two acre lot, just outside of town, if Laine likes it."

"Okay, we can do that. Did you meet with any of the plumbers or central air and heat companies yet? You know we are going to have to find some good ones to contract out with."

Hadn't he given Cole his itinerary? "Not yet, I have four meetings tomorrow and I also have a possible contract. The real-estate office I'm working with wants to do some major remodeling. They have four offices in this area."

"Cool."

"Yeah, cool. I'm at Laine's shop, so I'm hanging up on you. Try to keep Caroline out of jail and call me later."

Dev's good humor lasted until he opened the door to Flower Lane. He stopped dead in his tracks, the smile melting from his lips. The place was a disaster. Flowers littered the floor, along with shards of glass and ceramic from broken vases. Stuffed animals lay strewn from one side of the shop to the other and water covered the floor. The place looked like a twister had touched down inside. "What the...?" *Oh God, Lainey.* Dev's heart plummeted to his feet. His gaze darted around the shop as he inhaled deeply, trying to scent his mate over the heavy aroma of flowers.

Laine was sitting behind the counter, his head in his hands. He looked up and gave Dev a weak smile, but his eyes were a little on the watery side. "Hey. How did your meeting go?"

"Fuck that. What happened?" He walked over the debris and made a beeline to his mate. He stepped in-between Laine's legs, pulled him up and deposited him on the counter. It was waist high, making Dev's face level with Laine's chin. He hugged Laine tight enough to make Laine's breath huff out. "Are you all right? Lainey, what happened?" He pulled back to look into the teary amber eyes.

Laine blinked. He stared at the ceiling for a few seconds then looked back at Dev. "Victor's goons came to give us a message."

Dev groaned and squeezed his eyes shut. He'd known deep down something like this was going to happen.

Laine ran his fingers against the side of Dev's face. "It's not your fault. I started it. I'm the one who opened my mouth to protest their plans in the first place."

Dev hugged Laine again. "Ah, Lainey, it isn't either of our faults, this is not normal behavior. The man is a lunatic. He's a power-hungry tyrant and he has to be stopped." Dev truly believed that. People like Victor didn't stop, they kept on bullying until someone made them stop or someone died. Dev was not going to allow this to continue. Laine was his to protect and take care of and because of that alone Dev would've put a stop to this, even if he himself wasn't involved. No one was going to hurt Laine ever again. The man didn't have a mean bone in his body. He was obviously a joy to everyone around him. He was a florist for crying out loud. And damn it, he was already well on his way to being the center of Dev's world.

Laine snorted. "He doesn't fight fair, Dev."

He pulled back again, caressing Laine's face. "Then we won't either. He isn't getting away with this."

A tear streaked down Laine's face and he wiped it away quickly. "I don't want you hurt because of me."

Dev used his thumb to mop away another tear and kissed Laine's neck, which was the closest thing he could reach. "You're mine. Whatever affects you, now affects me too. And it isn't because of *you*. You didn't do anything wrong. Besides, they were going to jump me, remember?"

Laine's lower lip quivered. "If we fight back it will probably get worse."

Dev picked Laine up off the counter, giving him no choice but to wrap his legs around Dev's waist. "You let me worry about it. I promise you, I'll take care of it. You aren't going to have to put up with Victor and his bunch anymore."

Laine nodded and put his head down on Dev's shoulder.

Serena came out from the back and gave him a sad grin. "Why don't you take Lainey home? Beth and I will clean up this mess."

A small blonde-haired lady, who Dev hadn't seen before, came out of the back. "Yeah, take Lainey home. We'll close down for the day and clean up. We are getting a new shipment in tomorrow, so it's not that big of a loss. We still have a bunch in the back too, the only stuff damaged was out here."

Laine turned his head, probably to protest, but Dev didn't give him the chance. He pushed Laine's head back to his shoulder and rubbed his back. "Thank you, ladies." He gave them his cell number and left.

Laine lifted his head off Dev's shoulder, frowning at him. "I can walk."

"Yeah? Cause I've seen you walk, and—"

Laine groaned, but his lips twitched into a faint grin. "Hey, I warned you I was a bit of a klutz."

Dev set Laine on his feet, kissed his nose, then grabbed his hand. "That's all right. I have quite a fondness for clumsy redheads."

"Wow, Lainey. What in the world do you need this big a bed for?"

Laine glanced at his California king-sized bed and the man sitting on it, and grinned. "Good thing I have it. You wouldn't fit on a regular king."

"Yeah, that's true enough. That bed at the hotel sucked. I had to sleep diagonally."

Laine nodded, that much was true. Dev had thrashed around half the night, then finally picked Laine up and laid him on top of him so he could stretch out without crowding Laine off the bed. "I usually move around a lot. I'm not one to stay still when I sleep. That's a warning by the way. You'll likely wake up with bruises from sleeping with me."

"Then I guess I'll just have to let you sleep on top of me like last night. You didn't move around too much then."

Laine hung up another pair of Dev's slacks in the closet and reached for a shirt out of the suitcase. "That could work. Only, I don't know how much sleep either of us would actually get."

"Lainey, come sit down. You've been puttering around here since we walked in the door. You don't have to hang up my clothes."

"I can't sit." Laine sniffed. If he didn't stay busy until dinner, he'd start thinking about the shop again. And then he'd get all mad and weepy. "Your clothes will wrinkle."

"No, they won't. They've been in that suitcase for almost a week. And what if they do? I have a travel iron."

Laine shrugged and grabbed the last of Dev's pants. "It's no problem. I like the idea of your stuff being in my closet."

"Good, because a lot more of my stuff is going to be there until we can get a house built. Are you going to come back to Dallas with me when I have to go? Help me pack stuff up?"

Laine closed the closet. He needed to clean out a dresser drawer for Dev's socks and underwear. "Yeah. I can get Grammy to manage the shop for me for a few weeks." Maybe he could even afford to pay some security guards to hang out at the store and protect Grammy and the girls from Victor's goons.

He sighed and started towards the dresser. He didn't want to think about it yet.

Dev sat up on the bed, snagged Laine's arm and pulled him down. He landed with an "umph" on top of Dev.

Dev nipped his bottom lip. "Much better."

He gave Dev a weak smile, kissed his lips and tried to get up.

Dev tightened his hold. "Nope, I'm not letting you go. You've been moping around here since we got here. If all you were going to do is clean, we could have stayed and helped Serena and Beth. Talk to me. I know you're upset about the shop. You kept me from going and ripping Victor's head off by telling me you needed to come home. We're here, Victor is still in one piece and I'm not even stomping around throwing a temper tantrum, so talk to me."

Laine grinned. Yeah, Dev not killing Victor immediately was something. He'd wanted to...bad. Laine had stopped him by telling him that he didn't feel well and really needed to go home; which wasn't a lie, he hadn't—still didn't—feel well. So Dev had brought him here.

Laine dropped his head down on Dev's chest, listening to his mate's heartbeat. "I feel...violated. I know that sounds cliché, but I do."

"Yeah, I can imagine. If you'd let me kill Victor, you'd feel better."

"That's just the thing, Dev. What if you can't? He doesn't fight fair. He's probably just waiting on you. He probably had them destroy Flower Lane just so you'd come charging after him."

Dev nodded. "I'm sure that's *exactly* what he planned. I let you talk me out of going. I'm not stupid, Laine," Dev growled.

Laine lifted his head. "I didn't think you were. But I've dealt with Victor and—" Laine shook his head, the tears threatening. *Damn Victor.* "Let's just leave. Why don't I move to Texas with you?"

"If you run from this, you'll regret it."

"I've been running from *it* since it started. The only thing I regret is not running further. I should have moved years ago." He sat up, straddling Dev's hips, begging Dev to understand with his eyes. He didn't want his mate to think him a coward, but he'd rather Dev think him a wimp than to get killed.

Dev smiled and reached up, caressing Laine's cheek. "You have me now. You don't have to run. Besides, if you ran you'd spend all your time worried about the people you'd left here. You can't move everyone you care about."

Laine sighed and leaned into Dev's big hand. Dev was right. He would worry. That's why he hadn't split town in the first place. He had Grammy and Beth and Serena, and well, he had the rest of the pack. He liked his pack and took quite a bit of abuse to keep them from having to face it. He was a good Omega. He cared about people. Laine nodded and closed his eyes. And damn if the tears didn't start sliding out.

Dev pulled him down, pressing his head to that strong thick chest. "Shh. We'll fix it. You don't have to try and handle it on your own anymore. I'm here now." Dev kissed his forehead. Dev's hands started roaming.

It was nice. Dev had such good hands, strong but gentle. Laine's cock began to swell despite his piss-poor mood.

Laine had always had a healthy sex drive, but with Dev around? He couldn't remember ever coming as much as he had in the last twenty-four hours.

Dev nibbled on Laine's neck as he worked Laine's shirt up and off him. Immediately, Dev's mouth found his nipple rings.

The man was obsessed with his rings. Not that Laine was complaining, of course. He arched his back, pressing his chest into Dev's face.

"Mmm." Dev tugged the ring with his teeth, rolled Laine under him and stood up.

Laine groaned at the loss. Why was Dev stopping?

Dev unbuttoned Laine's pants and pulled them off his hips. He tapped Laine's hip and dipped his head. "Further up on the bed, Lainey."

Excitement raced through Laine. He scooted up into the middle of the bed like he was told. He loved that commanding voice, that tone Dev got when he expected Laine to comply. And comply he did. God, he loved domineering men. As long as they were also compassionate and fair. Someone who wouldn't take advantage of those weaker...someone like Dev. Dev took charge and made the decisions so Laine didn't have to. He could relax and concentrate on pleasure and pleasing. Laine loved to please, it's why he was such a great Omega. Or rather why he *would* be a great Omega if he had the right Alpha. Ugh, he didn't even want to think about Alphas...

"None of that." Dev shook his head. "You aren't allowed to think of anything right now. You are only allowed to feel." Dev crawled onto the bed, grabbed one of Laine's hands then the other. He positioned them both over Laine's head, holding them to the mattress.

Laine shivered, his cock getting even harder.

Dev chuckled and gently kissed Laine's lips. Laine tried to deepen the kiss, opening his mouth, even flicking Dev's lips with the tip of his tongue, but Dev pulled back.

"You like being held down?" Dev asked.

Laine nodded and a tiny whimper escaped. His hips pushed up into the air. Oh God, even the air on his prick felt good.

"You will tell me if you want me to let go."

Laine nodded again. "Just touch me."

"You really aren't in a position to be demanding things, Lainey." Dev winked.

The man was an evil tease. "Please, Dev?" Laine pleaded, gazing into those deep chocolatey brown eyes. Dev's face blurred. Laine blinked and Dev was sans color.

"Fuck, I don't know what's sexier, you begging or your eyes shifting." Dev used the thumb on his free hand to open Laine's mouth. He dipped forward and ran his tongue over the ends of Laine's canines.

Laine whimpered and bucked his hips, his whole body a tingly ball of sensation. He was close to blowing without Dev even touching him. He wanted to kiss Dev, to get in on the action, but he couldn't. It just felt too good. He closed his eyes, relaxing into Dev's ministrations, just lying there with his mouth open letting Dev have his way. Oh, it felt so good. Who would ever have thought someone caressing your teeth with their tongue could be such a turn-on? Not that it ever took too much to turn Laine on. His gums tingled. "Uhh..." His balls drew closer to his body and both his top and bottom canines lengthened. Laine gasped, his eyes flew open as Dev leaned back.

Dev's eyes were also lupine. He grinned and dipped his head to capture a nipple ring. He sucked and licked at Laine's nipple while his free hand wrapped around Laine's throbbing prick. He started tugging, jerking Laine off.

Laine's back arched up off the bed, his head thrashing side to side. He moaned and grunted and whimpered like crazy, but Dev didn't seem to mind. Laine was in absolute heaven.

Dev held his arms firmly, not allowing Laine to stop the ministrations. He bit down around Laine's nipple, his longer canine teeth pinching a tad.

Laine came unglued, his balls pulled tight, his voice came out in a ragged groan as his whole body stiffened. He cried out, staring into Dev's eyes and shot. Hot semen splashed against his stomach.

"That's it, Lainey, come for me." Dev stayed there and whispered encouraging, naughty words to him as he stroked his dick.

It felt like forever until he came down from the orgasmic high. When he did, Dev smiled at him.

Dev kissed him long and slow. He continued to stroke Laine's cock, not allowing him to go soft. When he pulled back he grinned at Laine, his teeth extended, his eyes still shifted.

Laine's own eyes had returned to normal, but seeing Dev's eyes and teeth made Laine's shift right back to their lupine equivalent.

Dev messaged Laine's wrists where he'd been squeezing, making sure they weren't sore. "You ready for round two?"

God, yes, always.

Dev chuckled.

Oh. He'd said that out loud. Laine shrugged. "Well, I am. Let me suck you?"

"Hell yes. Come 'ere." Dev let go of Laine's arms and got off the bed, standing beside it. He unfastened his pants, and pushed them out of the way, freeing his long, gorgeous cock.

Laine whimpered, licked his lips and crawled over to the edge of the bed. He intended on sitting on the edge, but once he got there, Dev rubbed his prick against Laine's face. "Suck it, now. Like that. Don't move."

Laine opened up and swallowed the nice piece of meat, staying on his hands and knees. He loved to suck dick. A day ago, giving him most any cock to play with would have made him a happy man. Now he only wanted this particular cock. He knew part of it was body chemistry, but he couldn't help thinking, even if he were human, Dev would've spoiled him for other men.

Dev groaned as Laine swallowed around his dick. His hands clenched and unclenched in Laine's hair.

Laine reached up with one hand and grabbed Dev's, pushing it against his head, encouraging Dev to get a hold.

Apparently that was the only encouragement Dev needed. He clutched Laine's head and started thrusting, fucking Laine's mouth.

The forcefulness was a huge turn-on to Laine. His damned cock was already leaking again. He was going to come just from giving Dev a blow job. Just like the first night. Oh man, Dev got to him. He was actually moving his hips.

Dev let go with one hand and bent over him. "Close, Lainey, close. Swallow it all, babe." His hand snaked down, encircling Laine's cock.

Laine nearly choked, it felt so good. He groaned around Dev's prick and kept working. His head bobbed up and down and took that long cock all the way down his throat. He wasn't sure who moaned louder when Dev started pumping his fist on Laine's prick.

Dev came first, but only by a few seconds.

Laine tasted the salty tangy flavor of his mate and joined him in climax. He shot into Dev's hand, on the bed and on his own thighs, as he swallowed Dev down. He didn't miss a drop. "Mmm..."

Dev finally let go of him and rested his chest over Laine's back. He kissed Laine's spine. "Feel better?"

Laine nodded and let Dev's dick slip out of his mouth. Now a snuggle and a nap were in order.

The doorbell rang.

They both groaned.

Dev stood, pulling his pants up. "God, Cole has terrible timing. Guess there goes the nap?"

Laine smiled. "I was just thinking the same thing."

Chapter Six

"Devlin, what do you think of the pack situation here? My Lainey isn't happy and hasn't been since that hooligan, Victor, took over the pack."

Dev turned away from the two redheads whispering across from him and looked at Laine's grandmother. "I don't care for it at all, Mrs. Campbell. How long has Victor been the pack Alpha, ma'am?"

The older woman patted Dev's hand and smiled. "Now, Devlin you're supposed to be calling me Grammy. We're family now." She took a sip of her ice tea and smiled at Laine and Caroline, who had their heads together giggling over something, then looked back to Dev. "He's only been in power a little over three years. George Marshal, the Alpha before Victor, was head of the pack for twenty-five years."

Cole snagged a nacho from the appetizer plate in the center of the table, his brow furrowed. "Grammy, how did Victor get the position? The traditional way? Or was he appointed or voted in?"

Grammy beamed at Cole, who'd remembered to use her nickname, and reached for a nacho. "I believe he challenged George in the traditional way, and George stepped down to avoid bloodshed."

"And no one stood up to him?" Cole asked as he picked up his beer.

Grammy finished chewing and shook her head. "No, Cole. No one wanted to cause a ruckus. We have a peaceful pack, or rather we *had* a peaceful pack, until Victor. My Edward was a Beta under George for many, many years. But Lainey? He wasn't strong enough to be anything other than Omega. Lainey wasn't born a wolf. Even though my Edward was, the gene skipped over my son Donald, Laine's father."

Interesting. Dev had never met a "made" werewolf before. He glanced at Laine and couldn't help but smile. Laine was laughing over something Caroline said. "How was Lainey made a wolf, Grammy?"

Grammy frowned and took a quick drink of her tea. "Edward saved him from the accident that killed his parents. Edward and I were following the three of them back from a day trip we all took up to Charlotte. A drunk driver sideswiped them and Donald and Elaine were killed instantly. Laine was an infant."

Cole let out a long, low whistle, shaking his head. "I'm sorry, Grammy, that must have been horrible. I'm guessing you saw the whole thing?"

Grammy nodded. "Yes, Cole, I did, but at least we saved Lainey, yes?"

Dev looked across at Laine again and smiled. "Yes, Grammy, at least you saved Lainey."

Laine peered up, his eyes wide. "Me? What are you guys talking about? Whatever Grammy is telling you, I didn't do it."

Dev chuckled.

Grammy laughed. "Are you accusing your grammy of lying, Lainey?"

Cole snagged the last nacho, grinning like an idiot. "Laine, I somehow doubt you're innocent. I've known you for"—he glanced down at his watch—"three hours and already I can tell you are pure mischief and probably as accident-prone as Caroline."

Caroline scoffed. "I am not accident-prone, Cole, you take that back." She raised a brow at Dev. "Dev?"

Dev held up his hands. "Oh, no, you aren't dragging me into this."

Grammy leaned forward and patted Caroline's hand. "It's quite all right, dear. If you are anything like my Lainey, you're a special young lady."

Caroline nodded, making her bright red hair fall over her shoulders. "See, I'm special."

Lainey giggled. "We'll remind them of that the next time either of us does something stupid."

Caroline frowned at Laine, but it was evident she was trying not to laugh. "Hush, Laine, you aren't helping our case."

Everyone laughed.

The waitress showed up with their food, quieting the conversation for a few minutes. Dev was having a blast. He really liked Laine's grandmother and Cole and Caroline seemed to like Laine. In fact, Laine and Caroline hadn't quit talking since they'd met this afternoon. Dev had been right on the money when he'd thought Laine and Caroline would become fast friends.

Laine looked up and met Dev's eyes while the waitress was handing out their steaks. He grinned, his eyes twinkling, and mouthed "thank you" at Dev.

Dev dipped his head, glad he'd put that expression on Laine's face. Laine loved his shop, and the whole ransacking and threat today had shaken him up pretty good. Laine had finally confessed that Victor directing his anger on Laine's *things* had him scared. Victor had always taken his anger out on *Laine*. Now, Laine was afraid it was a matter of time before Victor's rage spilled over to *someone* Laine cared about.

"Lainey, I have to tell you, I'm happy Dev found you." Caroline nodded, took a bite of her baked potato and a quick swig of tea. "I really thought he wouldn't have a mate or that maybe his mate would be a woman. Wouldn't that be a mess?"

Laine giggled and picked up the steak sauce from the middle of the table. "Oh Lord yes. I had the same fear for myself actually. Not that I don't like women, but..." Laine shrugged and tugged on the lid of the bottle. It was a new bottle and the little plastic thing was still attached. "I guess I would have dealt with it, if that had been the case, huh?" He tugged on the cap hard, it popped out of his hand, flying across the restaurant and hit a passing waiter.

Laine peeked behind him then snapped his head around, facing the table, his eyes wide as the waiter looked around to see what hit him. Caroline glanced at Laine, the bottle—still in Laine's hand—and back to Laine before she started laughing.

Laine smacked his forehead with his empty hand and groaned, but he too was laughing.

Dev and Cole exchanged looks and cracked up.

Grammy chuckled. "That's my boy."

Cole cut into his steak. "Reminds me of the time Caroline threw the ketchup bottle across a restaurant."

Caroline groaned and took a bite of steak.

Laine put some steak sauce on his plate and put the lidless bottle back. "Do tell."

Dev grinned, remembering the incident Cole was talking about. Caroline and Cole had been dating. "She was trying to put ketchup on her hamburger and she was shaking the bottle trying to get it to come out—"

"She got it to come out all right. After she lost her grip and it went sailing over her shoulder," Cole said.

A huge grin spread across Laine's face. He nudged Caroline with his shoulder. "How did you manage that?"

Cole chuckled. "She was shaking the hell out of it and it slipped. Ketchup went everywhere, and the bottle broke when it hit the floor. She got ketchup on her back, my arm and all over the people at the table next to us."

Grammy covered her mouth to muffle her laughter. "You two should keep them away from each other. That sounds exactly like something Laine would do. They could be quite a dangerous team."

Dev nodded. "I actually thought that this afternoon. Maybe we need to add to the company budget, Cole. We might need a 'bail Lainey and Caroline out of jail' fund or maybe a 'pay for things Lainey and Caroline break' fund."

Laine snorted, his eyes twinkling with mirth. "Oh, come on, we aren't that bad." His foot rubbed Dev's calf under the table.

Cole took a swig of his beer and kissed his wife's cheek. "If Laine drives anything like Caroline, we definitely need a 'traffic ticket' fund."

Caroline elbowed Cole and looked at Laine. "What kind of car do you drive, Lainey?"

Laine blushed and glanced towards Grammy.

Dev didn't know whether to laugh or cry. Apparently, Laine did drive as bad as Caroline. "Okay, Grammy, let me have it. Is he going to cost me an arm and a leg in insurance?"

Grammy beamed at him. "Only if you can get him insured, Devlin."

Cole started snickering.

"I'm not that bad," Laine protested. "I'm a good driver." He looked around the table. "Really." He sighed and shook his head, overlong red bangs falling in his eyes. "Things just have a way of jumping out in front of me."

Grammy grinned. "I've had to replace our garage door three times, our mailbox six times. I used to have to buy him a new set of tires every six months from him hitting and rubbing up against curbs. He's gone through a total of eight cars since the age of sixteen."

Dev's eyes shot wide, staring at Laine. "Good Lord, Lainey." Thank God Laine was a wolf and not easily killed. Not that that was going to keep Dev from worrying...much. He looked back to Grammy and very seriously asked, "Does Asheville have public transportation, Grammy?"

Cole laughed so hard his face turned red.

Caroline reached over and squeezed Laine's shoulder. "That settles it. I'll drive us to the mall tomorrow afternoon when the guys go on their business meetings."

Laine started giggling. "You're supposed to be on my side, Caroline." He mumbled something else and took a quick drink.

Dev arched a brow at his mate and ran his booted foot up Laine's leg. "What was that, Lainey?"

"I said, my car is in the shop anyway."

Everyone laughed, including Laine.

Laine excused himself while Grammy, Caroline and Cole were finishing up their desserts and Dev was waiting to pay the check. He couldn't remember the last time he'd had such a good time. He probably looked like a goober from smiling so big, but he couldn't help it. The evening had gone way better than he'd imagined. He'd known Grammy would love Dev. How could she not? Dev was just... Laine sighed. His mate was a wonderful man.

When Dev had told him that he'd invited Cole and Caroline, Laine had gotten a huge case of butterflies. He was terrified of not making a good impression on Dev's friends. Dev didn't have any family, Cole and Caroline were it, and it was important to Laine that they approved of him. He shook his head, chuckling to himself. He shouldn't have worried. Heck, they had come to town specifically to meet him. They'd been anxious to meet Dev's mate.

Dev had told them all at dinner how Caroline had always been setting him up on blind dates. From what Dev said, Caroline couldn't stand Dev being unattached. She had been convinced that because Dev was gay he wouldn't have a mate like all other werewolves, so she'd gone on a mission to find him one. According to Dev, the last blind date she'd set him up on, she hadn't even confirmed that the man was gay beforehand. She'd just invited the man to dinner telling him she wanted to introduce him to a "friend". Turned out that the man wasn't gay. Boy, what Laine wouldn't have given to see that. Dev and Cole sure got a kick out of the retelling of the story.

Laine opened the men's room door, bumping a man on his way out. "Excuse me."

The man kept walking.

Laine shrugged and went to the urinal. He did his business and zipped back up. He turned to go to the sink and ran smack dab into someone.

"Hello, Laine."

Fuck, fuck, fuck. Shit and damn. Laine peered up into Victor's eyes and glared. "Get out of my way, asshole."

Victor cupped Laine's chin and made a tsking sound. "Now, Lainey, is that any way to speak to your Alpha?"

Laine slapped at his hand and stepped back. "Don't touch me. You had your lackeys destroy my shop today. Wait till I tell Dev you're here." Laine was seething. No way was he going to stop Dev from busting this asshole up this time. The fucker had some nerve. Laine tried to step around Victor, but his arm was grabbed and he was jerked around and pulled up against Victor's chest. "Let go!"

Victor chuckled. "No, I don't think I will."

Laine struggled, flailing and jerking, to no avail. Victor was a lot bigger and stronger than him. *Damn.*

The larger man backed him up against the wall, chuckling, giving Laine even less room to maneuver. "I do like the way you struggle, Laine. You may be a wimp, but you're no coward."

"Fuck you."

"I tell you what, Laine. You let *me* fuck you and I'll take it easy on your loved ones. Speaking of which, where is your boyfriend?" Victor's mouth crashed down on his.

Laine wrenched his head to the side and used all his strength to escape the Alpha's arms.

Victor just laughed at him, holding on tight. "You know, if you'd have just kept your mouth shut—"

"Fuck you. If you weren't such an ass to everyone, I *would* have kept my mouth shut."

Again, Victor tried to kiss him.

The door creaked open and a gasp sounded as Laine managed to bite Victor's lip, drawing blood.

Victor howled and let go with one hand, raising it up, making a fist. "You little shit."

"I don't think so, asshole," a deep voice growled.

Victor was yanked away as his fist descended, missing Laine by several inches.

Laine blinked, watching Cole pummel the man's face. He sighed in relief. He hated to admit it, but he'd been getting a little concerned.

Finally, after several blows, Victor bolted towards the door. When he got there he turned to glare at Laine and pointed his finger. "You will regret this, Laine." He took off out the bathroom door.

Laine sagged against the wall, taking a deep breath.

"You okay, Lainey?" Cole came over to him.

He nodded. "Thanks, Cole."

Cole frowned. "The Alpha?"

Again Laine nodded. "Yeah, he—"

The bathroom door flew open and hit the wall with a loud bang. "Lainey!" Dev came running in, looking around. His gaze fell on Cole, then Laine. He rushed forward, pulling Laine into his arms, practically crushing him. "I saw Victor running out, I thought... Are you okay?"

"Yeah, thanks to Cole." He hugged Dev then leaned back. "I'm all right, really."

Dev glanced at Cole without loosening his grip on Laine. "You okay, buddy?"

"Yeah. I'm good. We have to stop this guy, Dev."

Dev nodded. "Yeah...yeah we do."

Chapter Seven

"Oh shit, oh shit, oh shit."

Dev sat up in bed blinking and looked around. Laine was nowhere in sight. Laine hadn't slept well last night. What the devil was the man doing up already?

"Oh shit, oh shit, oh shit."

Lainey. Dev grinned and pulled the covers off. Whatever it was Laine had gotten into must not be that dire. His refrain of "oh shit" was quiet and only slightly panicky. Nevertheless, Dev probably ought to check it out.

"Oh shit. Ooooh shit."

The smell of smoke combined with the rising alarm in Laine's voice had Dev hurrying his pace. The smell came from the other side of the condo.

Dev stepped through the kitchen door and stifled a laugh.

Laine was standing in front of the stove in a pair of white sleep pants. In front of him was a two foot flame rising from a skillet on the range. Actually, Laine wasn't standing, he was hopping from foot to foot, both arms—one with spatula in hand—flapping beside him. "Oh shit, oh shit," Laine chanted as he leaped from foot to foot.

Dev looked around for a lid to put over the frying pan. There weren't any sitting out on the counter. "Lainey—"

"Ack," Laine screamed and jumped around to face Dev, one hand flying to his chest, the other brandishing the spatula. "Jesus H. Christ, Dev, you scared the shit out of me."

Dev chuckled. "Where are the lids to the pots and pans?"

Laine used the utensil to point to the lower cabinet to Dev's left.

The smoke detector went off before he opened the cabinet door.

Laine screamed again, jumping almost a foot in the air.

Dev flinched as he scrounged under the cabinet and grabbed a lid that looked big enough. He passed Laine, who was still bouncing around, holding his hands to his ears now. Dev put the lid on the pan, dousing the flames, and turned the knob to kill the flame. "Open some windows."

"It's so loud." Laine ran over to the smoke detector and began beating it with the spatula.

Dev opened the window above the sink and the sliding glass door leading out to a balcony. He was naked, but oh well, the neighbors were just going to get an eyeful because he wanted that annoying beeping to stop.

Finally it did stop after Laine beat it into oblivion. Dev turned around to find Laine standing over the dead smoke detector, fanning his arms around, trying to get rid of the smoke, coughing.

It was too much for Dev. He started cackling. He laughed so hard tears filled his eyes. Laine was going to be the death of him.

"What?"

"Lainey, you're a mess. Am I going to have to ban you from cooking in addition to driving?"

Laine snorted then erupted into a fit of giggles. He threw his hands in the air and tossed the spatula in the sink. "How do you feel about going out to breakf— You're naked." Laine's gaze zeroed in on Dev's dick and he licked his lips.

Dev's cock decided to show off for his mate, filling instantly under that heated gaze. He sucked in a breath and immediately coughed. He fanned his arms, trying to move the air. "Come on, before we suffocate."

Laine put both of his hands on Dev's shoulders and dipped down, preparing to jump on Dev's back.

"Watch the—" He reached back to guide Laine's legs around him.

Laine's thighs and knees gripped Dev's hips, his feet never getting close to Dev's more tender anatomy. "Cock?" Laine kissed his cheek.

"Yeah." He pulled Laine's feet up and wrapped them around his waist, as Laine's arms enfolded his neck. Ooh, Laine's naked chest mashed against his back was nice. And, oh man, Laine was hard too. *Playtime.*

"Mmm, never fear. I wouldn't want to bruise it. I like the cock."

Dev chuckled. "You're nuts."

"Yup, like those too."

Dev grinned and turned his head to kiss Laine's cheek. He started walking back to the living room. He gave a quick glance to the sliding glass doors in the living room; Laine had pulled those curtains wide open too. Dev chuckled and shook his head. "If I'd known you had every curtain in the place opened, I'd have put some pants on."

"I like sunshine."

"I see. We're going to wake up tomorrow and find the complex empty and all your neighbors scared away."

Laine snorted. "More like they'll be knocking on my door wanting to know if the stud is taken."

"Now, I *know* you're nuts." He turned and dropped Laine on the bed.

Laine bounced then sprawled. He ended up spread out on the mattress, arms and legs wide, his gaze raking up and down Dev's body. "Absolutely certifiable. You don't mind do you?" He raised his hands up towards Dev.

"Nope, not at all. You're, however, at the moment, an overdressed nut." He grabbed the waistband of Laine's pj's and pulled them down.

Laine lifted his butt off the bed to assist, his thick cock hard and ready.

Dev lay down next to Laine on his side, his face even with Laine's hip, his head propped on his hand. He traced his finger up Laine's chiseled abs and back down, marveling at the way Laine's muscles jumped under his fingers. He looked up to find Laine's eyes closed, his bottom lip between his teeth. Dev's gaze trailed down Laine's body, past the gold hoops in his nipples— which Dev had to reach up and flick—past Laine's belly, to the nest of red curls above that thick, hard prick. He really was a beautiful man, slim and fit. His willowy form and ivory skin was such a contrast to Dev's own larger body and dark tan.

Dev leaned forward, tracing the hollow beside Laine's hipbone with his tongue.

Laine's head and shoulders shot off the bed, giggles sounding immediately.

Oooh, a ticklish spot. He pushed Laine back onto the bed and did it again.

Laine's hands flew to his hip, covering the spot, still giggling like mad. The man was just too damned cute.

Dev nuzzled Laine's hand and when he managed to nudge Laine's hand out of the way he licked again.

Laine bucked his hips off the bed. His cock bumped Dev's cheek.

Dev froze. He'd never been much of a cocksucker, but he had the sudden urge to taste Laine. He pushed Laine's hips down and grabbed that fat prick.

Laine hissed out a breath and relaxed back onto the bed. "Dev..."

"Shh..." Dev traced up one side of his mate's dick with his tongue then down the other side. He positioned himself over the redhead's groin, taking just the head between his lips. *Not bad.* Laine's skin was smooth and warm, salty.

"Dev, you don't have to."

"I want to."

Laine nodded. "Okay."

Dev gradually explored. He'd done this once or twice, but it had always been hurried, a case of feeling obliged, never for his own enjoyment. On this occasion he took his time, learning, enjoying his lover. Dev laved and nuzzled. He took one testicle in his mouth, then the other, before licking behind them. When he was ready to get serious and start sucking, Laine was squirming all over the place, his breath coming in pants.

Laine brought his hand up to his mouth, then all Dev heard was a whimper.

He looked up to find Laine biting his hand. "What are you doing?"

"Trying not to come." It came out in a squeak that had Dev holding back a grin. He didn't know anyone who could come as quickly as his mate. It was surprisingly sexy as all get out. The fact that Laine had such a short recovery period was pretty damned hot too.

Dev didn't even come that fast as a teenager. He knew some guys did, but he'd never been one of them. "Go ahead. I've complete faith you can get it up again."

"Mmm, okay." Laine dropped his hand back to his side.

Dev kissed his hand where Laine had left teeth marks, then sucked Laine's dick into his mouth. He squeezed the base in his palm. He couldn't go very far down without choking, but Laine didn't seem to care. Dev used his hand and mouth, watching Laine's reaction the whole time.

Laine's face scrunched together. It wouldn't be long. Laine's hips bucked up into his mouth, almost gagging him. Laine whimpered and begged.

Dev caught those slim hips, holding them still, and sucked the next time he moved up. That was all it took.

Laine's back arched off the bed, his begging and whimpering turned into grunts, as he shot in Dev's mouth.

Dev let the tangy flavor collect in his mouth then swallowed every drop.

"I...oh...uh...wow." Laine blinked down at him.

Dev grinned and slid up his mate's body to settle against him. He grabbed his own dick, rubbing it against Laine's hip. "Mmm, yeah, wow." He bent and kissed Laine's lips.

Laine's hands came up, his fingers tangling into Dev's hair, and he deepened the kiss. He moaned and turned his body to the side, pressing against Dev. He wrapped his hand around Dev's prick without breaking their kiss and stroked softly.

Damn, it felt good. Laine had great hands. Not as great as Laine's mouth or his ass, but still, nothing to shake a stick at.

He let go of his cock, allowing Laine to take over, and reached for Laine's nipples. When he found the little gold hoops, Laine moaned into his mouth. He tugged gently and twisted.

Laine's cock started hardening against Dev's thigh. And fuck if that wasn't hot. He loved knowing that he could get Laine hard again so quickly. His own cock jerked at Laine's renewed interest.

Laine pulled back breathlessly. "Let me suck you...please."

Dev dipped down and flicked the nipple ring with his tongue, then rolled onto his back, carrying Laine with him. "How about you ride me instead?"

"Oh yeah, I can do that. That works." Laine sat up and snatched the bottle of lube off the nightstand. "Want me to do it?"

Dev groaned. *Good Lord yes.* The thought of Laine with his fingers in his own ass made his cock twitch. Dev nodded and grabbed the pretty, eager cock, pumping lightly.

Dropping the bottle, Laine scrambled for it and flicked the lid open, getting some on his fingers before he closed it. He moaned and shut his eyes, sitting up a bit as he reached behind him. He looked beautiful, sensual, a fucking wet dream come to life, as he readied himself for Dev's cock.

"Fuck, honey." Dev gripped the prick in his hand a tad harder, pumped a little faster, as he watched Laine ride his own fingers.

Laine's eyes shot open, a look of surprise on his face. "Oh. Stop. Stop, stop, stop. Gonna come again."

Dev relented and let go of Laine's cock. He didn't want to but he really wanted to feel Laine come, squeezed tight around his dick. Dev nodded. "Hurry."

"Yeah." Laine grabbed Dev's prick, opened the bottle of lube, squirted some on the head then tossed the bottle aside. Dev started to tell Laine that he forgot to close the bottle but Laine's hands distracted him, slicking him up. Oh well, they'd clean up the mess later.

Laine bit his bottom lip, his amber eyes boring into Dev's as he lined Dev's prick up. He sank down slowly.

"Damn." Dev's breath caught. That tight little hole was like a vise pulling the head of his dick in. His eyes blurred, then suddenly the color was gone.

Laine gasped, his own irises spreading, swallowing up the white. His canine's slid down as he impaled himself on Dev's erection. "Dev..." His ass finally rested against Dev's hips. He sat still for several seconds trying to catch his breath.

Laine was concentrating on not losing his load, Dev could see it in his face. It didn't matter. Dev was pretty damned close himself. "Just move, Lainey, it's okay."

Laine nodded and raised himself up then back down. He found a steady, quick pace that had Dev's eyes rolling back in his head. It wasn't long before Laine's whole body went stiff and he was crying out above Dev.

The hot splash of semen hit Dev's abs and Laine's muscles constricted around him. Dev grabbed Laine's hips and thrust up into him, fucking Laine through his climax.

Laine's hoarse moan and the look of sheer bliss, coupled with the tight heat squeezing his cock plummeted Dev into his own orgasm.

Laine collapsed on top of him, out of breath.

Dev hugged him snugly, nuzzling his cheek against Laine's. Yeah, Victor was a dead man. No way was he going to lose Laine. Heck, he didn't even want Laine to be unhappy, therefore the Alpha had to go.

He rubbed Laine's slender back, relishing the feel of Laine's hot breath in his ear.

Laine turned his head and kissed Dev's ear, showing no signs of moving.

Not that Dev cared. Laine wasn't heavy, it was a comforting weight and feeling. If Laine was here with him, he was okay, not getting into mischief or getting attacked by psycho werewolf pack leaders.

Laine's breath evened out and slowed. He started snoring softly.

Dev continued to rub his back.

Laine needed the sleep. He'd been on edge ever since his run-in with Victor last night. He hadn't slept worth a damn. Dev knew because Laine tossed and turned all night, waking him several times. When Dev woke at three a.m. to find Laine still awake, he'd fucked Laine's pretty little ass into unconsciousness. God only knew what time the man had gotten up to cook, er, burn breakfast.

Dev chuckled, remembering the scene that greeted him in the kitchen this morning.

Laine wiggled a little on top of him and snuffled, jarred by his laughter.

Dev quickly slid out from under Laine and patted and rubbed his back until Laine settled back down. When Laine's snores started again, Dev got up and went to the bathroom. He picked up the open bottle of lube on the way, fortunately it hadn't dripped onto the floor.

He showered, shaved and grabbed a granola bar and orange juice for breakfast. While he ate, he cleaned up the mess Laine had made in the kitchen, then went back to check on Laine.

Laine was still sound asleep. No way was Dev waking him up. He grabbed the phone and called Cole, arranging for their meeting to take place an hour later. It would give Laine time to sleep before Caroline came and got him to go shopping, and it would give Dev time to get a few things straight with Victor.

Chapter Eight

Dev jogged down the steps, his truck keys in hand, and almost ran right in to an older man coming up.

The man stopped, surprised, and glanced up at Laine's front door. "Are you Devlin Johns?"

"Yes, sir, I am. Do I know you?" Dev knew he didn't, but the man obviously knew him, or at least *of* him.

"Good, you're very strong. A powerful wolf." The man extended his hand. "I'm George Marshal, I'm a friend of Margaret's."

"Who?" Wait, wasn't George the name of Laine's old pack Alpha? "You mean Grammy?" He shook the man's hand.

The older gentleman nodded his gray head. Dev guessed the man to be somewhere around Grammy's age, his early to mid-seventies. "Yes, Laine's grandmother."

"If you are wanting to speak to Lainey, he's—"

"No. I came to see you, Mr. Johns. It's about Margaret, er, Laine's grandmother."

"Is she all right?"

"Victor has Margaret."

Dev blinked. "He has Grammy? As in kidnapped Grammy?"

"Yes. I was on my way to Margaret's house this morning and saw them putting her in the car. I followed them to Peter's house. Then I came to get you. We have to go get her."

About a million and one things raced into Dev's head at once. Laine was going to be devastated. He had to tell Laine and he didn't want to see the hurt on Laine's face when he told him. He had to go get Grammy. He needed to know where Peter lived. Had George Marshal been sent by Victor to bait Dev? Dev didn't think so, the man seemed to be one of the good guys.

"I can't win against Victor, and neither can anyone else in my pack, but you can. I need your help. I have wolves that will help you, but...I need to know what your plans are. If you aren't going to go after Margaret, then I—"

"You bet your ass I'm going after Grammy." Dev winced. He hadn't meant to shout. "Sorry, Mr. Marshal. I've just had about all of Victor I can stand. I'd love any help you can offer."

Mr. Marshal smiled briefly. "Good, that's what I like to hear. You're a strong wolf and Margaret thinks you'd make an excellent Alpha. She had nothing but good things to say about you last night when I talked to her on the phone and that's good enough for me. I'm sick and tired of seeing the pack I built turn to shit. And please, call me George."

"Only if you call me Dev."

The older man dipped his head once in acknowledgement.

"What do you suggest? Is he unstable enough to hurt Grammy? He attacked Laine in the bathroom of the restaurant last night."

"Yes, I heard. No, I don't think he'll harm her, at least nothing permanent. He wants something. Laine is my best guess. He's been after that boy from the get-go."

"That would be my guess too, but he isn't getting Lainey. Nor Grammy for that matter. Let me call my...well I guess if I'm going to be Alpha, then Cole is my Beta."

"Margaret mentioned him too. Go ahead and call him." The older man tried to act like he was in control, but Dev heard the little quiver in his voice when he mentioned Margaret. The man clearly had feelings for Grammy.

Dev pushed in Cole's cell number. He wondered if Laine knew his grandmother was dating George? At least he thought that was the case. If it wasn't he'd eat his hat, then he'd see about playing matchmaker. George was obviously crazy about Grammy and seemed like a good, decent man.

Cole picked up the phone out of breath. "What?"

Oops. It sounded like Caroline was doing some pretty heavy breathing close to the phone as well. "I need you to come to Laine's apartment now."

"Okay give me—"

"Cole, this is an emergency."

Cole sighed, but Dev could hear rustling, like Cole was getting dressed. "Okay, be right there. What about Caroline?"

"Bring her with you." He wasn't going to take a chance of Victor snatching anyone else he cared about. Dev flipped his phone closed and met George's eyes. "Come on inside. Cole and Caroline are on their way and I've got to go wake Lainey."

George nodded and followed him inside.

Laine sat up when the door slammed. Oh man, he hadn't meant to fall asleep. He looked around for Dev, then realized it was more than likely Dev at the door. Who else would it be? No one else had keys except Grammy. *Oh shit.* Dev had several meetings today. Maybe it *was* Grammy.

Laine glanced at the bedroom door as he scrambled under the covers. He had them clutched to his chest like a reluctant virgin when Dev walked in, fully clothed. Laine let out a sigh of relief and dropped the covers. "Why are you back? Not that I care, but I thought you and Cole were going to meet with the realtor lady?" *Crap.* Laine peeked at the clock. Caroline was supposed to be here in three minutes. Laine jumped up and started for the bathroom. "Tell Caroline, I'll be—Oof." Dev caught him around the waist, halting his progress.

"Lainey..."

Uh-oh. He really did not like the tone of Dev's voice. "What's wrong?"

Dev sat on the edge of the bed, tugging Laine into his lap. "George Marshal is here and—"

"You're stalling. Just tell me."

"Victor kidnapped Grammy."

Laine shot to his feet. "What?"

Dev grabbed his hand and tried to pull him back.

He batted at Dev's hand. "He has Grammy? How?"

"He and his Betas snagged her this morning. She's at Peter's house..."

Dev kept talking but Laine didn't hear any of it. He shook his head. No, they couldn't have Grammy. Why would they want her? She wasn't a wolf. He walked around the bed and got the phone off the charger. He dialed Grammy's number.

Dev came up behind him and took the phone out of his hand. He pushed end and tossed it on the bed, then turned Laine towards him. He reached up and dried a tear Laine hadn't realized was there.

"We have to get her back, Dev."

Dev hugged him, his hand holding Laine's face to his chest. "We will Lainey. George is here and Cole and Caroline are on their way. We are going to decide the best way to get Grammy back." Dev cast a glance at the closed bedroom door and lowered his voice to barely a whisper. "Laine, I need to know now…is there any reason I shouldn't trust George?"

"No. George is a good man. You can trust him. He's been a friend of the family for years."

Dev nodded. "Let's get you a shower and some coffee while we wait on Cole and Caroline. It will make you feel a little better."

Laine started to protest, but Dev was right, he needed a clear head to help plan. He let Dev lead him into the bathroom. Dev started the shower for him and went to make coffee. Laine washed in a daze. He'd known Victor was up to something. Dev had kept him from tormenting Laine, so Victor had moved on to the next best thing. Would he hurt Grammy? Maybe he'd let Grammy go, if Laine agreed to take her place. What was he thinking? Victor wasn't going to back off after he got his pound of flesh. He was just itching to rough Laine up for the insolence he'd shown the other night.

Turning off the shower, Laine got out right as Dev came back into the bathroom. Dev grabbed the towel off the rack and held it open for him to step into.

"They're here, Lainey, and I've got the coffee made."

"Thanks." Laine went into the circle of his mate's arms and let Dev dry him off. He leaned into Dev's touch, thankful he had someone here for him.

Dev dried him and somehow managed to get him into the bedroom and dressed.

Laine's mind was going ninety-to-nothing, thinking about what-if and why and how? When he got to the living room, Cole, Caroline and George were all there.

Apparently, Cole and Caroline had been filled in and introduced to the former Alpha, because after George greeted Laine he immediately asked, "Has Victor called yet?"

"Called?" Laine glanced at the chair across from George and the empty spot next to Caroline. Then he crossed to Dev and sat on his lap. He didn't care what everyone else thought. He needed to be near Dev.

Dev pulled him into his arms, holding him close. "No, he hasn't."

Caroline shifted a little closer to her mate. "You mean like a demand for ransom?"

"Yes. That's what he means. As far as Victor knows, none of us know that he has Grammy." Dev looked over at George. "Or did he see you?"

George shook his head. "No, he didn't. I suspect he'll be calling shortly."

Laine didn't even want to think about what Victor would want for Grammy's safe return. He was positive it was going to be something he wasn't willing to pay. They...Dev was going to have to fight him. Laine sighed and rested his cheek against Dev. He did not want to ask Dev to do that.

Dev rubbed his arm. "We need to get our plan together before he calls. How many wolves can we count on to help out, to keep Victor's Betas out of the picture? I don't mind two or three wolves ganging up on the Betas to distract them while I take Victor, but I don't want anyone interfering with mine and Victor's fight."

Laine sat up, looking at Dev. "You're going to fight Victor?"

Dev smiled and caressed Laine's cheek. "You know there isn't any other way."

Laine nodded, he did know, but he still didn't have to like it. "I know."

"From what Dev has said, I can take, probably, two of the Betas but I can't take all four at the same time," Cole said.

George leaned forward. "Yes, you should be able to, but it would be better if we can keep them off of you so that you only have one at a time. And we should have enough wolves to do that."

Laine agreed not all the wolves would get involved, but they would support any movement against Victor. "No one likes Victor. We won't have to worry about any resistance except from the four Betas."

Dev kissed Laine's forehead. "Good, if we can get enough pack members to make sure it's a fair fight then that is all we need. I don't want them trying to help Cole or me fight. If I'm going to be Alpha, then it needs to be known that I got the position myself, in a fair fight."

George nodded. "I agree. Theoretically, you should be done fighting when you defeat Victor, but I won't swear to that. Peter is a cocky bastard and he might decide to challenge you."

"Then Cole should go after Peter first," Dev said.

Caroline frowned. "I don't like—"

The phone rang.

They all looked at it except Laine, who looked at Caroline. "I don't either, Caroline, but Dev is right. We don't have a choice. Victor has to be stopped."

Chapter Nine

"Lainey, there's no need for you to go."

Laine stopped dead in his tracks. *Oh, no way.* He did not hear that. "I am going to watch my mate's back and that is all I have to say about that."

Dev's hand landed on his shoulder and turned him around. "Lainey..."

"No, Dev. I need to go."

"No, babe, you don't."

Laine opened his mouth to argue, but Dev put a finger to his lips.

"Just listen. If I'm going to beat Victor, I need to concentrate. I can't do that if I'm worrying about you. And I *will* worry about you if you are there. I can't help it. You're my mate and my responsibility."

Laine shook his head. He wasn't a complete idiot. Laine knew his limitations, he wasn't a fighter, he knew that, but he could be there and be Dev's eyes. "I don't want to be a burden on you. But I need to go and help. I can watch your back. I can—"

"You could never be a burden. You're—"

Laine sighed. "But I am a burden, if you can't trust me."

Dev's lips landed on his in a heated kiss. Just as Laine was getting into it, Dev pulled back. "It has nothing to do with trust. I'd trust you with my life. And I'm not calling you a wimp either, you just aren't as strong as Victor or his goons. That's fact. I know you'd die trying, but that's just it, Lainey, I can't take that chance."

Wow. "I...I..." He couldn't not go and wonder how Dev was, wonder if things turned out okay. He had to go keep an eye on his mate. If he could just watch, he knew Dev would be okay. He could stay out of the fight, if that made Dev feel better, but—

"Promise me you'll stay here. I need you to do this for me, Laine."

Laine wasn't sure what made him do it, but he knew he couldn't promise and he couldn't lie, not to Dev, so he crossed his fingers and nodded.

Thankfully, Dev seemed satisfied with that. "I'll call you as soon as it's over, okay?"

"Okay."

Dev kissed him one last time and headed towards the front door of the condo.

"Dev?"

The big man stopped with his hand on the doorknob. "Yeah?" He turned to face Laine.

I love you. "Be careful."

Dev grinned. "I will. Caroline will be up in a second. Lock the door once she gets in."

Laine went to the door and watched Dev go down the stairs.

Cole and Caroline stood at the bottom of the stairs. Cole waved and Caroline started up the stairs. She stepped in the doorway and turned to watch Cole and Dev drive off in Dev's truck.

When Dev's taillights disappeared around the corner, Laine shut the door.

"How long should we give them before we follow?" Caroline asked.

Laine chuckled. "Caroline, if I liked women, I do believe I'd have to fight Cole for you." He kissed Caroline's freckled nose.

She hugged him. "I'm nervous, Lainey. I know they're strong and capable and all that crap, but I need to go."

Laine sighed. He knew how she felt, but he couldn't take her. Cole would never forgive him. And Dev would be pissed as hell. It was bad enough Laine was about to defy his mate and go, but he couldn't in good conscience take an unarmed, non-wolf into a fight for dominance. She didn't have the fast-healing abilities that wolves did. "Caroline—"

"Don't you dare." She pulled out of their hug and glared at him.

"All right. Give me the keys and come on. I'm driving." He snatched the keys out of Caroline's hands. He'd think of something by the time they got there. He knew damned well she wasn't going to leave it alone, any more than he would. If he left her, she'd find a way to follow, because that is exactly what he'd do. One thing he could say for Caroline, she was easy to figure out.

Caroline climbed into the passenger seat and gave him a hesitant look. "Are you sure you don't want me to drive?"

Laine groaned and started the engine. "Yes." He backed up, somehow managing to run up on the curb.

Caroline grabbed her seatbelt, putting it on, biting her lip. "I'm not saying a thing. Just get us there in one piece."

Sheesh. Yeah, getting them there in one piece was the easy part. Finding a way to restrain Caroline was...wait. *Restrain.*

That's what he had to do, he had to find a way to tie her up. "Caroline, is there any kind of rope in the car?"

"What do we need rope for?"

"A weapon?"

"No. Not unless there is something we can use for a weapon in the trunk."

Now, that was an even better idea, he'd lock her in the trunk. Laine hit another curb when he took a corner too fast, making Caroline squeak.

"Uh, Laine. I hate to be rude, but honey, you really do drive like shit."

Yep, she was *so* going in the trunk for that. She was supposed to be on his side.

Dev and Cole stepped out of the truck and looked around. They were fairly high up in altitude. It really was pretty out here. It helped to center his thoughts. He could smell several wolves, all through the trees. He could even pick out Victor's scent.

"I smell him." Cole stripped off his shirt. He pitched it in the bed of the truck and started on his shoes.

"Yeah, me too. You ready for this buddy? You know, you don't—"

"Don't even start that shit, Dev. We've been friends for over thirty years. Have I ever once not been there when you needed me?"

"Nope. Not once." And that was really all there was to say about that. He knew Cole was in this until the end. Dev toed off his boots and tossed them in the truck bed. "Hurry up. Let's get in there and find out what's what." They finished undressing in silence and stalked through the trees side by side.

Victor was still in human form as well. He stood in the middle of a circle of his Betas, the four other men already shifted. The rest of the pack, mostly in human form, remained off to the side.

George waited, fully clothed, in a line of wolves. Grammy was at his side, her hand in his. George caught Dev's gaze and gave him a nod.

Dev nodded back.

Several of the wolves near Grammy and George spread out, surrounding the Betas, growling.

Victor smiled at him. "As you can see, I lived up to my end of the deal. I gave the pathetic little Omega's granny back." He looked around, then lifted his nose, sniffing. He frowned at Dev. "Where is he? Where's Laine?"

"This is between you and me. Laine no longer has anything to do with this."

Victor snarled. "I want the Omega. I told you to bring him."

Dev held out his arms. "Beat me and you can have him."

Cole snorted beside him.

One of the wolves, Peter, growled and launched himself towards Dev and Cole.

Three of the wolves with George intercepted him.

"Here we go." Cole shifted and jumped into the fray. Immediately, one of the other Betas leapt in, followed by two more of the other pack members.

Victor glanced at them, shrugging. "Looks like you already have a bit of a following. I'm going to punish them once I kill you." Victor shifted.

Dev followed suit, actually managing to finish shifting before Victor.

Victor's eyes widened in surprise. Without further warning he and his remaining two Betas charged Dev.

Dev took out the first wolf easily, grabbing him by the throat. The man's neck squished between his teeth. Blood went everywhere. The wolf gurgled and Dev let go. He fell to the ground and shifted back to human form instantly, trying to heal himself. Dev's attention left him. He was no longer a threat. The man wasn't strong enough to shift again and rejoin the fight.

A sharp pain flared in Dev's side as the other Beta's teeth clamped down.

As Dev was trying to dislodge the Beta, Victor went for his throat.

Dev jerked out of reach.

Victor yelped and spun around ready to defend himself.

Out of the corner of his eye, Dev thought he caught a glimpse of red fur. *That better not be Lainey.* He shrugged off his second of panic and took advantage of Victor's distraction. He went for the Alpha's throat. He had Victor pinned to the ground, the other wolf still on his back, when Cole joined him, taking care of the pest clinging to his back.

Victor whimpered and lay still beneath Dev's teeth.

Dev let go and stepped back at the other man's surrender. He shifted, standing over Victor. "I want you out of here. I want you to take your Betas and leave Asheville. If I see any of you back here, I'll kill you on sight."

Victor gazed around, spotting his vanquished Betas. He dipped his head in defeat.

Dev looked, noticing the rest of the pack standing around. "Anyone have a problem with me being Alpha?"

Everyone shook their heads.

One man in the back shouted, "Welcome to the pack."

Another met his gaze and nodded. "As long as you keep Laine as Omega, you can stay."

Dev smiled. "I reckon I can do that. For those of you who haven't heard, Laine is my mate."

An older man chuckled. "Good, maybe you can keep him out of trouble."

"I wouldn't want to count on that, but I'll try." *Speaking of Laine...* Dev glanced around. He was positive he'd seen red fur. He sniffed the air.

Victor sprang from the ground, teeth bared, growling.

Dev reacted out of instinct. His right hand shifted, catching Victor up under the throat. His claws went all the way through Victor's neck. He debated holding him there for several seconds. The man certainly deserved to bleed to death, but Dev wasn't that cruel. He may regret it later, but he tossed Victor away, allowing the man to shift and heal himself. "This is your last warning, Victor. Next time I'll kill you."

Victor changed back, choking on his blood. He peered up at Dev, with wide, scared eyes, and nodded.

Peter and one of the other Betas came over and helped him up.

The pack started applauding.

Dev grinned and glanced over at Cole.

Cole shrugged. "I think you should've killed him."

Dev snorted.

Grammy rushed up and hugged his neck.

Dev stepped back, eyes wide. "Uh, Grammy, I'm naked."

She chuckled and patted his back. "Yes, dear, I can see that. My Lainey is a lucky man."

Cole and George smirked at him.

George nudged Cole's shoulder. "He's almost the same shade as Laine's hair."

Dev groaned and moved away from them. He was going to get dressed and go home. He needed to call Laine and let him know that—

Dev blinked and stared at the naked man in front of him. Oh yeah, that was definitely his Lainey. He'd know that ass anywhere. He stepped up behind the man and grabbed the back of his slim neck. "I thought I told you to stay home."

Laine squeaked, those red eyelashes fluttered and his amber eyes pleaded. "You did?"

"Oh, hell yeah, I did. Would you like to explain why you lied to me?"

Lainey gazed past him to Cole.

Dev turned his head in time to see Cole's smirk and shake his head. "Don't look at me for help."

He looked back at Laine and raised an eyebrow.

"I didn't actually lie, Dev."

"No?"

"I had my fingers crossed behind my back."

Dev opened his mouth then snapped it shut. What the hell could he say to that? He heard Cole, Grammy and George laughing behind him. And suddenly the ridiculousness of it hit him. He really, really should have expected something like that. He chuckled, wrapped his arm around Laine's shoulders, and got them moving towards their cars. The sooner they got clothes on, the better. "I'll remember that. It won't work again." He kissed Laine's forehead.

Laine beamed up at him. "I did good though, didn't I? I didn't actually get into a confrontation, and I stayed out of the way...mostly."

Dev shook his head. Yeah, at least Laine had stayed out of trouble. That in itself was a major feat. Dev squeezed his mate. "Yeah, Lainey, you did good." When they got to his truck, he and Cole got their clothes out of the bed and dressed. Surprisingly, Laine gathered his clothes from the truck too. He must have stripped there as well. Dev wondered briefly how Laine got here and why he didn't disrobe by the vehicle he came in, but quickly dismissed it in favor of watching Laine get dressed. Damn, the man looked good hopping around trying to get his pants on. Dev snapped his own pants and reached out and grabbed Laine's shoulder before he fell over.

Laine pulled his pants up and fastened them. "Thanks."

When they were finally all clothed again, Cole patted Laine on the back. "Hell, Lainey, I'm just impressed that Caroline didn't follow you."

Laine's pale face went paler and his eyes widened.

"Lainey, what's that banging noise?" Grammy asked.

Banging noise? Dev listened and sure enough...

Laine dropped his head in his hands. "I left Caroline in the trunk."

Dev blinked. "You, wh—" He couldn't help it, he started laughing. He couldn't even imagine. Then Cole fell against him, cackling. The man was laughing so hard he couldn't even stand. Which didn't help Dev's mirth any. Pretty soon he and Cole were both falling all over each other, laughing their fool heads off.

Poor Lainey didn't know whether to laugh with them or cry.

Grammy and George had no trouble deciding, they joined right in laughing.

Several minutes and a couple of tear-streaked faces later, Dev and Cole lay side by side in the bed of the truck with their legs hanging off the tailgate.

Grammy leaned over and kissed Dev's cheek, then Cole's. "George is taking me home, boys. Thank you, Devlin, I'm very proud to call you my grandson-in-law." She stood up, hugged Laine and patted his back. "Love you, dear." She was chuckling when she walked off.

George took her hand and waved. "See you later, boys."

Dev, Cole and Laine all waved.

Cole sat up, the last of his laughter gone, and patted a smiling Laine on the back. "You did good. Now, if I were you, I'd give me the keys and haul ass."

Laine looked at Dev, an eyebrow arched.

Dev grinned, on the verge of laughing again, stood up and hugged Laine. He took the keys from Laine's hand and tossed them to Cole. He kissed Laine on the lips and ushered him into the truck. "Come on, babe. Hell hath no fury and all that. And I have plans for your ass before Caroline takes a chunk out of it."

Laine scooted into the cab without a word. He leaned his head on Dev's shoulder as Dev started the truck and drove back down the mountain. "Thank you, Dev."

"You're more than welcome, love."

Laine nuzzled his shoulder. He was quiet for the longest time, then he asked, "How long do you think Caroline will stay mad?"

Dev chuckled, shaking his head. "Lainey, you're one of a kind."

Epilogue

One year later, Valentine's Day...

Dev walked into Flower Lane a little after five with a box of candy under his arm and a bag of food in the other. Lainey wasn't expecting him until six, so he'd managed at least a small surprise for their anniversary. He wished Laine didn't have to work late tonight, but at least he could hang out here with him.

Beth was on the phone at the front counter. She waved and pointed to the back.

Dev slipped up beside her and kissed her cheek before he went to find his mate. He'd grown attached to Flower Lane's employees in the last year. Dev grinned and stopped right outside the door at the sound of Caroline's voice.

"You owe me, Lainey!"

"No way. That was a year ago. You have more than paid me back for the trunk incident."

"Nope, not even close, but if you take me with you we'll call it even."

Dev leaned closer to the wall. He could hear them just fine but he had a sneaking suspicion they were about to start whispering. Sure enough, Laine's next words were barely audible.

"I'm doing this as a surprise for Dev. Besides, it's a gay club. How in the hell do you expect me to get you in there?"

Caroline snorted. "Well, duh, we'll tell them I'm in drag."

Dev blinked, holding back his laughter. Oh this was getting interesting.

"A pregnant drag queen?" Laine's voice rose just above a whisper.

"Why not?" Caroline hissed.

Yeah, why not, Lainey? This ought to be good. Dev smiled. He should go in and put a stop to their scheme already, but he was dying to hear how Laine got out of this one.

Laine groaned. "Okay, okay, here is what we'll do. You can dress up as a guy. Maybe we can disguise the baby as a beer belly. But, what are you going to do about Cole? It's Valentine's Day, I think he'll notice if you aren't home."

"Ooh, Lainey, you're a genius. Instead of pretending to go in drag, I really will go in drag. And don't worry about Cole, I'll think of something." Caroline giggled.

"I don't think it's called going in drag when it's a woman dressing as a man." Lainey sounded like he was really contemplating the situation.

"Why not?"

"I don't know."

Dev grinned, he could actually picture Laine shrugging.

As funny as it was, and as much as he hated ruining a surprise, he was going to have to put a stop to it, this had all the markings of trouble. He stepped into view, cleared his throat and strolled into the back.

Both conspirators had their backs to the door. Caroline was leaning over Laine's worktable watching him make a flower arrangement.

"No way in hell are you two going to that club. Caroline, go home."

Caroline whirled around, her red hair flying into her eyes, her pregnant belly knocking over a large metal vase Laine was filling with flowers.

When the vase fell, it landed right on Laine's foot, before it hit the linoleum with a clank. Flower petals littered the floor.

Laine's big amber eyes widened and he bit his bottom lip.

Dev had to give him credit, he stood there for a full ten seconds before he started howling like a banshee, hopping around on one foot. "Oww."

Caroline winced then looked at Dev and shrugged. "Oops." She jogged past Dev and out the door. "Call you later, Lainey. Happy anniversary."

Laine sat down on the floor holding his foot. "God, I can't wait until she has that baby. That is the third time today she's knocked something over on me."

Dev leaned against the doorjamb, grinning like an idiot. Thank God Lainey couldn't get pregnant. As clumsy as he was already, Dev would have to tie him up to keep him from killing himself.

Laine looked up from under his overlong auburn bangs. "I wasn't really going to take her, but—"

"Sure you weren't." Dev shoved away from the wall, set the food and candy on the worktable and offered his mate a hand.

Laine took his hand. "I wasn't...really. I've only got one extra pass and it's for you."

He pulled Laine to his feet. "*We* aren't going to that club either."

"But..." Laine's bottom lip pouted out just a tad, before he pulled it back in and scrunched up his face in confusion. "Hey, Dev?"

Uh-oh. Dev recognized that tone. Lainey was up to something. "Yeah?"

"Um...I love you."

Dev grinned. "Hey, Lainey?"

"Yeah?" Laine wrapped his arms around Dev's neck and pressed his cheek against Dev's, nuzzling just a little.

"I love you too, but the answer is still no. You're not going to that club."

"Damn." Laine's long lashes fluttered over his pretty gold eyes. "But I have a Valentine's surprise for you."

Dev groaned. "Can't you give it to me here?"

"Umm..." Laine kissed his temple and nuzzled his face against Dev's again. "No."

"Why not?"

Laine unwrapped his arms from Dev's neck and caught Dev's face in his palms. His bottom lip protruded again, but this time he didn't try to conceal the pout. "But, Dev..."

"Laine..."

Dropping his forehead against Dev's chest, Lainey grumbled, "They're having amateur night tonight during their annual Lupercalia festival at Ganymede's Grotto."

Amateur night? "For what?"

Looking up at Dev, he batted his lashes and grinned seductively. "If I tell you it will ruin the surprise."

Laine was so damned sexy, it very nearly distracted him, but Dev knew the man too well. If he didn't figure out what this was about now, he'd regret it later, when the shop closed and

Lainey wrangled him into going at the last minute. "What is the amateur night for?"

Laine bit his bottom lip and ran his hand up his chest tugging on one of his nipple rings through his shirt, an obvious ploy to divert if Dev had ever seen one. And it was working, his cock hardened right up. God, Laine was something. *The little minx.* "Lainey, spill it."

Laine's hand slid down, brushing over jeans and his very evident erection. "Stripping." He gripped his hard-on through his pants and slipped his other hand up under the green T-shirt, working his way towards the ring he'd just released.

Dev's cock jerked. Knowing Laine it would only be seconds before a nice wet cum stain appeared on the denim. It was extremely hot how easily Laine got off. Already the little whimpers were starting up, as Lainey rubbed harder on his cock and tugged on his ring underneath the shirt. Dev reached out towards him and—*Wait.* "You want to go watch regular people strip?"

Laine kept his hands busy, his hips pushed forward into his own touch. "No. I want to strip...for you."

If he hadn't known Laine so well, he'd have hit the roof. But this *was* his Lainey and Dev realized it wasn't some harebrained idea. Well yes, it was harebrained, but Laine had actually put some thought into this. Conflicting feelings raced through him. The idea of Laine naked was...well Laine naked was always a good thing, but Dev wasn't too keen on others seeing his mate without clothes. "This is my Valentine's Day present?"

Laine beamed at him. He dropped his hands, ceasing his groping, and nodded. "I've been taking lessons. You know Keegan? He works at Ganymede's Grotto. He comes into the shop to pick up their weekly flower order sometimes. We got to talking one day about gifts and his partner really likes to watch him dance. Then I remembered you mentioning that you'd been watching the strip show at Ganymede's Grotto last year before you went to meet Victor. So, since you got interrupted and didn't get to enjoy your last Valentine's Day, I thought I'd make it up to you. And Keegan offered to teach me to strip and I thought it would be the perfect gi—"

The man had been helping Laine take his clothes off? The dancer had seen his Lainey half-naked. Dev growled, his eyes narrowing on the little spitfire. Grabbing Laine's hand, Dev tugged him into his arms. He nestled Laine's sweet little belly against his boner and wrapped his arms around his back. "Mine."

Giggling, Laine ground his stomach against Dev. "Uh-huh. All yours. Can we go?"

"No."

Laine froze. "But—"

"No."

Laine's shoulders slumped.

Dev kissed his cheek. "Lainey, I had the best Valentine's Day ever last year. I met you. There is nothing to compensate for. But I won't argue if you want to strip for me at home later."

Laine went up on tiptoes to kiss Dev's chin. "It won't be as spectacular at home."

"Sure it will. And then after you're done..."

Jumping back, Laine turned towards him, his face once again radiant. "Oooh, I like that idea. Okay..." He looked around. "Music. We don't have a stereo in here. Humph. I'll just go get—"

He caught Laine before he could leave. "Whoa, wait a minute. Did you forget where we are? You can't do this here."

"Sure I can, this is where Keegan gave me lessons. I'll just lock the door."

Dev's eyes widened. Laine had been taking dancing lessons in the back of the shop?

Laine locked the door and pulled out a chair from a desk near the back. "Sit right there. I'll just hum."

Dev started to argue, but stopped himself. This ought to be interesting. "Okay."

"Ready?" One delicate red eyebrow arched at him.

"I'm ready."

Laine started humming. It was supposed to be a sexy little song, instead it was a bit off key sounding more like circus music. Slinking around the chair, Laine tripped over the vase Caroline had knocked over. He grimaced but kept on humming.

Dev's cock jerked. Why Laine's clumsiness turned him on, he didn't know, but it did. It was just part of his mate.

Laine grabbed the hem of his T-shirt. The circus tune came to a halt and the hip rolling slowed, long enough to get the shirt over his head...well almost over his head. He got hung up in it, with one arm still in the shirt and one arm out. "Shoot!" Laine fought free of the shirt. When he finally got it off his red hair was sticking up on one side. He brushed his hair out of his eyes and resumed dancing.

Dev barely held back a chuckle. Laine just wasn't coordinated enough to do two things at once.

Tossing his green shirt at Dev, Laine ran his hand down his sculpted belly. The twin nipple rings caught Dev's attention and Laine grinned knowingly.

Laine unbuttoned the snap on his jeans, doing a little hip thrust.

Dev rubbed his cock through his pants, never taking his eyes from the lithe figure in front of him. If Laine didn't hurry up, he was going to be the one coming with barely any stimulation. He had to be out of his mind contemplating having sex in the backroom of Lainey's shop, but that was exactly what he was going to do, if Laine would hustle.

A quick turn and a shake of Laine's pretty ass had Dev moaning. "Hurry up, Lainey."

Laine turned back around and unzipped his pants. He shimmied them off and stepped out of them with surprising grace. Under his jeans he wore silky white boxer shorts with tiny red hearts. His cock tented the material, straining towards Dev. There was already a little wet spot on the silk where the head of Laine's cock was. The smell of arousal made Dev's canines lengthen.

Dev groaned. Thank God he'd stopped Laine from doing this in public. He'd have a fight on his hands keeping all those pervy old men off his mate. Damn, Laine was something else.

Laine closed his eyes and trailed his hands down his chest, all the while swaying back and forth, and hooked his thumbs in his waistband. Snapping his eyes open, Laine revealed his wolf eyes, then he shoved the boxers down. His prick bobbed free, slapping against his lower abdomen. Wiggling, Laine let go and the silk fell to the floor around his ankles.

Fuck. Dev reached out a hand to his mate. "Come here, honey."

Laine stopped humming and stepped towards Dev. "Oof!" The metal vase skidded to a halt against the leg of the chair, breaking off more petals, and Laine hit the floor with a thud.

Dev scrambled up, reaching for his mate.

Big gold eyes peered up at him.

"Oops." Laine shrugged. "Forgot about the vase."

Laughter bubbled up inside him and he offered Laine a hand. "Lainey?"

"Yeah?"

Dev sat and pulled him onto his lap, kissing him on the lips. "I love you."

About the Author

J.L. Langley writes M/M erotic romance, among other things, and is fortunate to live with four of the most gorgeous males to walk the earth...okay, so one of those males is canine, but he is quite beautiful for a German Shepherd. J.L. was born and raised in Texas. Which is a good thing considering that Texas is full of cowboys and there is nothing better than a man in a pair of tight Wranglers and a cowboy hat as far as she's concerned.

To learn more about J.L. Langley, please visit http://www.jllangley.com/. Send an email to J.L. Langley at mailto:10star@jllangley.com or join her Yahoo! group to join in the fun with other readers as well as J.L.! http://groups.yahoo.com/group/the_yellow_rose

Look for these titles

Now Available
Willow Bend by Ally Blue
Love's Evolution by Ally Blue
A Year and A Day by Willa Okati
Unspoken by Willa Okati
The Letter by Willa Okati

Coming Soon:
What Hides Inside by Ally Blue
Fireflies by Ally Blue
Sex and Sexuality by Willa Okati
With Caution by J.L. Langley

Can two men from different worlds cut the ties binding them to heartaches past and present, and make a life together?

Willow Bend
© 2006 Ally Blue

For Paul Gordon, the little town of Willow Bend, South Carolina is the perfect place to start over. A place where he can move on after his lover's death, alone and anonymous.

Cory Saunders is just trying to survive. Between working two jobs and caring for his ailing mother, it's all he can do to keep his head above water.

When Paul and Cory meet, their mutual attraction is undeniable. When the intense physical attraction starts to blossom into something deeper, neither wants to admit to what's happening. Cory doesn't have time for a relationship, and Paul isn't sure he's ready for one. But sometimes, what you thought you couldn't have turns out to be exactly what you need.

Warning: this title contains explicit male/male sex and graphic language.

Available now in ebook and print from Samhain Publishing.

Love is the journey of a lifetime.

Love's Evolution
© 2006 Ally Blue

Chris Tucker is a cultured and sophisticated gentleman. Matt Gallagher is a pierced and tattooed wild child. Not exactly the pair you'd expect to become a couple. But the sparks fly between them from the moment they meet, and the fire never goes out.

Through the first rush of attraction to falling in love, through jealousy and sexual experimentation and a life-threatening injury, the bond they share grows and deepens. Come along with Matt and Chris on their journey, and share their joys and heartaches, from their first hello to happily ever after and everything in between.

Warning, this title contains the following: explicit homoerotic sex, graphic language, and M/M/M ménage a trois.

Available now in ebook and print from Samhain Publishing.

Love can conquer anything...even death.

A Year and a Day
© *2006 Willa Okati*

After being separated from his lover, Ash, no one and nothing is going to stand in Slate's way when it comes to getting him back. He plans on using magics he's unfamiliar with to call Ash back to his side — but he doesn't think about the consequences. Nothing matters but getting his lover back in his arms again.

However, once they're reunited, Slate and Ash are determined to stay together no matter what the cost. After all, true love can conquer anything...even death.

Warning: This title contains explicit sex, graphic language, and male/male erotic romance.

Available now in ebook from Samhain Publishing.

Sometimes a kiss is worth more than a thousand words.

Unspoken
© 2006 Willa Okati

Once a famous vocalist, Ian has become mute through a mysterious set of circumstances that no doctor can explain. He has people he can call on, but what he really needs is a best friend, a companion, a lover. The very person he's been looking for is about to arrive on his doorstep.

At a low point, Ian encounters a strange man in his garden—a wandering musician, like the bards of older times. Andy accepts Ian for who he is, lack of voice included, and reassures Ian that love itself is one of the greatest forms of expression.

Will Ian coax Andy to stay, save him, and share with him a love that will not be denied, even if it goes unspoken?

Warning: This novella contains graphic depictions of male/male encounters and adult language.

Available now in ebook from Samhain Publishing.

Fly Away

Discover the Talons Series

5 STEAMY NEW PARANORMAL ROMANCES
TO HOOK YOU IN

Kiss Me Deadly, by Shannon Stacey
King of Prey, by Mandy M. Roth
Firebird, by Jaycee Clark
Caged Desire, by Sydney Somers
Seize the Hunter, by Michelle M. Pillow

AVAILABLE IN EBOOK—COMING SOON IN PRINT!

WWW.SAMHAINPUBLISHING.COM

GREAT
cheap
fun

Discover eBooks!
THE FASTEST WAY TO GET THE HOTTEST NAMES

Get your favorite authors on your favorite reader, long before they're
out in print! Ebooks from Samhain go wherever you go, and work with
whatever you carry—Palm, PDF, Mobi, and more.

Samhain
Publishing, Ltd.

WWW.SAMHAINPUBLISHING.COM

Printed in the United States
88138LV00006B/1-27/A